Library
Brevard Junior College
Cocoa, Florida

RUSSIAN SILHOUETTES

RUSSIAN SILHOUETTES

MORE STORIES OF RUSSIAN LIFE

BY

ANTON TCHEKOFF
(ANTON PAVLOVICH CHEKHOV)

TRANSLATED FROM THE RUSSIAN BY
MARIAN FELL

Short Story Index Reprint Series

BOOKS FOR LIBRARIES PRESS
FREEPORT, NEW YORK

Copyright © 1915 by Charles Scribner's Sons

Copyright © renewed 1943 by Olivia Fell Vans Agnew

Reprinted 1970 by arrangement with
Charles Scribner's Sons

INTERNATIONAL STANDARD BOOK NUMBER:
0-8369-3744-9

LIBRARY OF CONGRESS CATALOG CARD NUMBER:
72-142260

PRINTED IN THE UNITED STATES OF AMERICA

CONTENTS

STORIES OF CHILDHOOD

The Boys	3
Grisha	14
A Trifle from Real Life	20
The Cook's Wedding	29
Shrove Tuesday	38
In Passion Week	46
An Incident	54
A Matter of Classics	63
The Tutor	68
Out of Sorts	73

STORIES OF YOUTH

A Joke	79
After the Theatre	86
Volodia	91
A Naughty Boy	111
Bliss	115
Two Beautiful Girls	119

CONTENTS

LIGHT AND SHADOW

	PAGE
THE CHORUS GIRL	135
THE FATHER OF A FAMILY	144
THE ORATOR	151
IONITCH	157
AT CHRISTMAS TIME	187
IN THE COACH HOUSE	195
LADY N——'S STORY	205
A JOURNEY BY CART	212
THE PRIVY COUNCILLOR	227
ROTHSCHILD'S FIDDLE	255
A HORSEY NAME	272
THE PETCHENEG	278
THE BISHOP	295

STORIES OF CHILDHOOD

THE BOYS

"VOLODIA is here!" cried some one in the courtyard.

"Voloditchka is here!" shrieked Natalia, rushing into the dining-room.

The whole family ran to the window, for they had been expecting their Volodia for hours. At the front porch stood a wide posting sleigh with its troika of white horses wreathed in dense clouds of steam. The sleigh was empty because Volodia was already standing in the front entry untying his hood with red, frost-bitten fingers. His schoolboy's uniform, his overcoat, his cap, his goloshes, and the hair on his temples were all silvery with frost, and from his head to his feet he exhaled such a wholesome atmosphere of cold that one shivered to be near him. His mother and aunt rushed to kiss and embrace him. Natalia fell down at his feet and began pulling off his goloshes. His sisters shrieked, doors creaked and banged on every side, and his father came running into the hall in his shirt-sleeves waving a pair of scissors and crying in alarm:

"Is anything the matter? We expected you yesterday. Did you have a good journey? For heaven's sake, give him a chance to kiss his own father!"

"Bow, wow, wow!" barked the great black dog, My Lord, in a deep voice, banging the walls and furniture with his tail.

All these noises went to make up one great, joyous clamour that lasted several minutes. When the first burst of joy had subsided the family noticed that, beside Volodia, there was still another small person in the hall. He was wrapped in scarfs and shawls and hoods and was standing motionless in the shadow cast by a huge fox-skin coat.

"Volodia, who is that?" whispered Volodia's mother.

"Good gracious!" Volodia exclaimed recollecting himself. "Let me present my friend Tchetchevitsin. I have brought him from school to stay with us."

"We are delighted to see you! Make yourself at home!" cried the father gaily. "Excuse my not having a coat on! Allow me!—Natalia, help Mr. Tcherepitsin to take off his things! For heaven's sake, take that dog away! This noise is too awful!"

A few minutes later Volodia and his friend were sitting in the dining-room drinking tea, dazed by their noisy reception and still rosy with cold. The wintry rays of the sun, piercing the frost and snow on the window-panes, trembled over the samovar and bathed themselves in the slop-basin. The room was warm, and the boys felt heat and cold jostling one another in their bodies, neither wanting to concede its place to the other.

"Well, Christmas will soon be here!" cried Volodia's

father, rolling a cigarette. "Has it seemed long since your mother cried as she saw you off last summer? Time flies, my son! Old age comes before one has time to heave a sigh. Mr. Tchibisoff, do help yourself! We don't stand on ceremony here!"

Volodia's three sisters, Katia, Sonia, and Masha, the oldest of whom was eleven, sat around the table with their eyes fixed on their new acquaintance. Tchetchevitsin was the same age and size as Volodia, but he was neither plump nor fair like him. He was swarthy and thin and his face was covered with freckles. His hair was bristly, his eyes were small, and his lips were thick; in a word, he was very plain, and, had it not been for his schoolboy's uniform, he might have been taken for the son of a cook. He was taciturn and morose, and he never once smiled. The girls immediately decided that he must be a very clever and learned person. He seemed to be meditating something, and was so busy with his own thoughts that he started if he were asked a question and asked to have it repeated.

The girls noticed that Volodia, who was generally so talkative and gay, seldom spoke now and never smiled and on the whole did not seem glad to be at home. He only addressed his sisters once during dinner and then his remark was strange. He pointed to the samovar and said:

"In California they drink gin instead of tea."

He, too, seemed to be busy with thoughts of his

own, and, to judge from the glances that the two boys occasionally exchanged, their thoughts were identical.

After tea the whole family went into the nursery, and papa and the girls sat down at the table and took up some work which they had been doing when they were interrupted by the boys' arrival. They were making decorations out of coloured paper for the Christmas tree. It was a thrilling and noisy occupation. Each new flower was greeted by the girls with shrieks of ecstasy, of terror almost, as if it had dropped from the sky. Papa, too, was in raptures, but every now and then he would throw down the scissors, exclaiming angrily that they were blunt. Mamma came running into the nursery with an anxious face and asked:

"Who has taken my scissors? Have you taken my scissors again, Ivan?"

"Good heavens, won't she even let me have a pair of scissors?" answered papa in a tearful voice, throwing himself back in his chair with the air of a much-abused man. But the next moment he was in raptures again.

On former holidays Volodia had always helped with the preparations for the Christmas tree, and had run out into the yard to watch the coachman and the shepherd heaping up a mound of snow, but this time neither he nor Tchetchevitsin took any notice of the coloured paper, neither did they once visit the stables.

THE BOYS

They sat by a window whispering together, and then opened an atlas and fell to studying it.

"First, we must go to Perm," whispered Tchetchevitsin. "Then to Tyumen, then to Tomsk, and then—then to Kamschatka. From there the Eskimos will take us across Behring Strait in their canoes, and then—we shall be in America! There are a great many wild animals there."

"Where is California?" asked Volodia.

"California is farther down. If once we can get to America, California will only be round the corner. We can make our living by hunting and highway robbery."

All day Tchetchevitsin avoided the girls, and, if he met them, looked at them askance. After tea in the evening he was left alone with them for five minutes. To remain silent would have been awkward, so he coughed sternly, rubbed the back of his right hand with the palm of his left, looked severely at Katia, and asked:

"Have you read Mayne Reid?"

"No, I haven't— But tell me, can you skate?"

Tchetchevitsin became lost in thought once more and did not answer her question. He only blew out his cheeks and heaved a sigh as if he were very hot. Once more he raised his eyes to Katia's face and said:

"When a herd of buffalo gallop across the pampas the whole earth trembles and the frightened mustangs kick and neigh."

Tchetchevitsin smiled wistfully and added:

"And Indians attack trains, too. But worst of all are the mosquitoes and the termites."

"What are they?"

"Termites look something like ants, only they have wings. They bite dreadfully. Do you know who I am?"

"You are Mr. Tchetchevitsin!"

"No, I am Montezuma Hawkeye, the invincible chieftain."

Masha, the youngest of the girls, looked first at him and then out of the window into the garden, where night was already falling, and said doubtfully:

"We had Tchetchevitsa (lentils) for supper last night."

The absolutely unintelligible sayings of Tchetchevitsin, his continual whispered conversations with Volodia, and the fact that Volodia never played now and was always absorbed in thought—all this seemed to the girls to be both mysterious and strange. Katia and Sonia, the two oldest ones, began to spy on the boys, and when Volodia and his friend went to bed that evening, they crept to the door of their room and listened to the conversation inside. Oh! what did they hear? The boys were planning to run away to America in search of gold! They were all prepared for the journey and had a pistol ready, two knives, some dried bread, a magnifying-glass for lighting fires, a compass, and four roubles. The girls discovered that the boys would have to walk several thousand miles, fighting on the way with savages and tigers, and that they would then find gold and ivory, and slay their enemies. Next, they would turn pirates, drink gin, and at last marry beautiful wives and settle down to cultivate a plantation. Volodia and Tchetchevitsin both talked at once and kept interrupting one another from excitement. Tchetchevitsin called himself "Montezuma Hawkeye," and Volodia "my Paleface Brother."

"Be sure you don't tell mamma!" said Katia to Sonia as they went back to bed. "Volodia will bring us gold and ivory from America, but if you tell mamma she won't let him go!"

Tchetchevitsin spent the day before Christmas Eve studying a map of Asia and taking notes, while Volodia roamed about the house refusing all food, his face looking tired and puffy as if it had been stung by a bee. He stopped more than once in front of the icon in the nursery and crossed himself saying:

"O Lord, forgive me, miserable sinner! O Lord, help my poor, unfortunate mother!"

Toward evening he burst into tears. When he said good night he kissed his father and mother and sisters over and over again. Katia and Sonia realized the significance of his actions, but Masha, the youngest, understood nothing at all. Only when her eye fell upon Tchetchevitsin did she grow pensive and say with a sigh:

"Nurse says that when Lent comes we must eat peas and Tchetchevitsa."

Early on Christmas Eve Katia and Sonia slipped quietly out of bed and went to the boys' room to see them run away to America. They crept up to their door.

"So you won't go?" asked Tchetchevitsin angrily. "Tell me, you won't go?"

"Oh, dear!" wailed Volodia, weeping softly. "How can I go? I'm so sorry for mamma!"

"Paleface Brother, I beg you to go! You promised me yourself that you would. You told me yourself how nice it would be. Now, when everything is ready, you are afraid!"

"I—I'm not afraid. I—I am sorry for mamma."

"Tell me, are you going or not?"

"I'm going, only—only wait a bit, I want to stay at home a little while longer!"

"If that is the case, I'll go alone!" Tchetchevitsin said with decision. "I can get along perfectly well without you. I want to hunt and fight tigers! If you won't go, give me my pistol!"

Volodia began to cry so bitterly that his sisters could not endure the sound and began weeping softly themselves. Silence fell.

"Then you won't go?" demanded Tchetchevitsin again.

"I—I'll go."

"Then get dressed!"

And to keep up Volodia's courage, Tchetchevitsin began singing the praises of America. He roared like a tiger, he whistled like a steamboat, he scolded, and promised to give Volodia all the ivory and gold they might find.

The thin, dark boy with his bristling hair and his freckles seemed to the girls to be a strange and wonderful person. He was a hero to them, a man without fear, who could roar so well that, through the closed door, one might really mistake him for a tiger or a lion.

When the girls were dressing in their own room, Katia cried with tears in her eyes:

"Oh, I'm so frightened!"

All was quiet until the family sat down to dinner at two o'clock, and then it suddenly appeared that the boys were not in the house. Inquiries were made in the servants' quarters and at the stables, but they were not there. A search was made in the village, but they could not be found. At tea time they were still missing, and when the family had to sit down to supper without them, mamma was terribly anxious and was even crying. That night another search was made in the village and men were sent down to the river with lanterns. Heavens, what an uproar arose!

Next morning the policeman arrived and went into the dining-room to write something. Mamma was crying.

Suddenly, lo and behold! a posting sleigh drove up to the front door with clouds of steam rising from its three white horses.

"Volodia is here!" cried some one in the courtyard.

"Voloditchka is here!" shrieked Natalia, rushing into the dining-room.

My Lord barked "Bow, wow, wow!" in his deep voice.

It seemed that the boys had been stopped at the hotel in the town, where they had gone about asking every one where they could buy gunpowder. As he entered the hall, Volodia burst into tears and flung his arms round his mother's neck. The girls trembled with terror at the thought of what would happen next, for they heard papa call Volodia and Tchetchevitsin into his study and begin talking to them. Mamma wept and joined in the talk.

"Do you think it was right?" papa asked, chiding them. "I hope to goodness they won't find it out at school, because, if they do, you will certainly be expelled. Be ashamed of yourself, Master Tchetchevitsin! You are a bad boy. You are a mischief-maker and your parents will punish you. Do you think it was right to run away? Where did you spend the night?"

"In the station!" answered Tchetchevitsin proudly.

Volodia was put to bed, and a towel soaked in vinegar was laid on his head. A telegram was despatched, and next day a lady arrived, Tchetchevitsin's mamma, who took her son away.

As Tchetchevitsin departed his face looked haughty

and stern. He said not a word as he took his leave of the girls, but in a copy-book of Katia's he wrote these words for remembrance:

"Montezuma Hawkeye."

GRISHA

GRISHA, a chubby little boy born only two years and eight months ago, was out walking on the boulevard with his nurse. He wore a long, wadded burnoose, a large cap with a furry knob, a muffler, and wool-lined goloshes. He felt stuffy and hot, and, in addition, the waxing sun of April was beating directly into his face and making his eyelids smart.

Every inch of his awkward little figure, with its timid, uncertain steps, bespoke a boundless perplexity.

Until that day the only universe known to Grisha had been square. In one corner of it stood his crib, in another stood nurse's trunk, in the third was a chair, and in the fourth a little icon lamp. If you looked under the bed you saw a doll with one arm and a drum; behind nurse's trunk were a great many various objects: a few empty spools, some scraps of paper, a box without a lid, and a broken jumping-jack. In this world, besides nurse and Grisha, there often appeared mamma and the cat. Mamma looked like a doll, and the cat looked like papa's fur coat, only the fur coat did not have eyes and a tail. From the world which was called the nursery a door led to a place where people dined and drank tea. There stood Grisha's high chair and there hung the clock made to wag its pendulum and strike. From the dining-room one could pass into another room with big red chairs; there, on the floor, glowered a dark stain for which people still shook their forefingers at Grisha. Still farther beyond lay another room, where one was not allowed to go, and in which one sometimes caught glimpses of papa, a very mysterious person! The functions of mamma and nurse were obvious: they dressed Grisha, fed him, and put him to bed; but why papa should be there was incomprehensible. Aunty was also a puzzling person. She appeared and disappeared. Where did she go? More than once Grisha had looked for her under the bed, behind the trunk, and under the sofa, but she was not to be found.

In the new world where he now found himself, where the sun dazzled one's eyes, there were so many papas and mammas and aunties that one scarcely knew which one to run to. But the funniest and oddest things of all were the horses. Grisha stared at their moving legs and could not understand them at all. He looked up at nurse, hoping that she might help him to solve the riddle, but she answered nothing.

Suddenly he heard a terrible noise. Straight toward him down the street came a squad of soldiers marching in step, with red faces and sticks under their arms. Grisha's blood ran cold with terror and he looked up anxiously at his nurse to inquire if this were not dangerous. But nursie neither ran away nor cried, so he decided it must be safe. He followed the soldiers with his eyes and began marching in step with them.

Across the street ran two big, long-nosed cats, their tails sticking straight up into the air and their tongues lolling out of their mouths. Grisha felt that he, too, ought to run, and he started off in pursuit.

"Stop, stop!" cried nursie, seizing him roughly by the shoulder. "Where are you going? Who told you to be naughty?"

But there sat a sort of nurse with a basket of oranges in her lap. As Grisha passed her he silently took one.

"Don't do that!" cried his fellow wayfarer, slapping his hand and snatching the orange away from him. "Little stupid!"

Next, Grisha would gladly have picked up some of the slivers of glass that rattled under his feet and glittered like icon lamps, but he was afraid that his hand might be slapped again.

"Good day!" Grisha heard a loud, hoarse voice say over his very ear, and, looking up, he caught sight of a tall person with shiny buttons.

To his great joy this man shook hands with nursie; they stood together and entered into conversation. The sunlight, the rumbling of the vehicles, the horses, the shiny buttons, all struck Grisha as so amazingly

GRISHA

new and yet unterrifying, that his heart overflowed with delight and he began to laugh.

"Come! Come!" he cried to the man with the shiny buttons, pulling his coat tails.

"Where to?" asked the man.

"Come!" Grisha insisted. He would have liked to say that it would be nice to take papa and mamma and the cat along, too, but somehow his tongue would not obey him.

In a few minutes nurse turned off the boulevard and led Grisha into a large courtyard where the snow still lay on the ground. The man with shiny buttons followed them. Carefully avoiding the puddles and lumps of snow, they picked their way across the courtyard, mounted a dark, grimy staircase, and entered a room where the air was heavy with smoke and a strong smell of cooking. A woman was standing over a stove frying chops. This cook and nurse embraced one another, and, sitting down on a bench with the man, began talking in low voices. Bundled up as he was, Grisha felt unbearably hot.

"What does this mean?" he asked himself, gazing about. He saw a dingy ceiling, a two-pronged oven fork, and a stove with a huge oven mouth gaping at him.

"Ma-a-m-ma!" he wailed.

"Now! Now!" his nurse called to him. "Be good!"

The cook set a bottle, two glasses, and a pie on the

table. The two women and the man with the shiny buttons touched glasses and each had several drinks. The man embraced alternately the cook and the nurse. Then all three began to sing softly.

Grisha stretched his hand toward the pie, and they gave him a piece. He ate it and watched his nurse drinking. He wanted to drink, too.

"Give, nursie! Give!" he begged.

The cook gave him a drink out of her glass. He screwed up his eyes, frowned, and coughed for a long time after that, beating the air with his hands, while the cook watched him and laughed.

When he reached home, Grisha explained to mamma, the walls, and his crib where he had been and what he had seen. He told it less with his tongue than with his hands and his face; he showed how the sun had shone, how the horses had trotted, how the terrible oven had gaped at him, and how the cook had drunk.

That evening he could not possibly go to sleep. The soldiers with their sticks, the great cats, the horses, the bits of glass, the basket of oranges, the shiny buttons, all this lay piled on his brain and oppressed him. He tossed from side to side, chattering to himself, and finally, unable longer to endure his excitement, he burst into tears.

"Why, he has fever!" cried mamma, laying the palm of her hand on his forehead. "What can be the reason?"

"The stove!" wept Grisha. "Go away, stove!"

"He has eaten something that has disagreed with him," mamma concluded.

And, shaken by his impressions of a new life apprehended for the first time, Grisha was given a spoonful of castor-oil by mamma.

A TRIFLE FROM REAL LIFE

NIKOLAI ILITCH BELAYEFF was a young gentleman of St. Petersburg, aged thirty-two, rosy, well fed, and a patron of the race-tracks. Once, toward evening, he went to pay a call on Olga Ivanovna with whom, to use his own expression, he was dragging through a long and tedious love-affair. And the truth was that the first thrilling, inspiring pages of this romance had long since been read, and that the story was now dragging wearily on, presenting nothing that was either interesting or novel.

Not finding Olga at home, my hero threw himself upon a couch and prepared to await her return.

"Good evening, Nikolai Ilitch!" he heard a child's voice say. "Mamma will soon be home. She has gone to the dressmaker's with Sonia."

On the divan in the same room lay Aliosha, Olga's son, a small boy of eight, immaculately and picturesquely dressed in a little velvet suit and long black stockings. He had been lying on a satin pillow, mimicking the antics of an acrobat he had seen at the circus. First he stretched up one pretty leg, then another; then, when they were tired, he brought his arms into play, and at last jumped up galvanically, throwing himself on all fours in an effort to stand on his head. He went through all these motions with the most serious face in the world, puffing like a martyr, as if he himself regretted that God had given him such a restless little body.

"Ah, good evening, my boy!" said Belayeff. "Is that you? I did not know you were here. Is mamma well?"

Aliosha seized the toe of his left shoe in his right hand, assumed the most unnatural position in the world, rolled over, jumped up, and peeped out at Belayeff from under the heavy fringes of the lampshade.

"Not very," he said shrugging his shoulders. "Mamma is never really well. She is a woman, you see, and women always have something the matter with them."

From lack of anything better to do, Belayeff began scrutinizing Aliosha's face. During all his acquaintance with Olga he had never bestowed any consideration upon the boy or noticed his existence at all. He had seen the child about, but what he was doing there Belayeff, somehow, had never cared to think.

Now, in the dusk of evening, Aliosha's pale face and fixed, dark eyes unexpectedly reminded Belayeff of Olga as she had appeared in the first pages of their romance. He wanted to pet the boy.

"Come here, little monkey," he said, "and let me look at you!"

The boy jumped down from the sofa and ran to Belayeff.

"Well," the latter began, laying his hand on the boy's thin shoulder. "And how are you? Is everything all right with you?"

"No, not very. It used to be much better."

"In what way?"

"That's easy to answer. Sonia and I used to learn only music and reading before, but now we have French verses, too. You have cut your beard!"

"Yes."

"So I noticed. It is shorter than it was. Please let me touch it—does that hurt?"

"No, not a bit."

"Why does it hurt if you pull one hair at a time, and not a bit if you pull lots? Ha! Ha! I'll tell you something. You ought to wear whiskers! You could shave here on the sides, here, and here you could let the hair grow——"

The boy nestled close to Belayeff and began to play with his watch-chain.

"Mamma is going to give me a watch when I go to school, and I am going to ask her to give me a chain just like yours— Oh, what a lovely locket! Papa has a locket just like that; only yours has little stripes on it, and papa's has letters. He has a portrait of mamma in his locket. Papa wears another watch-chain now made of ribbon."

"How do you know? Do you ever see your papa?"

"I—n-no—I——"

Aliosha blushed deeply at being caught telling a fib

and began to scratch the locket furiously with his nail. Belayeff looked searchingly into his face and repeated:

"Do you ever see your papa?"

"N-no!"

"Come, tell me honestly! I can see by your face that you are not telling the truth. It's no use quibbling now that the cat is out of the bag. Tell me, do you see him? Now then, as between friends!"

Aliosha reflected.

"You won't tell mamma?" he asked.

"What an idea!"

"Honour bright?"

"Honour bright!"

"Promise!"

"Oh, you insufferable child! What do you take me for?"

Aliosha glanced around, opened his eyes wide, and said:

"For heaven's sake don't tell mamma! Don't tell a soul, because it's a secret. I don't know what would happen to Sonia and Pelagia and me if mamma should find out. Now, listen. Sonia and I see papa every Thursday and every Friday. When Pelagia takes us out walking before dinner we go to Anfel's confectionery and there we find papa already waiting for us. He is always sitting in the little private room with the marble table and the ash-tray that's made like a goose without a back."

"What do you do in there?"

"We don't do anything. First we say how do you do, and then papa orders coffee and pasties for us. Sonia likes pasties with meat, you know, but I can't abide them with meat. I like mine with cabbage or eggs. We eat so much that we have a hard time eating our dinner afterward so that mamma won't guess anything."

"What do you talk about?"

"With papa? Oh, about everything. He kisses us and hugs us and tells us the funniest jokes. Do you know what? He says that when we grow bigger he is going to take us to live with him. Sonia doesn't want to go, but I wouldn't mind. Of course it would be lonely without mamma, but I could write letters to her. Isn't it funny, we might go and see her then on Sundays, mightn't we? Papa says, too, he is going to buy me a pony. He is such a nice man! I don't know why mamma doesn't ask him to live with her and why she won't let us see him. He loves mamma very much. He always asks how she is and what she has been doing. When she was ill he took hold of his head just like this—and ran about the room. He always asks us whether we are obedient and respectful to her. Tell me, is it true that we are unfortunate?"

"H'm—why do you ask?"

"Because papa says we are. He says we are unfortunate children, and that he is unfortunate, and that mamma is unfortunate. He tells us to pray to God for her and for ourselves."

A TRIFLE FROM REAL LIFE 25

Aliosha fixed his eyes on the figure of a stuffed bird, and became lost in thought.

"Well, I declare—" muttered Belayeff. "So, that's what you do, you hold meetings at a confectioner's? And your mamma doesn't know it?"

"N-no. How could she? Pelagia wouldn't tell her for the world. Day before yesterday papa gave us pears. They were as sweet as sugar. I ate two!"

"H'm. But—listen to me, does papa ever say anything about me?"

"About you? What shall I say?" Aliosha looked searchingly into Belayeff's face and shrugged his shoulders. "Nothing special," he answered.

"Well, what does he say, for instance?"

"You won't be angry if I tell you?"

"What an idea! Does he abuse me?"

"No, he doesn't abuse you, but, you know, he is angry with you. He says that it is your fault that mamma is unhappy, and that you have ruined mamma. He is such a funny man! I tell him that you are kind and that you never scold mamma, but he only shakes his head."

"So he says I have ruined her?"

"Yes—don't be angry, Nikolai Ilitch!"

Belayeff rose and began pacing up and down the room.

"How strange this is—and how ridiculous!" he muttered shrugging his shoulders and smiling sarcastically. "It is all *his* fault and yet he says *I* have ruined her! What an innocent baby this is! And so he told you I had ruined your mother?"

"Yes, but—you promised not to be angry!"

"I'm not angry and—and it is none of your business anyway. Yes, this is—this is really ridiculous! Here I have been caught like a mouse in a trap, and now it seems it is all my fault!"

The door-bell rang. The boy tore himself from Belayeff's arms and ran out of the room. A moment later a lady entered with a little girl. It was Aliosha's mother, Olga Ivanovna. Aliosha skipped into the room behind her, singing loudly and clapping his hands. Belayeff nodded and continued to walk up and down.

"Of course!" he muttered. "Whom should he blame but me? He has right on his side! He is the injured husband."

"What is that you are saying?" asked Olga Ivanovna.

"What am I saying? Just listen to what your young hopeful here has been preaching. It appears that I am a wicked scoundrel and that I have ruined you and your children. You are all unhappy, and I alone am frightfully happy. Frightfully, frightfully happy!"

"I don't understand you, Nikolai. What is the matter?"

"Just listen to what this young gentleman here has to say!" cried Belayeff pointing to Aliosha.

Aliosha flushed and then grew suddenly pale and his face became distorted with fear.

"Nikolai Ilitch!" he whispered loudly. "Hush!"

Olga Ivanovna looked at Aliosha in surprise, and then at Belayeff, and then back again at Aliosha.

"Ask him!" Belayeff continued. "That idiot of yours, Pelagia, takes them to a confectioner's and arranges meetings there between them and their papa. But that isn't the point. The point is that papa is the victim, and that I am an abandoned scoundrel who has wrecked the lives of both of you!"

"Nikolai Ilitch!" groaned Aliosha. "You gave me your word of honour!"

"Leave me alone!" Belayeff motioned to him impatiently. "This is more important than words of honour. This hypocrisy, these lies are intolerable!"

"I don't understand!" cried Olga Ivanovna, the tears glistening in her eyes. "Listen, Aliosha," she asked, turning to her son. "Do you really see your father?"

But Aliosha did not hear her, his eyes were fixed with horror on Belayeff.

"It cannot be possible!" his mother exclaimed, "I must go and ask Pelagia."

Olga Ivanovna left the room.

"But Nikolai Ilitch, you gave me your word of honour!" cried Aliosha trembling all over.

Belayeff made an impatient gesture and went on pacing the floor. He was absorbed in thoughts of the wrong that had been done him, and, as before, was unconscious of the boy's presence: a serious, grown-up person like him could not be bothered with little boys. But Aliosha crept into a corner and told Sonia with horror how he had been deceived. He trembled and hiccoughed and cried. This was the first time in his life that he had come roughly face to face with deceit; he had never imagined till now that there were things in this world besides pasties and watches and sweet pears, things for which no name could be found in the vocabulary of childhood.

THE COOK'S WEDDING

GRISHA, a little urchin of seven, stood at the kitchen door with his eye at the keyhole, watching and listening. Something was taking place in the kitchen that seemed to him very strange and that he had never seen happen before. At the table on which the meat and onions were usually chopped sat a huge, burly peasant in a long coachman's coat. His hair and beard were red, and a large drop of perspiration hung from the tip of his nose. He was holding his saucer on the outstretched fingers of his right hand and, as he supped his tea, was nibbling a lump of sugar so noisily that the goose-flesh started out on Grisha's back. On a grimy stool opposite him sat Grisha's old nurse, Aksinia. She also was drinking tea; her mien was serious and at the same time radiant with triumph. Pelagia, the cook, was busy over the stove and seemed to be endeavouring to conceal her face by every possible means. Grisha could see that it was fairly on fire, burning hot, and flooded in turn with every colour of the rainbow from dark purple to a deathly pallor. The cook was constantly catching up knives, forks, stove-wood, and dish-rags in her trembling hands, and was bustling about and grumbling and making a great racket without accomplishing anything. She did not once glance toward the table at which the other two were sitting, and replied to the nurse's questions abruptly and roughly without ever turning her head in their direction.

"Drink, drink, Danilo!" the nurse was urging the driver. "What makes you always drink tea? Take some vodka!"

And the nurse pushed the bottle toward her guest, her face assuming a malicious expression.

"No, ma'am, I don't use it. Thank you, ma'am," the driver replied. "Don't force me to drink it, goody Aksinia!"

"What's the matter with you? What, you a driver and won't drink vodka? A single man ought to drink! Come, have a little!"

The driver rolled his eyes at the vodka and then at the malicious face of the nurse, and his own face assumed an expression no less crafty than hers.

"No, no; you'll not catch me, you old witch!" he seemed to be saying.

"No, thank you; I don't drink," he answered aloud. "That foolishness won't do in our business. A workman can drink if he wants to because he never budges from the same place, but we fellows live too much in public. Don't we now? Supposing I were to go into an inn and my horse were to break away, or, worse still, supposing I were to get drunk and, before I knew it, were to go to sleep and fall off the box? That's what happens!"

THE COOK'S WEDDING

"How much do you make a day, Danilo?"

"That depends on the day. There are days and days. A coachman's job isn't worth much now. You know yourself that drivers are as thick as flies, hay is expensive, travellers are scarce and are always wanting to go everywhere on horseback. But, praise be to God, we don't complain. We keep ourselves clothed and fed and we can even make some one else happy—(here the driver cast a look in Pelagia's direction)—if they want us to!"

Grisha did not hear what was said next. His mamma came to the door and sent him away to the nursery to study.

"Be off to your lessons, you have no business to be here!" she exclaimed.

On reaching the nursery, Grisha took up "Our Mother Tongue," and tried to read, but without success. The words he had just overheard had raised a host of questions in his mind.

"The cook is going to be married," he thought. "That is strange. I don't understand why she wants to be married. Mamma married papa and Cousin Vera married Pavel Andreitch, but papa and Pavel Andreitch have gold watch-chains and nice clothes and their boots are always clean. I can understand any one marrying them. But this horrid driver with his red nose and his felt boots—ugh! And why does nursie want poor Pelagia to marry?"

When her guest had gone, Pelagia came into the

house to do the housework. Her excitement had not subsided. Her face was red and she looked startled. She scarcely touched the floor with her broom and swept out every corner at least five times. She lingered in the room where Grisha's mamma was sitting. Solitude seemed to be irksome to her and she longed to pour out her heart in words and to share her impressions with some one.

"Well, he's gone!" she began, seeing that mamma would not open the conversation.

"He seems to be a nice man," said mamma without looking up from her embroidery. "He is sober and steady looking."

"My lady, I won't marry him!" Pelagia suddenly screamed. "I declare I won't!"

"Don't be silly, you're not a baby! Marriage is a serious thing, and you must think it over carefully and not scream like that for no reason at all. Do you like him?"

"Oh, my lady!" murmured Pelagia in confusion. "He does say such things—indeed he does!"

"She ought to say outright she doesn't like him," thought Grisha.

"What a goose you are! Tell me, do you like him?"

"He's an old man, my lady! Hee, hee!"

"Listen to her!" the nurse burst out from the other end of the room. "He isn't forty yet! You mustn't look a gift-horse in the mouth! Marry him and have done with it!"

THE COOK'S WEDDING

"I won't marry him! I won't, I won't!" screamed Pelagia.

"Then you're a donkey, you are! What in the world are you after, anyhow? Any other woman but you would be down on her knees to him, and you say you won't marry him! She's running after Grisha's tutor, she is, my lady; she's setting her cap at him! Ugh, the shameless creature!"

"Had you ever seen this Danilo before to-day?" her mistress asked Pelagia.

"How could I have seen him before to-day? This was the first time. Aksinia picked him up somewhere—bad luck to him! Why must I have him thrown at my head?"

That day the whole family kept their eyes fixed on Pelagia's face as she was serving the dinner and teased her about the driver. Pelagia blushed furiously and giggled with confusion.

"What a shameful thing it must be to get married!" thought Grisha. "What a horribly shameful thing!"

The whole dinner was too salty, blood was oozing from the half-cooked chickens, and, to complete the disaster, Pelagia kept dropping the knives and forks and dishes as if her hands had been a pair of rickety shelves. No one blamed her, however, for every one knew what her state of mind must be.

Once only did papa angrily throw down his napkin and exclaim to mamma:

"What is this craze you have for match-making?

Can't you let them manage it for themselves if they want to get married?"

After dinner the neighbouring cooks and maids kept flitting in and out of the kitchen, and were whispering together there until late in the evening. Heaven knows how they had scented the approaching wedding! Waking up at midnight, Grisha heard his nurse and the cook murmuring together in his nursery behind the curtain. The nurse was trying to convince the cook of something, and the latter was alternately sobbing and giggling. When he fell asleep, Grisha saw in his dreams Pelagia being spirited away by the Evil One and a witch.

Next day quiet reigned once more, and from that time forward life in the kitchen jogged on as if there were no such thing in the world as a driver. Only nurse would don her new shawl from time to time and sally forth for a couple of hours, evidently to a conference, with a serious and triumphant expression on her face. Pelagia and the driver did not see one another, and if any one mentioned his name to her she would fly into a rage and exclaim:

"Bad luck to him! As if I ever thought of him at all—ugh!"

One evening, while Pelagia and the nurse were busily cutting out clothes in the kitchen, mamma came in and said:

"Of course you may marry him, Pelagia, that is your own affair, but I want you to understand that I

THE COOK'S WEDDING

can't have him living here. You know I don't like to have men sitting in the kitchen. Remember that! And I can't ever let you go out for the night."

"What do you take me for, my lady?" screamed Pelagia. "Why do you cast him into my teeth? Let him fuss all he wants to! What does he mean by hanging himself round my neck, the——"

Looking into the kitchen one Sunday morning, Grisha was petrified with astonishment. The room was packed to overflowing; the cooks from all the neighbouring houses were there with the house porter, two constables, a sergeant in his gold lace, and a boy named Filka. This Filka was generally to be found hanging about the wash-house playing with the dogs, but to-day he was washed and brushed and dressed in a gold-tinsel cassock and was carrying an icon in his hands. In the middle of the kitchen stood Pelagia in a new gingham dress with a wreath of flowers on her head. At her side stood the driver. The young couple were flushed and perspiring, and were blinking their eyes furiously.

"Well, it's time to begin," said the sergeant after a long silence.

A spasm passed over Pelagia's features and she began to bawl. The sergeant picked up a huge loaf of bread from the table, pulled the nurse to his side, and commenced the ceremony. The driver approached the sergeant and flopped down on his knees before him, delivering a smacking kiss on his hand. Pelagia went mechanically after him and also flopped down on her knees. At last the outside door opened, a gust of white mist blew into the kitchen, and the assembly streamed out into the courtyard.

"Poor, poor woman!" thought Grisha, listening to the cook's sobs. "Where are they taking her? Why don't papa and mamma interfere?"

After the wedding they sang and played the concertina in the laundry until night. Mamma was annoyed because nurse smelled of vodka and because, with all these weddings, there never was any one to put on the samovar. Pelagia had not come in when Grisha went to bed that night.

"Poor woman, she is crying out there somewhere in the dark," he thought. "And the driver is telling her to shut up!"

Next morning the cook was back in the kitchen again. The driver came in for a few minutes. He thanked mamma, and, casting a stern look at Pelagia, said:

"Keep a sharp eye on her, my lady! And you, too, Aksinia, don't let her alone; make her behave herself. No nonsense for her! And please let me have five roubles of her wages, my lady, to buy myself a new pair of hames."

Here, then, was a fresh puzzle for Grisha! Pelagia had been free to do as she liked and had been responsible to no one, and now suddenly, for no reason at all, along came an unknown man who seemed somehow to

THE COOK'S WEDDING

have acquired the right to control her actions and her property! Grisha grew very sad. He was on the verge of tears and longed passionately to be kind to this woman, who, it seemed to him, was a victim of human violence. He ran into the storeroom, picked out the largest apple he could find there, tiptoed into the kitchen, and, thrusting the apple into Pelagia's hand, rushed back as fast as his legs could carry him.

SHROVE TUESDAY

"HERE, Pavel, Pavel!" Pelagia Ivanovna cried, rousing her husband from a nap. "Do go and help Stepa! He is sitting there crying again over his lessons. It must be something he can't understand."

Pavel Vasilitch got up, made the sign of the cross over his yawning mouth, and said meekly:

"Very well, dear."

The cat sleeping beside him also jumped up, stretched its tail in the air, arched its back, and half-closed its eyes. The mice could be heard scuttling behind the hangings. Having put on his slippers and dressing-gown, Pavel Vasilitch passed into the dining-room all ruffled and heavy with sleep. A second cat that had been sniffing at a plate of cold fish on the window-sill jumped to the floor as he entered, and hid in the cupboard.

"Who told you to go smelling that?" Pavel Vasilitch cried with vexation, covering the fish with a newspaper. "You're more of a pig than a cat!"

A door led from the dining-room into the nursery. There, at a table disfigured with deep gouges and stains, sat Stepa, a schoolboy of ten with tearful eyes

SHROVE TUESDAY

and a petulant face. He was hugging his knees to his chin and swaying backward and forward like a Chinese idol with his eyes fixed angrily on the schoolbook before him.

"So you're learning your lessons, eh?" asked Pavel Vasilitch, yawning and taking his seat at the table beside him. "That's the way, sonny. You've had your play and your nap, and you've eaten your pancakes, and to-morrow will be Lent, a time of repentance; so now you're at work. The happiest day must have an end. What do those tears mean? Are your lessons getting the better of you? It's hard to do lessons after eating pancakes! That's what ails you, little sonny!"

"Why do you laugh at the child?" calls Pelagia Ivanovna from the next room. "Show him how to do his lessons, instead of making fun of him! Oh, what a trial he is! He'll be sure to get a bad mark to-morrow!"

"What is it you don't understand?" asked Pavel Vasilitch of Stepa.

"This here, how to divide these fractions," the boy answered crossly. "The division of fractions by fractions."

"H'm, you little pickle, that's easy, there's nothing about it to understand. You must do the sum right, that's all. To divide one fraction by another you multiply the numerator of the first by the denominator of the second in order to get the numerator of the quotient. Very well. Now the denominator of the first——"

"I know that already!" Stepa interrupted him, flicking a nutshell off the table. "Show me an example."

"An example? Very well, let me have a pencil. Now, then, listen to me. Supposing that we want to divide seven-eighths by two-fifths. Very well, then the proposition is this: we want to divide these two fractions by one another— Is the samovar boiling?"

"I don't know."

"Because it's eight o'clock and time for tea. Very well, now listen to me. Supposing that we divide seven-eighths not by two-fifths, but by two, that is by the numerator only. What is the answer?"

"Seven-sixteenths."

"Splendid! Good boy! Now, then, sonny, the trick is this: as we have divided—let me see—as we have divided it by two, of course—wait a minute, I'm getting muddled myself. I remember when I was a boy at school we had a Polish arithmetic master named Sigismund Urbanitch, who used to get muddled over every lesson. He would suddenly lose his wits while he was in the midst of demonstrating a proposition, blush to the roots of his hair, and rush about the classroom as if the devil were after him. Then he would blow his nose four or five times and burst into tears. But we were generous to him, we used to pretend not

SHROVE TUESDAY 41

to notice it, and would ask him whether he had the toothache. And yet we were a class of pirates, of cutthroats, I can tell you, but, as you see, we were generous. We boys weren't puny like you when I was a youngster; we were great big chaps, you never saw such great strapping fellows! There was Mamakin, for instance, in the third grade. Lord! What a giant he was! Why, that colossus was seven feet high! The whole house shook when he walked across the floor and he would knock the breath out of your body if he laid his hand on your shoulder. Not only we boys, but even the masters feared him. Why Mamakin would sometimes——"

Pelagia Ivanovna's footsteps resounded in the next room. Pavel Vasilitch winked at the door and whispered:

"Mother's coming, let's get to work! Very well, then, sonny," he continued, raising his voice. "We want to divide this fraction by that one. All right. To do that we must multiply the numerator of the first by——"

"Come in to tea!" called Pelagia Ivanovna.

Father and son left their arithmetic and went in to tea. Pelagia Ivanovna was already seated at the dining-table with the silent aunt and another aunt who was deaf and dumb and old granny Markovna, who had assisted Stepa into the world. The samovar was hissing and emitting jets of steam that settled in large, dark shadows upon the ceiling. The cats came in from the hall, sleepy, melancholy, their tails standing straight up in the air.

"Do have some preserves with your tea, Markovna!" said Pelagia Ivanovna turning to the old dame. "Tomorrow will be Lent, so you must eat all you can."

Markovna helped herself to a large spoonful of jam, raised it to her lips, and swallowed it with a sidelong glance at Pavel Vasilitch. Next moment a sweet smile broke over her face, a smile almost as sweet as the jam itself.

"These preserves are perfectly delicious!" she exclaimed. "Did you make them yourself, Pelagia Ivanovna, dearie?"

"Yes, of course, who else could have made them? I do everything myself. Stepa, darling, was your tea too weak for you? Mercy, you've finished it already! Come, hand me your cup, sweetheart, and let me give you some more."

"That young Mamakin I was telling you about, sonny," continued Pavel Vasilitch, turning to Stepa, "couldn't abide our French teacher. 'I'm a gentleman!' he used to exclaim. 'I won't be lorded over by a Frenchman!' Of course he used to be flogged for it, and badly flogged, too. When he knew he was in for a thrashing he used to jump through the window and take to his heels, not showing his nose in school after that for five or six days. Then his mother would go to the head master and beg him for pity's sake to find her Mishka and give the scoundrel a thrashing, but

SHROVE TUESDAY 43

the head master used to say: 'That's all very well, madam, but no five of our men can hold that fellow!'"

"My goodness, what dreadful boys there are in the world!" whispered Pelagia Ivanovna, fixing terrified eyes on her husband. "His poor mother!"

A silence followed—Stepa yawned loudly as he contemplated the Chinaman on the tea-caddy whom he had seen at least a thousand times before. Markovna and the two aunts sipped their tea primly from their saucers. The air was close and oppressive with the heat of the stove. The lassitude that comes to the satiated body when it is forced to continue eating was depicted on the faces and in the movements of the family. The samovar had been taken away and the table had been cleared, but they still continued to sit about the board. Pelagia Ivanovna jumped up from time to time and ran into the kitchen with a look of horror on her face to confer with the cook about supper. The aunts both sat motionless in the same position, dozing with their hands folded on their chests and their lack-lustre eyes fixed on the lamp. Markovna kept hiccoughing every minute and asked each time:

"I wonder what makes me hiccough? I don't know what I could have eaten or drunk—hick!"

Pavel Vasilitch and Stepa leaned over the table side by side with their heads together, poring over the pages of the *Neva Magazine* for the year 1878.

" 'The monument to Leonardo da Vinci in front of

the Victor Emmanuel Museum at Milan.' Look at that, it's like a triumphal arch! And there are a man and a lady, and there are some more little people——"

"That looks like one of the boys at our school," Stepa said.

"Turn over the page— 'The Proboscis of the House Fly as Seen through the Microscope.' Goodness what a fly! I wonder what a bedbug would look like under the microscope, eh? How disgusting!"

The ancient hall clock coughed rather than struck ten times, as if it were afflicted with a cold. Into the dining-room came Anna the cook and fell flop at her master's feet.

"Forgive me my sins, master, for Christ's sake!" she cried and got up again very red in the face.

"Forgive me mine, too, for Christ's sake!" answered Pavel Vasilitch calmly.

Anna then fell down at the feet of every member of the family in turn and asked forgiveness for her sins, omitting only Markovna, who, not being high-born, was unworthy of a prostration.

Another half-hour passed in silence and peace. The *Neva* was tossed aside onto the sofa and Pavel Vasilitch, with one finger raised aloft, was reciting Latin poetry he had learned in his youth. Stepa was watching his father's finger with its wedding-ring and dozing as he listened to the words he could not understand. He rubbed his heavy eyes with his fist but they kept closing tighter and tighter each time.

"I'm going to bed!" he said at last, stretching and yawning.

"What? To bed?" cried Pelagia Ivanovna. "Won't you eat your meat for the last time before Lent?"

"I don't want any meat."

"Have you taken leave of your senses?" his startled mother exclaimed. "How can you say that? You won't have any meat after to-night for the whole of Lent!"

Pavel Vasilitch was startled, too.

"Yes, yes, sonny," he cried. "Your mother will give you nothing but Lenten fare for seven weeks after to-night. This won't do. You must eat your meat!"

"But I want to go to bed!" whimpered Stepa.

"Then bring in the supper quick!" cried Pavel Vasilitch in a flutter. "Anna, what are you doing in there, you old slow-coach? Come quick and bring in the supper!"

Pelagia Ivanovna threw up her hands and rushed into the kitchen as if the house were afire.

"Hurry! Hurry!" rang through the house. "Stepa wants to go to bed! Anna! Oh, heavens, what is the matter? Hurry!"

In five minutes the supper was on the table. The cats appeared once more, stretching and arching their backs, with their tails in the air. The family applied themselves to their meal. No one was hungry, all were surfeited to the point of bursting, but they felt it was their duty to eat.

IN PASSION WEEK

"RUN, the church-bells are ringing! Be a good boy in church and don't play! If you do, God will punish you!"

My mother slipped a few copper coins into my hand and then forgot all about me, as she ran into the kitchen with an iron that was growing cold. I knew I should not be allowed to eat or drink after confession, so before leaving home I choked down a crust of bread and drank two glasses of water. Spring was at its height. The street was a sea of brown mud through which ruts were already in process of being worn; the housetops and sidewalks were dry, and the tender young green of springtime was pushing up through last year's dry grass under the fence rows. Muddy rivulets were babbling and murmuring down the gutters in which the sun did not disdain to lave its rays. Chips, bits of straw, and nutshells were floating swiftly down with the current, twisting and turning and catching on the dirty foam flakes. Whither, whither were they drifting? Would they not be swept from the gutter into the river, from the river into the sea, and from the sea into the mighty ocean? I tried to

IN PASSION WEEK

picture to myself the long and terrible journey before them, but my imagination failed even before reaching the river.

A cab drove by. The cabman was clucking to his horse and slapping the reins, unaware of two street-urchins hanging from the springs of his little carriage. I wanted to join these boys, but straightway remembered that I was on my way to confession, whereupon the boys appeared to me to be very wicked sinners indeed.

"God will ask them on the Last Judgment Day why they played tricks on a poor cabman," I thought. "They will begin to make excuses, but the devil will grab them and throw them into eternal fire. But if they obey their fathers and mothers and give pennies and bread to the beggars, God will have mercy on them and will let them into Paradise."

The church porch was sunny and dry. Not a soul was there; I opened the church door irresolutely and entered the building. There, in the dim light more fraught with melancholy and gloom for me than ever before, I became overwhelmed by the consciousness of my wickedness and sin. The first object that met my sight was a huge crucifixion with the Virgin and St. John the Baptist on either side of the cross. The lustres and shutters were hung with mourning black, the icon lamps were glimmering faintly, and the sun seemed to be purposely avoiding the church windows. The Mother of God and the favourite Disciple were depicted in profile silently gazing at that unutterable agony upon the cross, oblivious of my presence. I felt that I was a stranger to them, paltry and vile; that I could not help them by word or deed; that I was a horrid, worthless boy, fit only to chatter and be naughty and rough. I called to mind all my acquaintances, and they all seemed to me to be trivial and silly and wicked, incapable of consoling one atom the terrible grief before me. The murky twilight deepened, the Mother of God and John the Baptist seemed very lonely.

Behind the lectern where the candles were sold stood the old soldier Prokofi, now churchwarden's assistant.

His eyebrows were raised and he was stroking his beard and whispering to an old woman.

"The service will begin directly after vespers this evening. There will be prayers after matins to-morrow at eight o'clock. Do you hear me? At eight o'clock."

Between two large pillars near the rood-screen the penitents were standing in line waiting their turn for confession. Among them was Mitka, a ragged little brat with an ugly, shaven head, protruding ears, and small, wicked eyes. He was the son of Nastasia the washerwoman, and was a bully and a thief who filched apples from the fruit-stalls and had more than once made away with my knuckle-bones. He was now staring crossly at me and seemed to be exulting in the fact that he was going to confession before me. My

IN PASSION WEEK   49

heart swelled with rage and I tried not to look at him. From the bottom of my soul I was furious that this boy's sins were about to be forgiven.

In front of him stood a richly dressed lady with a white plume in her hat. Clearly she was deeply agitated and tensely expectant, and one of her cheeks was burning with a feverish flush.

I waited five minutes, ten minutes—then a well-dressed young man with a long, thin neck came out from behind the screen. He had on high rubber goloshes, and I at once began dreaming of the day when I should buy a pair of goloshes like his for myself. I decided that I would certainly do so. And now came the lady's turn. She shuddered and went behind the screen.

Through a crack I could see her approach the altar, prostrate herself, rise, and bow her head expectantly without looking at the priest. The priest's back was turned toward the screen, and all I could see of him was his broad shoulders, his curly grey hair, and the chain around his neck from which a cross was suspended. Sighing, without looking at the lady, he began nodding his head and whispering rapidly, now raising, now lowering his voice. The lady listened meekly, guiltily almost, with downcast eyes, and answered him in a few words.

"What can be her sin?" I wondered, looking reverently at her beautiful, gentle face. "Forgive her, God, and make her happy!"

But now the priest was covering her head with the stole.

"I, Thy unworthy servant," his voice rang out, "by the power vouchsafed me, forgive this woman and absolve her from sin——"

The lady prostrated herself once more, kissed the cross, and retired. Both her cheeks were flushed now, but her face was calm, and unclouded, and joyous.

"She is happy now," I thought, my eye wandering from her to the priest pronouncing the absolution. "But how happy he must be who is able to forgive sin!"

It was Mitka's turn next, and my heart suddenly boiled over with hatred for the little thief. I wanted to go behind the screen ahead of him, I wanted to be first. Mitka noticed the movement, and hit me on the head with a candle. I paid him back in his own coin, and for a moment sounds of panting and the breaking of candles were heard in the church. We were forcibly parted, and my enemy nervously and stiffly approached the altar and bowed to the ground, but what happened after that I was unable to see. All I could think of was that I was going next, after Mitka, and at that thought the objects around me danced and swam before my eyes. Mitka's protruding ears grew larger than ever and melted into the back of his neck, the priest swayed, and the floor rocked under my feet.

The priest's voice rang out:

"I, Thy unworthy servant——"

IN PASSION WEEK 51

I found myself moving toward the screen. My feet seemed to be treading on air. I felt as if I were floating. I reached the altar, which was higher than my head. The weary, dispassionate face of the priest flashed for a moment across my vision, but after that I saw only his blue-lined sleeves and one corner of the stole. I felt his near presence, smelled the odour of his cassock, and heard his stern voice, and the cheek that was turned toward him began to burn. I lost much of what he said from excitement, but I answered him earnestly, in a voice that sounded to me as if it were not my own. I thought of the lonely Mother of God, and the Disciple, and the crucifixion, and my mother, and wanted to cry and ask for forgiveness.

"What is your name?" asked the priest, laying the stole over my head.

How relieved I now felt, and how light of heart! My sins were gone, I was sanctified. I could enter into Paradise. It seemed to me that I exhaled the same odour as the priest's cassock, and I sniffed my sleeve as I came out from behind the screen and went to the deacon to register. The dim half-light of the church no longer struck me as gloomy, and I could now look calmly and without anger at Mitka.

"What is your name?" asked the deacon.

"Fedia."

"Fedia, what?"

"I don't know."

"What is your daddy's name?"

"Ivan."

"And his other name?"

I was silent.

"How old are you?"

"Nine years old."

On reaching home I went straight to bed to avoid seeing my family at supper. Shutting my eyes, I lay thinking of how glorious it would be to be martyred by Herod or some one; to live in a desert feeding bears like the hermit Seraphim; to pass one's life in a cell with nothing to eat but wafers; to give away all one possessed to the poor; to make a pilgrimage to Kief. I could hear them laying the table in the dining-room; supper would soon be ready! There would be pickles and cabbage pasties and baked fish—oh, how hungry I was! I now felt willing to endure any torture whatsoever, to live in the desert without my mother, feeding bears out of my own hands, if only I could have just one little cabbage pasty first!

"Purify my heart, O God!" I prayed, pulling the bedclothes up over my head. "O guardian angels, save me from sin!"

Next morning, Thursday, I woke with a heart as serene and joyful as a spring day. I walked gaily and manfully to church, conscious that I was now a communicant and that I was wearing a beautiful and expensive shirt made from a silk dress left me by my grandmamma. Everything in church spoke of joy and happiness and springtime. The Mother of God and

John the Baptist looked less sad than they had the evening before, and the faces of the communicants were radiant with anticipation. The past, it seemed was all forgiven and forgotten. Mitka was there, washed and dressed in his Sunday best. I looked cheerfully at his protruding ears, and, to show that I bore him no malice, I said:

"You look fine to-day. If your hair didn't stick up so and you weren't so poorly dressed one might almost think your mother was a lady instead of a washerwoman. Come and play knuckle-bones with me on Easter Day!"

Mitka looked suspiciously at me and secretly threatened me with his fist.

The lady of yesterday was radiantly beautiful. She wore a light-blue dress fastened with a large, flashing brooch shaped like a horseshoe.

I stood and admired her, thinking that when I grew to be a man I should certainly marry a woman like her, but, remembering suddenly that to think of marriage was shameful, I stopped, and moved toward the choir where the deacon was already reading the prayers that concluded the service.

AN INCIDENT

IT was morning. Bright rays of sunlight were streaming into the nursery through the lacy curtain that the frost had drawn across the panes of the windows. Vania, a boy of six with a shaven head and a nose like a button, and his sister Nina, a chubby, curly-haired girl of four, woke from their sleep and stared crossly at one another through the bars of their cribs.

"Oh, shame, shame!" grumbled nursie. "All good folks have had breakfast by now and your eyes are still half-closed!"

The sun's rays were chasing each other merrily across the carpet, the walls, and the tail of nursie's dress, and seemed to be inviting the children to a romp, but they did not notice the sun, they had waked in a bad humour. Nina pouted, made a wry face, and began to whine:

"Tea, nursie, I want my tea!"

Vania frowned and wondered how he could manage to quarrel and so find an excuse to bawl. He was already winking his eyes and opening his mouth when mamma's voice came from the dining-room saying:

"Don't forget to give the cat some milk; she has kittens now!"

Vania and Nina pulled long faces and looked du-

AN INCIDENT

biously at one another; then they both screamed, jumped out of bed, and scampered into the kitchen as they were, barefooted and in their little nightgowns, filling the air with shrill squeals as they ran.

"The cat has kittens! The cat has kittens!" they shrieked.

Under a bench in the kitchen stood a box, the same box which Stepan used for carrying coal when fires were lighted in the fire-places. Out of this box peered the cat. Profound weariness was manifested in her face, and her green eyes with their narrow black pupils wore an expression both languid and sentimental. One could see from her mien that if "he," the father of her children, were but with her, her happiness would be complete. She opened her mouth wide and tried to mew but her throat only emitted a wheezing sound. The squeaking of her kittens came from inside the box.

The children squatted down on their heels near the box, motionless, holding their breath, their eyes riveted on the cat. They were dumb with wonder and amazement and did not hear their nurse as she grumblingly pursued them. Unaffected pleasure shone in the eyes of both.

In the lives and education of children domestic animals play a useful if inconspicuous part. Who does not remember some strong, noble watch-dog of his childhood, some petted spaniel, or the birds that died in captivity? Who does not recall the stupid, arrogant turkeys, and the meek old tabby-cats that were always ready to forgive us even when we stepped on their tails for fun and caused them the keenest pain? I sometimes think that the loyalty, patience, capacity for forgiveness, and fidelity of our domestic animals have a far greater and more potent influence over the minds of children than the long discourses of some pale, prosy German tutor or the hazy explanations of a governess who tries to tell them that water is compounded of oxygen and hydrogen.

"Oh, how tiny they are!" cried Nina, staring at the kittens round-eyed and breaking into a merry peal of laughter— "They look like mice!"

"One, two, three—" counted Vania. "Three kittens. That means one for me and one for you and one for some one else."

"Murrm-murr-r-r-m," purred the cat, flattered at receiving so much attention. "Murr-r-m."

When they were tired of looking at the kittens, the children took them out from under the cat and began squeezing and pinching them; then, not satisfied with this, they wrapped them in the hems of their nightgowns and ran with them into the drawing-room.

Their mother was sitting there with a strange man. When she saw the children come in not dressed, not washed, with their nightgowns in the air she blushed and looked sternly at them.

"For shame! Let your nightgowns down!" she cried. "Go away or else I shall have to punish you!"

But the children heeded neither the threats of their

AN INCIDENT

mother nor the presence of the stranger. They laid the kittens down on the carpet and raised their voices in shrill vociferation. The mother cat roamed about at their feet and mewed beseechingly. A moment later the children were seized and borne off into the nursery to be dressed and fed and to say their prayers, but their hearts were full of passionate longing to have done with these prosaic duties as quickly as possible and to escape once more into the kitchen.

Their usual games and occupations faded into the background.

By their arrival in the world the kittens had eclipsed everything else and had taken their place as the one engrossing novelty and passion of the day. If Vania or Nina had been offered a ton of candy or a thousand pennies for each one of the kittens they would have refused the bargain without a moment's hesitation. They sat over the kittens in the kitchen until the very moment for dinner, in spite of the vigorous protests of their nurse and of the cook. The expression on their faces was serious, absorbed, and full of anxiety. They were worrying not only over the present, but also over the future of the kittens. They decided that one should stay at home with the old cat to console its mother, the second should go to the cottage in the country, and the third should live in the cellar where there were so many rats.

"But why don't they open their eyes?" Nina puzzled. "They are blind, like beggars!"

Vania, too, was perturbed by this phenomenon. He set to work to open the eyes of one of the kittens, and puffed and snuffled over his task for a long time, but the operation proved to be unsuccessful. The children were also not a little worried because the kittens obstinately refused all meat and milk set before them. Their grey mother ate everything that was put under their little noses.

"Come on, let's make some little houses for the kitties!" Vania suggested. "Then they can live in their own separate homes and the old kitty can come and visit them."

They put hat-boxes in various corners of the kitchen, and the kittens were transferred to their new homes. But this family separation proved to be premature. With the same imploring, sentimental look on her face, the cat made the round of the boxes and carried her babies back to their former nest.

"Kitty is their mother," Vania reflected. "But who is their father?"

"Yes, who is their father?" Nina repeated.

"They *must* have a father," both decided.

Vania and Nina debated for a long time as to who should be the father of the kittens. At last their choice fell upon a large dark-red horse with a broken tail who had been thrown into a cupboard under the stairs and there lay awaiting his end in company with other rubbish and broken toys. This horse they dragged forth and set up beside the box.

AN INCIDENT

"Mind now!" the children admonished him. "Stand there and see they behave themselves!"

Shortly before dinner Vania was sitting at the table in his father's study dreamily watching a kitten that lay squirming on the blotting-paper under the lamp. His eyes were following each movement of the little creature and he was trying to force first a pencil and then a match into its mouth. Suddenly his father appeared beside the table as if he had sprung from the floor.

"What's that?" Vania heard him ask in an angry voice.

"It's—it's a little kitty, papa."

"I'll show you a little kitty! Look what you've done, you bad boy, you've messed up the whole blotter!"

To Vania's intense surprise, his papa did not share his affection for kittens. Instead of going into raptures and rejoicing over it with him, he pulled Vania's ear and shouted:

"Stepan! Come and take this nasty thing away!"

At dinner, too, a scandal occurred. During the second course the family suddenly heard a faint squeaking. A search for the cause was made and a kitten was discovered under Nina's apron.

"Nina, leave the table at once!" cried her father angrily. "Stepan, throw the kittens into the slop-barrel this minute! I won't have such filth in the house!"

Vania and Nina were horrified. Apart from its cruelty, death in the slop-barrel threatened to deprive the old cat and the wooden horse of their children, to leave the box deserted, and to upset all their plans for the future, that beautiful future in which one cat would take care of its old mother, one would live in the country, and the third would catch rats in the cellar. The children began to cry and to beg for the lives of the kittens. Their father consented to spare them on condition that the children should under no circumstances go into the kitchen or touch the kittens.

When dinner was over, Vania and Nina roamed disconsolately through the house, pining for their pets. The prohibition to enter the kitchen had plunged them in gloom. They refused candy when it was offered them and were cross and rude to their mother. When their Uncle Peter came in the evening they took him aside and complained to him of their father who wanted to throw the kittens into the slop-barrel.

"Uncle Peter," they begged. "Tell mamma to have the kittens brought into the nursery! Do tell her!"

"All right, all right!" their uncle consented to get rid of them.

Uncle Peter seldom came alone. There generally appeared with him Nero, a big black Dane with flapping ears and a tail as hard as a stick. He was a silent and gloomy dog, full of the consciousness of his own dignity. He ignored the children and thumped them with his

AN INCIDENT

tail as he stalked by them as if they had been chairs. The children cordially hated him, but this time practical considerations triumphed over sentiment.

"Do you know what, Nina?" said Vania, opening his eyes very wide. "Let's make Nero their father instead of the horse! The horse is dead and he is alive."

They waited all the evening for the time to come when papa should sit down to his whist and Nero might be admitted into the kitchen. At last papa began playing. Mamma was busy over the samovar and was not noticing the children—the happy moment had come!

"Come on!" Vania whispered to his sister.

But just then Stepan came into the room and announced with a smile:

"Madame, Nero has eaten the kittens!"

Nina and Vania paled and looked at Stepan in horror.

"Indeed he has!" chuckled the butler. "He has found the box and eaten every one!"

The children imagined that every soul in the house would spring up in alarm and fling themselves upon that wicked Nero. But instead of this they all sat quietly in their places and only seemed surprised at the appetite of the great dog. Papa and mamma laughed. Nero walked round the table wagging his tail and licking his chops with great self-satisfaction. Only the cat was uneasy. With her tail in the air she roamed through the house, looking suspiciously at every one and mewing pitifully.

"Children, it's ten o'clock! Go to bed!" cried mamma.

Vania and Nina went to bed crying and lay for a long time thinking about the poor, abused kitty and that horrid, cruel, unpunished Nero.

A MATTER OF CLASSICS

BEFORE going to take his Greek examination, Vania Ottopeloff devoutly kissed every icon in the house. He felt a load on his chest and his blood ran cold, while his heart beat madly and sank into his boots for fear of the unknown. What would become of him to-day? Would he get a B or a C? He asked his mother's blessing six times over, and, as he left the house, he begged his aunt to pray for him. On his way to school he gave two copecks to a beggar, hoping that these two coins might redeem him from ignorance and that God would not let those numeral nouns with their terrible "Tessarakontas" and "Oktokaidekas" get in his way.

He came back from school late, at five o'clock, and went silently to his room to lie down. His thin cheeks were white and dark circles surrounded his eyes.

"Well? What happened? What did you get?" asked his mother coming to his bedside.

Vania blinked, made a wry face, and burst into tears. Mamma's jaw dropped, she grew pale and threw up her hands, letting fall a pair of trousers which she had been mending.

"What are you crying for? You have failed, I suppose?" she asked.

"Yes, I've—I've been plucked. I got a C."

"I knew that would happen, I had a presentiment that it would!" his mother exclaimed. "The Lord have mercy on us! What did you fail in?"

"In Greek— Oh, mother—they asked me the future of Phero and, instead of answering Oisomai, I answered Opsomai; and then—and then the accent is not used if the last syllable is a diphthong, but—but I got confused, I forgot that the alpha was long and put on the accent. Then we had to decline Artaxerxes and I got muddled and made a mistake in the ablative—so he gave me a C— Oh, I'm the unhappiest boy in the whole world! I worked all last night—I have got up at four every morning this week——"

"No, it is not you who are unhappy, you good-for-nothing boy, it is I! You have worn me as thin as a rail, you monster, you thorn in my flesh, you wicked burden on your parents! I have wept for you, I have broken my back working for you, you worthless trifler, and what is my reward? Have you learned a thing?"

"I—I study—all night—you see that yourself——"

"I have prayed God to send death to deliver me, poor sinner, but death will not come. You bane of my existence! Other people have decent children, but my only child isn't worth a pin. Shall I beat you? I would if I could, but where shall I get the strength to do it? Mother of God, where shall I get the strength?"

Mamma covered her face with the hem of her dress and burst into tears. Vania squirmed with grief and

A MATTER OF CLASSICS

pressed his forehead against the wall. His aunt came in.

"There, now, I had a presentiment of this!" she exclaimed, turning pale and throwing up her hands as she guessed at once what had happened. "I felt low in my mind all this morning; I knew we should have trouble, and here it is!"

"You viper! You bane of my existence!" exclaimed Vania's mother.

"Why do you abuse him?" the boy's aunt scolded the mother, nervously pulling off the coffee-coloured kerchief she wore on her head. "How is he to blame? It is your fault! Yours! Why did you send him to that school? What sort of lady are you? Do you want to climb up among the gentlefolk? Aha! You will certainly get there at this rate! If you had done as I told you, you would have put him into business as I did my Kuzia. There's Kuzia now making five hundred roubles a year. Is that such a trifle that you can afford to laugh at it? You have tortured yourself and tortured the boy with all this book-learning, worse luck to it! See how thin he is! Hear him cough! He is thirteen years old and he looks more like ten."

"No, Nastenka, no, darling, I haven't beaten that tormentor of mine much, and beating is what he needs. Ugh! You Jesuit! You Mohammedan! You thorn in my flesh!" she cried, raising her hand as if to strike her son. "I should thrash you if I had the strength. People used to say to me when he was still little: 'Beat him! Beat him!' But I didn't listen to them, unhappy woman that I am! So now I have to suffer for it. But wait a bit, I'll have your ears boxed! Wait a bit——"

His mother shook her fist at him and went weeping into the room occupied by her lodger, Eftiki Kuporosoff. The lodger was sitting at his table reading "Dancing Self-Taught." This Kuporosoff was considered a clever and learned person. He spoke through his nose, washed with scented soap that made every one in the house sneeze, ate meat on fast-days, and was looking for an enlightened wife; for these reasons he thought himself an extremely intellectual lodger. He also possessed a tenor voice.

"Dear me!" cried Vania's mother, running into his room with the tears streaming down her cheeks. "Do be so very kind as to thrash my boy! Oh, *do* do me that favour! He has failed in his examinations! Oh, misery me! Can you believe it, he has failed! I can't punish him myself on account of being so weak and in bad health, so do thrash him for me! Be kind, be chivalrous and do it for me, Mr. Kuporosoff! Have mercy on a sick woman!"

Kuporosoff frowned and heaved a very deep sigh through his nostrils. He reflected, drummed on the table with his fingers, sighed once more, and went into Vania's room.

"Look here!" he began his harangue. "Your parents are trying to educate you, aren't they, and give

A MATTER OF CLASSICS

you a start in life, you miserable young man? Then why do you act like this?"

He held forth for a long time, he made quite a speech. He referred to science, and to darkness and light.

"Yes, indeed, young man!" he exclaimed from time to time.

When he had concluded, he took off his belt and caught hold of Vania's ear.

"This is the only way to treat you!" he exclaimed.

Vania knelt down obediently and put his head on Kuporosoff's knees. His large pink ears rubbed against Kuporosoff's new brown-striped trousers.

Vania made not a sound. That evening at a family conclave it was decided to put him into business at once.

THE TUTOR

THE high-school boy Gregory Ziboroff condescendingly shakes hands with little Pete Udodoff. Pete, a chubby youngster of twelve with bristling hair, red cheeks, and a low forehead, dressed in a little grey suit, bows and scrapes, and reaches into the cupboard for his books. The lesson begins.

According to an agreement made with Udodoff, the father, Ziboroff is to help Pete with his lessons for two hours each day, in return for which he is to receive six roubles a month. He is preparing the boy for the second grade of the high-school. He prepared him for the first grade last year, but little Pete failed to pass his examinations.

"Very well," begins Ziboroff lighting a cigarette. "You had the fourth declension to study. Decline fructus!"

Peter begins to decline it.

"There, you haven't studied again!" cries Ziboroff rising. "This is the sixth time I have given you the fourth declension to learn, and you can't get it through your head! For heaven's sake, when will you ever begin to study your lessons?"

"What, you haven't studied again?" exclaims a

THE TUTOR

wheezing voice in the next room and Pete's papa, a retired civil servant, enters. "Why haven't you studied? Oh, you little donkey! Just think, Gregory, I had to thrash him again yesterday!"

Sighing profoundly, Udodoff sits down beside his son and opens the boy's ragged grammar. Ziboroff begins examining Pete before his father, thinking to himself: "I'll just show that stupid father what a stupid son he has!" The high-school boy is seized with the fury of the examiner and is ready to beat the little red-cheeked numskull before him, he hates and despises him so. He is even annoyed when the youngster hits on the right answer to one of his questions. How odious this little Pete seems to him!

"You don't even know the second declension! You don't even know the first! This is the way you learn your lessons! Come, tell me, what is the vocative of meus filius?"

"The vocative of meus filius? Why the vocative of meus filius is—it is——"

Pete stares hard at the ceiling and moves his lips inaudibly. No answer comes.

"What is the dative of dea?"

"Deabus—filiabus!" Pete bursts out.

Old Udodoff nods approvingly. The high-school boy, who was not expecting a correct answer, feels annoyed.

"What other nouns have their dative in abus?" he asks.

It appears that anima, the soul, has its dative in abus, something that is not to be found in any grammar.

"What a melodious language Latin is!" observes Udodoff. "Alontron—bonus—anthropos—how marvellous! It is all very important!" he concludes with a sigh.

"The old brute is interrupting the lesson," thinks Ziboroff. "Sitting over us like an inspector—I hate to be bossed! Now, then!" he cries to Pete. "You must learn that same lesson over again for next time. Next we'll do some arithmetic. Fetch your slate! I want you to do this problem."

Pete spits on his slate and rubs it dry with his sleeve. His tutor picks up the arithmetic and dictates the following problem to him.

"'If a merchant buys 138 yards of cloth, some of which is black and some blue, for 540 roubles, how many yards of each did he buy if the blue cloth cost 5 roubles a yard and the black cloth 3?' Repeat what I have just said."

Peter repeats the problem and instantly and silently begins to divide 540 by 138.

"What are you doing? Wait a moment! No, no, go ahead! Is there a remainder? There ought not to be. Here, let me do it!"

Ziboroff divides 540 by 138, and finds that it goes three times and something over. He quickly rubs out the sum.

"How queer!" he thinks, ruffling his hair and flushing. "How should it be done? H'm—this is an indeterminate equation and not a sum in arithmetic at all——"

The tutor looks in the back of the book and finds that the answer is 75 and 63.

"H'm—that's queer. Ought I to add 5 and 3 and divide 540 by 8? Is that right? No that's not it. Come, do the sum!" he says to Pete.

"What's the matter with you? That's an easy problem!" cries Udodoff to Peter. "What a goose you are, sonny! Do it for him, Mr. Ziboroff!"

Gregory takes the pencil and begins figuring. He hiccoughs and flushes and pales.

"The fact is, this is an algebraical problem," he says. "It ought to be solved with x and y. But it can be done in this way, too. Very well, I divide this by this, do you understand? Now then, I subtract it from this, see? Or, no, let me tell you, suppose you do this sum yourself for to-morrow. Think it out alone!"

Pete smiles maliciously. Udodoff smiles, too. Both realize the tutor's perplexity. The high-school boy becomes still more violently embarrassed, rises, and begins to walk up and down.

"That sum can be done without the help of algebra," says Udodoff, sighing and reaching for the counting board. "Look here!"

He rattles the counting board for a moment, and produces the answer 75 and 63, which is correct.

"That's how we ignorant folks do it."

The tutor falls a prey to the most unbearably painful sensations. He looks at the clock with a sinking heart, and sees that it still lacks an hour and a quarter to the end of the lesson. What an eternity that is!

"Now we will have some dictation," he says.

After the dictation comes a lesson in geography; after that, Bible study; after Bible study, Russian—there is so much to learn in this world! At last the two hours' lesson is over, Ziboroff reaches for his cap, condescendingly shakes hands with little Pete, and takes his leave of Udodoff.

"Could you let me have a little money to-day?" he asks timidly. "I must pay my school bill to-morrow. You owe me for six months' lessons."

"Oh, do I really? Oh, yes, yes—" mutters Udodoff. "I would certainly let you have the money with pleasure, but I'm sorry to say I haven't any just now. Perhaps in a week—or two."

Ziboroff acquiesces, puts on his heavy goloshes, and goes out to give his next lesson.

OUT OF SORTS

SIMON PRATCHKIN, a commissioner of the rural police, was walking up and down the floor of his room trying to smother a host of disagreeable sensations. He had gone to see the chief of police on business the evening before, and had unexpectedly sat down to a game of cards at which he had lost eight roubles. The amount was a trifle, but the demons of greed and avarice were whispering in his ear the accusation that he was a spendthrift.

"Eight roubles—a mere nothing!" cried Pratchkin, trying to drown the voices of the demons. "People often lose more than that without minding it at all. Besides, money is made to spend. One trip to the factory, one visit to Piloff's tavern, and eight roubles would have been but a drop in a bucket!"

"It is winter; horse and peasant——"

monotonously murmured Pratchkin's son Vania, in the next room.

"Down the road triumphant go—triumphant go——"

"Triumphant!" Pratchkin went on, pursuing the train of his thoughts. "If he had been stuck for a dozen roubles he wouldn't have been so triumphant! What is he so triumphant about? Let him pay his debts on time! Eight roubles—what a trifle! That's not eight thousand roubles. One can always win eight roubles back again."

> "And the pony trots his swiftest
> For he feels the coming snow—
> For he feels the coming snow."

"Well, he wouldn't be likely to go at a gallop, would he? Was he supposed to be a race-horse? He was a hack, a broken-down old hack! Foolish, drunken peasants always want to go at breakneck speed, and then, when they fall into an ice-hole, or down a precipice, some one has to haul them out and doctor them. If I had my way, I'd prescribe a kind of turpentine for them that they wouldn't forget in a hurry! And why did I lead a low card? If I had led the ace of clubs, I wouldn't have fallen into a hole myself——"

> "O'er the furrows soft and crumbling
> Flies the sleigh so free and wild—
> O'er the furrows soft and crumbling——"

"Crumbling—crumbling furrows—what stuff that is! People will let those writers scribble anything. It was that ten-spot that made all the trouble. Why the devil did it have to turn up just at that moment?"

> "When a little boy comes tumbling—comes tumbling
> Down the road a merry child—a merry child."

"If the boy was running he must have been overeating himself and been naughty. Parents never will put their children to work. Instead of playing, that boy ought to have been splitting kindling, or reading the Bible—and I hadn't the sense to come away! What an ass I was to stay after supper! Why didn't I have my meal and go home?"

"At the window stands his mother,
  Shakes her finger—shakes her finger at the boy——"

"She shakes her finger at him, does she? The trouble with her is, she is too lazy to go out-of-doors and punish him. She ought to catch him by his little coat and give him a good spanking. It would do him more good than shaking her finger at him. If she doesn't take care, he will grow up to be a drunkard. Who wrote that?" asked Pratchkin aloud.

"Pushkin, papa."

"Pushkin? H'm. What an ass he is! People like that simply write without knowing themselves what they are saying."

"Papa, here's a peasant with a load of flour!" cried Vania.

"Let some one take charge of it!"

The arrival of the flour failed to cheer Pratchkin. The more he tried to console himself, the more poignant grew his sense of loss, and he regretted those eight roubles as keenly as if they had in reality been eight thousand. When Vania finished studying his lesson and silence fell, Pratchkin was standing gloomily at the window, his mournful gaze fixed upon the snow-drifts in the garden. But the sight of the snowdrifts only opened wider the wound in his breast. They reminded him of yesterday's expedition to the chief of police. His spleen rose and embittered his heart. The need to vent his sorrow reached such a pitch that it would brook no delay. He could endure it no longer.

"Vania!" he shouted. "Come here and let me whip you for breaking that window-pane yesterday!"

STORIES OF YOUTH

A JOKE

IT was noon of a bright winter's day. The air was crisp with frost, and Nadia, who was walking beside me, found her curls and the delicate down on her upper lip silvered with her own breath. We stood at the summit of a high hill. The ground fell away at our feet in a steep incline which reflected the sun's rays like a mirror. Near us lay a little sled brightly upholstered with red.

"Let us coast down, Nadia!" I begged. "Just once! I promise you nothing will happen."

But Nadia was timid. The long slope, from where her little overshoes were planted to the foot of the ice-clad hill, looked to her like the wall of a terrible, yawning chasm. Her heart stopped beating, and she held her breath as she gazed into that abyss while I urged her to take her seat on the sled. What might not happen were she to risk a flight over that precipice! She would die, she would go mad!

"Come, I implore you!" I urged her again. "Don't be afraid! It is cowardly to fear, to be timid."

At last Nadia consented to go, but I could see from her face that she did so, she thought, at the peril of her life. I seated her, all pale and trembling, in the little sled, put my arm around her, and together we plunged into the abyss.

The sled flew like a shot out of a gun. The riven wind lashed our faces; it howled and whistled in our ears, and plucked furiously at us, trying to wrench our heads from our shoulders; its pressure stifled us; we felt as if the devil himself had seized us in his talons, and were snatching us with a shriek down into the infernal regions. The objects on either hand melted into a long and madly flying streak. Another second, and it seemed we must be lost!

"I love you, Nadia!" I whispered.

And now the sled began to slacken its pace, the howling of the wind and the swish of the runners sounded less terrible, we breathed again, and found ourselves at the foot of the mountain at last. Nadia, more dead than alive, was breathless and pale. I helped her to her feet.

"Not for anything in the world would I do that again!" she said, gazing at me with wide, terror-stricken eyes. "Not for anything on earth. I nearly died!"

In a few minutes, however, she was herself again, and already her inquiring eyes were asking the question of mine:

"Had I really uttered those four words, or had she only fancied she heard them in the tumult of the wind?"

I stood beside her smoking a cigarette and looking attentively at my glove.

She took my arm and we strolled about for a long time at the foot of the hill. It was obvious that the riddle gave her no peace. Had I spoken those words or not? It was for her a question of pride, of honour, of happiness, of life itself, a very important question, the most important one in the whole world. Nadia looked at me now impatiently, now sorrowfully, now searchingly; she answered my questions at random and waited for me to speak. Oh, what a pretty play of expression flitted across her sweet face! I saw that she was struggling with herself; she longed to say something, to ask some question, but the words would not come; she was terrified and embarrassed and happy.

"Let me tell you something," she said, without looking at me.

"What?" I asked.

"Let us—let us slide down the hill again!"

We mounted the steps that led to the top of the hill. Once more I seated Nadia, pale and trembling, in the little sled, once more we plunged into that terrible abyss; once more the wind howled, and the runners hissed, and once more, at the wildest and most tumultuous moment of our descent, I whispered:

"I love you, Nadia!"

When the sleigh had come to a standstill, Nadia threw a backward look at the hill down which we had just sped, and then gazed for a long time into my face, listening to the calm, even tones of my voice. Every inch of her, even her muff and her hood, every line of her little frame expressed the utmost uncertainty. On her face was written the question:

"What can it have been? Who spoke those words? Was it he, or was it only my fancy?"

The uncertainty of it was troubling her, and her patience was becoming exhausted. The poor girl had stopped answering my questions, she was pouting and ready to cry.

"Had we not better go home?" I asked.

"I—I love coasting!" she answered with a blush. "Shall we not slide down once more?"

She "loved" coasting, and yet, as she took her seat on the sled, she was as trembling and pale as before and scarcely could breathe for terror!

We coasted down for the third time and I saw her watching my face and following the movements of my lips with her eyes. But I put my handkerchief to my mouth and coughed, and when we were half-way down I managed to say:

"I love you, Nadia!"

So the riddle remained unsolved! Nadia was left pensive and silent. I escorted her home, and as she walked she shortened her steps and tried to go slowly, waiting for me to say those words. I was aware of the struggle going on in her breast, and of how she was forcing herself not to exclaim:

"The wind could not have said those words! I don't want to think that it said them!"

Next day I received the following note:

"If you are going coasting, to-day, call for me. N."

Thenceforth Nadia and I went coasting every day, and each time that we sped down the hill on our little sled I whispered the words:

"I love you, Nadia!"

Nadia soon grew to crave this phrase as some people crave morphine or wine. She could no longer live without hearing it! Though to fly down the hill was as terrible to her as ever, danger and fear lent a strange fascination to those words of love, words which remained a riddle to torture her heart. Both the wind and I were suspected; which of us two was confessing our love for her now seemed not to matter; let the draught but be hers, and she cared not for the goblet that held it!

One day, at noon, I went to our hill alone. There I perceived Nadia. She approached the hill, seeking me with her eyes, and at last I saw her timidly mounting the steps that led to the summit. Oh, how fearful, how terrifying she found it to make that journey alone! Her face was as white as the snow, and she shook as if she were going to her doom, but up she climbed, firmly, without one backward look. Clearly she had determined to discover once for all whether those wondrously sweet words would reach her ears if I were not there. I saw her seat herself on the sled with a pale face and lips parted with horror, saw her shut her eyes and push off, bidding farewell for ever to this world. "zzzzzzz!" hissed the runners. What did she hear? I know not—I only saw her rise tired and trembling from the sled, and it was clear from her expression that she could not herself have said what she had heard; on her downward rush terror had robbed her of the power of distinguishing the sounds that came to her ears.

And now, with March, came the spring. The sun's rays grew warmer and brighter. Our snowy hillside grew darker and duller, and the ice crust finally melted away. Our coasting came to an end.

Nowhere could poor Nadia now hear the beautiful words, for there was no one to say them; the wind was silent and I was preparing to go to St. Petersburg for a long time, perhaps for ever.

One evening, two days before my departure, I sat in the twilight in a little garden separated from the garden where Nadia lived by a high fence surmounted by iron spikes. It was cold and the snow was still on the ground, the trees were lifeless, but the scent of spring was in the air, and the rooks were cawing noisily as they settled themselves for the night. I approached the fence, and for a long time peered through a chink in the boards. I saw Nadia come out of the house and stand on the door-step, gazing with anguish and longing at the sky. The spring wind was blowing directly into her pale, sorrowful face. It reminded her of the wind that had howled for us on the hillside when she had heard those four words, and with that recollection her face grew very sad indeed, and the tears rolled down her cheeks. The poor child held out her arms as if to implore the wind to bring those words to her ears once more. And I, waiting for a gust to carry them to her, said softly:

"I love you, Nadia!"

Heavens, what an effect my words had on Nadia! She cried out and stretched forth her arms to the wind, blissful, radiant, beautiful. . . .

And I went to pack up my things. All this happened a long time ago. Nadia married, whether for love or not matters little. Her husband is an official of the nobility, and she now has three children. But she has not forgotten how we coasted together and how the wind whispered to her:

"I love you, Nadia!"

That memory is for her the happiest, the most touching, the most beautiful one of her life.

But as for me, now that I have grown older, I can no longer understand why I said those words and why I jested with Nadia.

AFTER THE THEATRE

WHEN Nadia Zelenia came home with her mother from the theatre, where they had been to see "Evgeni Onegin," and found herself in her own room once more, she took off her dress, loosened her hair, and hastened to sit down at her desk in her petticoat and little white bodice, to write a letter in the style of Tatiana.

"I love you," she wrote, "but you do not, no, you do not love me!"

As she wrote this she began to laugh.

She was only sixteen and had never been in love in her life. She knew that the officer Gorni and the student Gruzdieff both loved her, but now, after seeing the opera, she did not want to believe it. How attractive it would be to be wretched and spurned! It was, somehow, so poetical, so beautiful and touching, when one loved while the other remained cold and indifferent! Onegin was arresting because he did not love Tatiana, but Tatiana was enchanting because she loved so ardently. Had they both loved one another equally well and been happy, might not both have been uninteresting?

"No longer think that you love me," Nadia continued, thinking of Gorni. "I cannot believe it. You

AFTER THE THEATRE

are clever and serious and wise; you are a very talented man, and may have a brilliant future before you. I am a stupid, frivolous girl and you know yourself that I should only hinder you in your life. You were attracted to me, it is true; you thought you had found your ideal in me, but that was a mistake. Already you are asking yourself: why did I ever meet that girl? Only your kindness prevents you from acknowledging this."

Nadia began to feel very sorry for herself, she burst into tears and continued:

"If it were not so hard to leave mamma and my brother, I should take the veil and go away to the ends of the earth. Then you would be free to love some one else."

Nadia's tears now prevented her from seeing what she was writing; little rainbows were trembling across the table, the floor, and the ceiling, and it seemed to her as though she were looking through a prism. To go on writing was impossible, so she threw herself back in her chair and began thinking of Gorni.

Goodness, how attractive, how fascinating men were! Nadia remembered the beautiful expression that came over Gorni's face when he was talking of music. How humble, how engaging, how gentle he then looked, and what efforts he made not to let his voice betray the passion he felt! Emotion must be concealed in society where haughtiness and chilly indifference are the marks of good breeding and a good education, so he would try to hide his feelings, but in vain. Every one knew that he loved music madly. Endless arguments about music and the bold criticisms of Philistines kept his nerves constantly on edge, so that he appeared to be timid and silent. He played the piano beautifully, and if he had not been an officer he would certainly have become a musician.

The tears dried on Nadia's cheeks. She remembered that Gorni had proposed to her at a symphony concert and had later repeated his proposal downstairs by the coat rack, where they were standing in a strong draught.

"I am very glad that you have at last come to know Gruzdieff," she went on. "He is a very clever man and you are sure to be friends. He came to see us yesterday evening and stayed until two. We were all in raptures over him, and I was sorry that you had not come, too. He talked wonderfully."

Nadia laid her arms on the table and rested her head upon them, and her hair fell over the letter. She remembered that Gruzdieff was in love with her, too, and that he had as much right to her letter as Gorni had. On second thoughts, would it not be better to send it to him? A causeless happiness stirred in her breast; at first it was tiny, and rolled gently about there like a small rubber ball; then it grew larger and fuller, and at last gushed up like a fountain. Nadia forgot Gorni and Gruzdieff, and her thoughts grew confused, but her rapture rose and rose, until it flowed

AFTER THE THEATRE

from her breast into her hands and feet, and a fresh, gentle breeze seemed to be fanning her head and stirring her hair. Her shoulders shook with soft laughter; the table shook, the lamp-chimney trembled, and tears gushed from her eyes over the letter. She was powerless to control her laughter, so she hastened to think of something funny to prove that her mirth was not groundless.

"Oh, what a ridiculous poodle!" she cried, feeling a little faint from laughing. "What a ridiculous poodle!"

She remembered that Gruzdieff had romped with their poodle Maxim yesterday after tea, and had told her a story of a very intelligent poodle, who chased a jackdaw around a garden. The jackdaw had turned round while the poodle was chasing him, and said:

"You scoundrel, you!"

Not knowing that it was a trained bird, the poodle had been dreadfully dismayed; he had slunk away in perplexity and had afterward begun to howl.

"Yes, I think I shall have to love Gruzdieff," Nadia decided, and she tore up the letter.

So she began to muse on the student, and on his love and hers, but her thoughts were soon rambling, and she found herself thinking of many things: of her mother, of the street, of the pencil, and of the piano. . . . She thought of all this with pleasure, and everything seemed to her to be beautiful and good, but her happiness told her that this was not all, there was a great deal more to come in a little while, which would be much better even than this. Spring would soon be here, and then summer would come, and she would go with her mother to Gorbiki, and there Gorni would come on his holidays, and would take her walking in the garden and make love to her.

Gruzdieff would come, too; he would play croquet and bowls with her, and tell her funny and thrilling stories. She longed for the garden, the darkness, the clear sky, and the stars. Once more her shoulders shook with laughter; the room seemed to her to be filled with the scent of lavender, and a twig tapped against the window-pane.

She went across to the bed, sat down, and, not knowing what to do because of the great happiness that filled her heart, she fixed her eyes on the little icon that hung at the head of her bed, and murmured:

"Oh! Lord! Lord! Lord!"

VOLODIA

ONE Sunday evening in spring Volodia, a plain, shy, sickly lad of seventeen, was sitting, a prey to melancholy, in a summer-house on the country place of the Shumikins. His gloomy reflections flowed in three different channels. In the first place, to-morrow, Monday, he would have to take an examination in mathematics. He knew that if he did not pass he would be expelled from school, as he had already been two years in the sixth grade. In the second place, his pride suffered constant agony during his visits to the Shumikins, who were rich people with aristocratic pretensions. He imagined that Madame Shumikin and her nieces looked down upon his mother and himself as poor relations and dependents, and that they made fun of his mother and did not respect her. He had once overheard Madame Shumikin saying on the terrace to her cousin Anna Feodorovna that she was still pretending to be young, and that she never paid her debts and had a great hankering after other people's shoes and cigarettes. Every day Volodia would implore his mother not to go to the Shumikins' again. He painted for her the humiliating rôle which she played among these people, he entreated her and spoke rudely to her, but the spoiled, frivolous woman, who had wasted two fortunes in her day, her own and her husband's, yearned for high life and refused to understand him, so that twice every week Volodia was obliged to accompany her to the hated house.

In the third place, the lad could not free himself for a moment from a certain strange, unpleasant feeling that was entirely new to him. He imagined himself to be in love with Anna Feodorovna, the cousin and guest of Madame Shumikin. Anna Feodorovna was a talkative, lively, laughing little lady of thirty; healthy, rosy, and strong, with plump shoulders, a plump chin, and an eternal smile on her thin lips. She was neither pretty nor young. Volodia knew this perfectly well, and for that very reason he was unable to refrain from thinking of her, from watching her as she bent her plump shoulders over her croquet mallet, or, as she, after much laughter and running up and down-stairs, sank all out of breath into a chair, and with half-closed eyes pretended that she felt a tightness and strangling across the chest. She was married, and her husband was a staid architect who came down into the country once a week, had a long sleep, and then returned to the city. This feeling on Volodia's part began with an unreasoning hatred of the architect, and a sensation of joy whenever he returned to the city.

And now, as he sat in the summer-house thinking about to-morrow's examination and his mother, whom every one laughed at, he felt a great longing to see

Nyuta, as the Shumikins called Anna Feodorovna, and to hear her laughter and the rustling of her dress. This longing did not resemble the pure, poetic love of which he had read in novels, and of which he dreamed every night as he went to bed. It was a strange and incomprehensible thing, and he was ashamed and afraid of it as of something wicked and wrong which he hardly dared to acknowledge even to himself.

"This is not love," he thought. "One does not fall in love with a woman of thirty. It is simply a little intrigue; yes, it is a little intrigue."

Thinking about intrigues, he remembered his invincible shyness, his lack of a moustache, his freckles, his little eyes, and pictured himself standing beside Nyuta. The contrast was impossible. So he hastened to imagine himself handsome and bold and witty, dressed in the latest fashion. . . .

In the very heat of his imaginings, as he sat huddled in a dark corner of the summer-house with his eyes fixed on the ground, he heard light footsteps approaching. Some one was hurrying down the garden path. The footsteps ceased and a figure clad in white gleamed in the doorway.

"Is any one there?" asked a woman's voice.

Volodia recognised the voice and raised his head in alarm.

"Who is there?" asked Nyuta, stepping into the summer-house. "Ah, is it you, Volodia? What are you doing in there? Brooding? How can you always be brooding and brooding? It's enough to drive you crazy!"

Volodia rose and looked at Nyuta in confusion. She was on her way back from the bath-house; a Turkish towel hung across her shoulders, and a few damp locks of hair had escaped from under her white silk kerchief and were clinging to her forehead. She exhaled the cool, damp odour of the river, and the scent of almond soap. The upper button of her blouse was undone, so that her neck and throat were visible to the lad.

"Why don't you say something?" asked Nyuta, looking Volodia up and down. "It is rude not to answer when a lady speaks to you. What a stick-in-the-mud you are, Volodia, always sitting and thinking like some stodgy old philosopher, and never opening your mouth! You have no vim in you, no fire! You are horrid, really! A boy of your age ought to live, and frisk, and chatter, and fall in love, and make love to the ladies."

Volodia stared at the towel which she was holding in her plump, white hand and pondered.

"He won't answer!" cried Nyuta in surprise. "This is too strange, really! Listen to me, be a man! At least smile! Bah! What a horrid dry-as-dust you are!" she laughed. "Volodia, do you know what makes you such a boor? It's because you never make love. Why don't you do it? There are no girls here, I know, but what is to prevent you from making love to a woman? Why don't you make love to me, for instance?"

Volodia listened to her and rubbed his forehead in intense, painful irresolution.

"It is only proud people who never speak and like to be alone," Nyuta continued, pulling his hand down from his forehead. "You are proud, Volodia. Why do you squint at me like that? Look me in the eye, if you please. Now then, stick-in-the-mud!"

Volodia made up his mind to speak. In an effort to smile he stuck out his lower lip, blinked his eyes, and his hand again went to his head.

"I—I love you!" he exclaimed.

Nyuta raised her eyebrows in astonishment and burst out laughing.

"What is this I hear?" she chanted as singers do in an opera when they hear a terrible piece of news. "What? What did you say? Say it again! Say it again!"

"I—I love you!" Volodia repeated.

And involuntarily, without premeditation and not realising what he was doing, he took a step toward Nyuta and seized her arm above the wrist. Tears started into his eyes, and the whole world seemed to turn into a huge Turkish towel smelling of the river.

"Bravo, bravo!" he heard a laughing voice cry approvingly. "Why don't you say something? I want to hear you speak! Now, then!"

Seeing that he was permitted to hold her arm,

Volodia looked into Nyuta's laughing face and awkwardly, uneasily, put both arms around her waist, bringing his wrists together behind her back. As he held her thus, she put her hands behind her head showing the dimples in her elbows, and, arranging her hair under her kerchief, she said in a quiet voice:

"I want you to become bright and agreeable and charming, Volodia, and this you can only accomplish through the influence of women. Why, what a horrid cross face you have! You ought to laugh and talk. Honestly, Volodia, don't be a stick! You are young yet; you will have plenty of time for philosophising later on. And now, let me go. I'm in a hurry to get back. Let me go, I tell you!"

She freed herself without effort, and went out of the summer-house singing a snatch of song. Volodia was left alone. He smoothed his hair, smiled, and walked three times round the summer-house. Then he sat down and smiled again. He felt an unbearable sense of mortification, and even marvelled that human shame could reach such a point of keenness and intensity. The feeling made him smile again and wring his hands and whisper a few incoherent phrases.

He felt humiliated because he had just been treated like a little boy, and because he was so shy, but chiefly because he had dared to put his arms around the waist of a respectable married woman, when neither his age nor, as he thought, his social position, nor his appearance warranted such an act.

VOLODIA

He jumped up and, without so much as a glance behind him, hurried away into the depths of the garden, as far away from the house as he could go.

"Oh, if we could only get away from here at once!" he thought, seizing his head in his hands. "Oh, quickly, quickly!"

The train on which Volodia and his mother were to go back to town left at eight-forty. There still remained three hours before train time, and he would have liked to have gone to the station at once without waiting for his mother.

At eight o'clock he turned toward the house. His whole figure expressed determination and seemed to be proclaiming: "Come what may, I am prepared for anything!" He had made up his mind to go in boldly, to look every one straight in the face, and to speak loudly no matter what happened.

He crossed the terrace, passed through the drawing-room and the living-room, and stopped in the hall to catch his breath. He could hear the family at tea in the adjoining dining-room; Madame Shumikin, his mother, and Nyuta were discussing something with laughter.

Volodia listened.

"I assure you I could scarcely believe my eyes!" Nyuta cried. "I hardly recognised him when he began to make love to me, and actually—will you believe it?—put his arms around my waist! He has quite a way with him! When he told me that he loved me, he had the look of a wild animal, like a Circassian."

"You don't say so!" cried his mother, rocking with long shrieks of laughter. "You don't say so! How like his father he is!"

Volodia jumped back, and rushed out into the fresh air.

"How can they all talk about it?" he groaned, throwing up his arms and staring with horror at the sky. "Aloud, and in cold blood, too! And mother laughed! Mother! Oh, God, why did you give me such a mother? Oh, why?"

But enter the house he must, happen what might. He walked three times round the garden, and then, feeling more composed, he went in.

"Why didn't you come in to tea on time?" asked Madame Shumikin sternly.

"Excuse me, it—it is time for me to go—" Volodia stammered, without raising his eyes. "Mother, it is eight o'clock!"

"Go along by yourself, dear," answered his mother languidly. "I am spending the night here with Lily. Good-by, my boy, come, let me kiss you."

She kissed her son and said in French:

"He reminds one a little of Lermontov, doesn't he?"

Volodia managed to take leave of the company somehow without looking any one in the face, and ten minutes later he was striding along the road to the station, glad to be off at last. He now no longer felt frightened or ashamed, and could breathe deeply and freely once more.

Half a mile from the station he sat down on a stone by the wayside and began looking at the sun, which was now half hidden behind the horizon. A few small lights were already gleaming here and there near the station, and a dim green ray shone out, but the train had not yet appeared. It was pleasant to sit there quietly, watching the night slowly creeping across the fields. The dim summer-house, Nyuta's light footsteps, the smell of the bath-house, her laughter, and her waist—all these things rose up before Volodia's fancy with startling vividness, and now no longer seemed terrible and significant to him as they had a few hours before.

"What nonsense! She did not pull her hand away; she laughed when I put my arm around her waist," he thought. "Therefore she must have enjoyed it. If she had not liked it she would have been angry——"

Volodia was vexed now at not having been bolder. He regretted that he was stupidly running away, and was convinced that, were the same circumstances to occur again, he would be more manly and look at the thing more simply——

But it would not be hard to bring those circumstances about. The Shumikins always strolled about the garden for a long time after supper. If Volodia were to go walking with Nyuta in the dark—there would be the chance to re-enact the same scene!

"I'll go back and leave on an early train to-morrow morning," he decided. "I'll tell them I missed this train."

So he went back. Madame Shumikin, his mother, Nyuta, and one of the nieces were sitting on the terrace playing cards. When Volodia told them his story about having missed the train they were uneasy lest he should be late for his examination, and advised him to get up early next morning. Volodia sat down at a little distance from the card-players, and during the whole game kept his eyes fixed on Nyuta. He had already determined on a plan. He would go up to Nyuta in the dark, take her hand, and kiss her. It would not be necessary for either to speak; they would understand one another without words.

But the ladies did not go walking after supper; they continued their game instead. They played until one o'clock, and then all separated for the night.

"How stupid this is!" thought Volodia, with annoyance. "But never mind, I'll wait until to-morrow. To-morrow in the summer-house—never mind!"

He made no effort to go to sleep, but sat on the edge of his bed with his arms around his knees and thought. The idea of the examination was odious to him. He had already made up his mind that he was going to be expelled, and that there was nothing terrible about that. On the contrary, it was a good thing, a very good thing. To-morrow he would be as free as a bird. He would leave off his schoolboy's uniform for civilian clothes, smoke in public, and come over here to make love to Nyuta whenever he liked. He would be a young man. As for what people called his career and his future, that was perfectly clear. Volodia would not enter the government service, but would become a telegraph operator or have a drug store, and become a pharmaceutist. Were there not plenty of careers open to a young man? An hour passed, two hours passed, and he was still sitting on the edge of his bed and thinking——

At three o'clock, when it was already light, his door was cautiously pushed open and his mother came into the room.

"Aren't you asleep yet?" she asked with a yawn. "Go to sleep, go to sleep. I've just come in for a moment to get a bottle of medicine."

"For whom?"

"Poor Lily is ill again. Go to sleep, child, you have an examination to-morrow."

She took a little bottle out of the closet, held it to the window, read the label, and went out.

"Oh, Maria, that isn't it!" he heard a woman's voice exclaim. "That is Eau de Cologne, and Lily wants morphine. Is your son awake? Do ask him to find it!"

The voice was Nyuta's. Volodia's heart stopped beating. He hastily put on his trousers and coat and went to the door.

"Do you understand? I want morphine!" explained Nyuta in a whisper. "It is probably written in Latin. Wake Volodia, he will be able to find it!"

Volodia's mother opened the door, and he caught sight of Nyuta. She was wearing the same blouse she had worn when she came from the bath-house. Her hair was hanging loose, and her face looked sleepy and dusky in the dim light.

"There, Volodia is awake!" she exclaimed. "Volodia, do get me the morphine out of the closet, there's a good boy. What a nuisance Lily is! She always has something the matter with her."

The mother murmured something, yawned, and went away.

"Come, find it!" cried Nyuta. "What are you standing there for?"

Volodia went to the closet, knelt down, and began searching among the bottles of medicine and pill-boxes there. His hands were trembling and cold chills were running down his chest and back. He aimlessly seized bottles of ether, carbolic acid, and various boxes of herbs in his shaking hands, spilling and scattering the contents. The smell overpowered him and made his head swim.

"Mother has gone—" he thought. "That's good—good."

"Hurry!" cried Nyuta.

"Just a moment—there, this must be it!" said Volodia having deciphered the letters "morph—" on one of the labels. "Here it is!"

Nyuta was standing in the doorway with one foot in the hall and one in Volodia's room. She was twisting up her hair—which was no easy matter, for it was long and thick—and was looking vacantly at Volodia. In the dim radiance shed by the white, early morning sky, with her full blouse and her flowing hair, she looked to him superb and entrancing. Fascinated, trembling from head to foot, and remembering with delight how he had embraced her in the summer-house, he handed her the bottle and said:

"You are——"

"What?" she asked smiling.

He said nothing; he looked at her, and then, as he had done in the summer-house, he seized her hand.

"I love you—" he whispered.

Volodia felt as if the room and Nyuta, and the dawn, and he himself had suddenly rushed together into a keen, unknown feeling of happiness for which he was ready to give his whole life and lose his soul for ever, but half a minute later it all suddenly vanished.

"Well, I must go—" said Nyuta, looking contemptuously at Volodia. "What a pitiful, plain boy you are— Bah, you ugly duckling!"

How hideous her long hair, her full blouse, her footsteps and her voice now seemed to him!

"Ugly duckling!" he thought. "Yes, I am indeed ugly—everything is ugly."

The sun rose; the birds broke into song; the sound of the gardener's footsteps and the creaking of his wheelbarrow rose from the garden. The cows lowed and the notes of a shepherd's pipe trembled in the air. The sunlight and all these manifold sounds proclaimed that somewhere in the world there could be found a life that was pure, and gracious, and poetic. Where was it? Neither Volodia's mother, nor any one of the people who surrounded the boy had ever spoken of it to him.

When the man servant came to call him for the morning train, he pretended to be asleep.

"Oh, to thunder with it all!" he thought.

He got up at eleven. As he brushed his hair before the mirror he looked at his plain face, so pale after his sleepless night, and thought:

"She is quite right. I really am an ugly duckling."

When his mother saw him and seemed horrified at his not having gone to take his examination, Volodia said:

"I overslept, mamma, but don't worry; I can give them a certificate from the doctor."

Madame Shumikin and Nyuta woke at one o'clock. Volodia heard the former throw open her window with a bang, and heard Nyuta's ringing laugh answer her rough voice. He saw the dining-room door flung open and the nieces and dependents, among whom was his mother, troop in to lunch. He saw Nyuta's freshly washed face, and beside it the black eyebrows and beard of the architect, who had just come.

Nyuta was in Little Russian costume, and this was not becoming to her and made her look clumsy. The architect made some vulgar, insipid jests, and Volodia thought that there were a terrible lot of onions in the stew that day. He also thought that Nyuta was laughing loudly and looking in his direction on purpose to let him understand that the memory of last night did not worry her in the least, and that she scarcely noticed the presence at table of the ugly duckling.

At four o'clock Volodia and his mother drove to the station. The lad's sordid memories, his sleepless night, and the pangs of his conscience aroused in him a feeling of painful and gloomy anger. He looked at his mother's thin profile, at her little nose, and at the rain-coat that had been a gift to her from Nyuta, and muttered:

"Why do you powder your face? It does not become you at all! You try to look pretty, but you don't pay your debts, and you smoke cigarettes that aren't yours! It's disgusting! I don't like you, no, I don't, I don't!"

So he insulted her, but she only rolled her eyes in terror and, throwing up her hands, said in a horrified whisper:

"What are you saying? Heavens, the coachman will hear you! Do hush, he can hear everything!"

"I don't like you! I don't like you!" he went on, struggling for breath. "You are without morals or heart. Don't dare to wear that rain-coat again, do you hear me? If you do, I'll tear it to shreds!"

"Control yourself, child!" wept his mother. "The coachman will hear you!"

"Where is my father's fortune? Where is your own? You have squandered them both. I am not ashamed of my poverty, but I am ashamed of my mother. I blush whenever the boys at school ask me about you."

The village was two stations from town. During the whole journey Volodia stood on the platform of the car, trembling from head to foot, not wanting to go inside because his mother, whom he hated, was sitting there. He hated himself, and the conductor, and the smoke of the engine, and the cold to which he ascribed the shivering fit that had seized him. The heavier his heart grew, the more convinced he became that somewhere in the world there must be people who lived a pure, noble, warm-hearted, gracious life, full of love, and tenderness, and merriment, and freedom. He felt this and suffered so keenly from the thought that one of the passengers looked intently at him, and said:

"You must have a toothache!"

Volodia and his mother lived with a widow who rented a large apartment and let rooms to lodgers. His mother had two rooms, one with windows where her own bed stood, and another adjoining it, which was small and dark, where Volodia lived. A sofa, on which he slept, was the only furniture of this little room; all

the available space was taken up by trunks full of
dresses, and by hat-boxes and piles of rubbish which
his mother had seen fit to collect. Volodia studied his
lessons in his mother's room, or in the "parlour,"
as the large room was called, where the lodgers assembled before dinner and in the evening.

On reaching home, Volodia threw himself down on
his sofa and covered himself with a blanket, hoping
to cure his shivering fit. The hat-boxes, the trunks,
and the rubbish, all proclaimed to him that he had
no room of his own, no corner in which he could take
refuge from his mother, her guests, and the voices
that now assailed his ears from the parlour. His
school satchel and the books that lay scattered about
the floor reminded him of the examination he had
missed. Quite unexpectedly there rose before his
eyes a vision of Mentone, where he had lived with his
father when he was seven years old. He recalled
Biarritz, and two little English girls with whom he had
played on the beach. He vainly tried to remember the
colour of the sky, and the ocean, and the height of the
waves, and how he had then felt; the little English
girls flashed across his vision with all the vividness of
life, but the rest of the picture was confused and
gradually faded away.

"It is too cold here," Volodia thought. He got up,
put on his overcoat, and went into the parlour.

The inmates of the house were assembled there at
tea. His mother, an old maid music teacher with

horn spectacles, and Monsieur Augustin, a fat Frenchman, who worked in a perfume factory, were sitting near the samovar.

"I haven't had dinner to-day," his mother was saying. "I must send the maid for some bread."

"Duniash!" shouted the Frenchman.

It appeared that the maid had been sent on an errand by her mistress.

"Oh, no matter!" said the Frenchman, smiling broadly. "I go for the bread myself! Oh, no matter!"

He laid down his strong, reeking cigar in a conspicuous place, put on his hat, and went out.

When he had gone, Volodia's mother began telling the music teacher of her visit to Madame Shumikin's, and of the enthusiastic reception she had had there.

"Lily Shumikin is a relative of mine, you know," she said. "Her husband, General Shumikin, was a cousin of my husband's. She was the Baroness Kolb before her marriage."

"Mother, that isn't true!" cried Volodia exasperated. "Why do you lie so?"

Now he knew that his mother was not lying, and that in her account of General Shumikin and Baroness Kolb there was not a word of untruth, but he felt none the less as if she were lying. The tone of her voice, the expression of her face, her glance—all were false.

"It's a lie!" Volodia repeated, bringing his fist down on the table with such a bang that the cups and saucers rattled and mamma spilled her tea. "What makes you talk about generals and baronesses? It's all a lie!"

The music teacher was embarrassed and coughed behind her handkerchief, as if she had swallowed a crumb. Mamma burst into tears.

"How can I get away from here?" thought Volodia.

He was ashamed to go to the house of any of his school friends. Once more he unexpectedly remembered the two little English girls. He walked across the parlour and into Monsieur Augustin's room. There the air smelled strongly of volatile oils and glycerine soap. Quantities of little bottles full of liquids of various colours cluttered the table, the window-sills, and even the chairs. Volodia took up a paper and read the heading: "Le Figaro." The paper exhaled a strong and pleasant fragrance. He picked up a revolver that lay on the table.

"There, there, don't mind what he says!" the music teacher was consoling his mother in the next room. "He is still young, and young men always do foolish things. We must make up our minds to that."

"No, Miss Eugenia, he has been spoiled," moaned his mother. "There is no one who has any authority over him, and I am too weak to do anything. Oh, I am very unhappy."

Volodia put the barrel of the revolver into his mouth, felt something which he thought was the trigger, and pulled— Then he found another little hook and pulled again. He took the revolver out of his mouth and examined the lock. He had never held a firearm in his hands in his life.

"I suppose this thing ought to be raised," he thought. "Yes, I think that is right."

Monsieur Augustin entered the parlour laughing and began to recount some adventure he had had on the way. Volodia once more put the barrel into his mouth, seized it between his teeth, and pulled a little hook he felt with his fingers. A shot rang out—something hit him with tremendous force in the back of the neck, and he fell forward upon the table with his face among the bottles and glasses. He saw his father wearing a high hat with a wide silk band, because he was wearing mourning for some lady in Mentone, and felt himself suddenly seized in his arms and fall with him into a very deep, black abyss.

Then everything grew confused and faded away.

A NAUGHTY BOY

IVAN LAPKIN, a youth of pleasing exterior, and Anna Zamblitskaya, a girl with a tip-tilted nose, descended the steep river bank and took their seats on a bench at its foot. The bench stood at the water's edge in a thicket of young willows. It was a lovely spot. Sitting there, one was hidden from all the world and observed only by fish and the daddy-longlegs that skimmed like lightning across the surface of the water. The young people were armed with fishing-rods, nets, cans containing worms, and other fishing appurtenances. They sat down on the bench and immediately began to fish.

"I am glad that we are alone at last," began Lapkin glancing behind him. "I have a great deal to say to you, Miss Anna, a very great deal. When first I saw you—you've got a bite!—I realized at last the reason for my existence. I knew that you were the idol at whose feet I was to lay the whole of an honourable and industrious life—that's a big one biting! On seeing you I fell in love for the first time in my life. I fell madly in love!— Don't pull yet, let it bite a little longer!— Tell me, dearest, I beg you, if I may aspire, not to a return of my affection—no, I am not worthy of that, I dare not even dream of it—but tell me if I may aspire to—pull!" With a shriek, Anna jerked the arm that held the fishing-rod into the air; a little silvery-green fish dangled glistening in the sunlight.

"Goodness gracious, it's a perch! Oh, oh, be quick, it's coming off!"

The perch fell off the hook, flopped across the grass toward its native element, and splashed into the water.

Somehow, while pursuing it, Lapkin accidentally seized Anna's hand instead of the fish and accidentally pressed it to his lips. Anna pulled it away, but it was too late, their lips accidentally met in a kiss. It all happened accidentally. A second kiss succeeded the first, and then followed vows and the plighting of troth. Happy moments! But perfect bliss does not exist on earth, it often bears a poison in itself, or else is poisoned by some outside circumstances. So it was in this case. When the young people had exchanged kisses they heard a sudden burst of laughter. They looked at the river in stupefaction; before them, up to his waist in water, stood a naked boy: it was Kolia, Anna's schoolboy brother! He stood there smiling maliciously with his eyes fixed on the young people.

"Aha! You're kissing one another, are you? All right, I'll tell mamma!"

"I hope that, as an honourable boy—" faltered Lapkin, blushing. "To spy on us is mean, but to sneak is low, base, vile. I am sure that, as a good and honourable boy, you——"

"Give me a rouble and I won't say anything!"

A NAUGHTY BOY

answered the honourable boy. "If you don't, I'll tell on you——"

Lapkin took a rouble from his pocket and gave it to Kolia. The boy seized it in his wet hand, whistled, and swam away. The young couple exchanged no more kisses on that occasion.

Next day Lapkin brought Kolia a box of paints from town and a ball; his sister gave him all her old pill-boxes. They next had to present him with a set of studs with little dogs' heads on them. The bad boy obviously relished the game and began spying on them so as to get more presents. Wherever Lapkin and Anna went, there he went too. He never left them to themselves for a moment.

"The little wretch!" muttered Lapkin grinding his teeth. "So young and yet so great a rascal! What will become of us?"

All through the month of June Kolia tormented the unhappy lovers. He threatened them with betrayal, he spied on them, and then demanded presents; he could not get enough, and at last began talking of a watch. The watch was given him.

Once during dinner, while the waffles were on the table, he burst out laughing, winked, and said to Lapkin:

"Shall I tell them, eh?"

Lapkin blushed furiously and put his napkin into his mouth instead of a waffle. Anna jumped up from the table and ran into another room.

The young people remained in this situation until the end of August when the day at last came on which Lapkin proposed for Anna's hand. Oh, what a joyful day it was! No sooner had he spoken with his sweetheart's parents and obtained their consent to his suit, than Lapkin rushed into the garden in search of Kolia. He nearly wept with exultation on finding him, and caught the wicked boy by the ear. Anna came running up, too, looking for Kolia, and seized him by the other ear. The pleasure depicted on the faces of the lovers when Kolia wept and begged for mercy was well worth seeing.

"Dear, good, sweet angels, I won't do it again! Ouch, ouch! Forgive me!" Kolia implored them.

They confessed afterward that during all their courtship they had never once experienced such bliss, such thrilling rapture, as they did during those few moments when they were pulling the ears of that wicked boy.

BLISS

IT was midnight. Suddenly Mitia Kuldaroff burst into his parents' house, dishevelled and excited, and went flying through all the rooms. His father and mother had already gone to rest; his sister was in bed finishing the last pages of a novel, and his schoolboy brothers were fast asleep.

"What brings you here?" cried his astonished parents. "What is the matter?"

"Oh, don't ask me! I never expected anything like this! No, no, I never expected it! It is—it is absolutely incredible!"

Mitia burst out laughing and dropped into a chair, unable to stand on his feet from happiness.

"It is incredible! You can't imagine what it is! Look here!"

His sister jumped out of bed, threw a blanket over her shoulders, and went to her brother. The schoolboys woke up——

"What's the matter with you? You look like a ghost."

"It's because I'm so happy, mother. I am known all over Russia now. Until to-day, you were the only people who knew that such a person as Dimitri Kuldaroff existed, but now all Russia knows it! Oh, mother! Oh, heavens!"

Mitia jumped up, ran through all the rooms, and dropped back into a chair.

"But what has happened? Talk sense!"

"You live like wild animals, you don't read the news, the press is nothing to you, and yet there are so many wonderful things in the papers! Everything that happens becomes known at once, nothing remains hidden! Oh, how happy I am! Oh, heavens! The newspapers only write about famous people, and now there is something in them about me!"

"What do you mean? Where is it?"

Papa turned pale. Mamma glanced at the icon and crossed herself. The schoolboys jumped out of bed and ran to their brother in their short nightshirts.

"Yes, sir! There is something about me in the paper! The whole of Russia knows it now. Oh, mother, keep this number as a souvenir; we can read it from time to time. Look!"

Mitia pulled a newspaper out of his pocket and handed it to his father, pointing to an item marked with a blue pencil.

"Read that!"

His father put on his glasses.

"Come on, read it!"

Mamma glanced at the icon once more, and crossed herself. Papa cleared his throat, and began:

"At 11 p. m., on December 27, a young man by the name of Dimitri Kuldaroff——"

"See? See? Go on!"

"A young man by the name of Dimitri Kuldaroff, coming out of a tavern on Little Armourer Street, and being in an intoxicated condition——"

"That's it, I was with Simion Petrovitch! Every detail is correct. Go on! Listen!"

"——being in an intoxicated condition, slipped and fell under the feet of a horse belonging to the cabman Ivan Drotoff, a peasant from the village of Durinka in the province of Yuknofski. The frightened horse jumped across Kuldaroff's prostrate body, pulling the sleigh after him. In the sleigh sat Stepan Lukoff, a merchant of the Second Moscow Guild of Merchants. The horse galloped down the street, but was finally stopped by some house porters. For a few moments Kuldaroff was stunned. He was conveyed to the police station and examined by a doctor. The blow which he had sustained on the back of the neck——"

"That was from the shaft, papa. Go on! Read the rest!"

"——the blow which he had sustained on the back of the neck was pronounced to be slight. The victim was given medical assistance."

"They put cold-water bandages round my neck. Do you believe me now? What do you think? Isn't it great? It has gone all over Russia by now! Give me the paper!"

Mitia seized the paper, folded it, and put it into his pocket, exclaiming:

"I must run to the Makaroffs, and show it to them! And the Ivanoffs must see it, too, and Natalia, and Anasim—I must run there at once! Good-bye!"

Mitia crammed on his cap and ran blissfully and triumphantly out into the street.

TWO BEAUTIFUL GIRLS

I

WHEN I was a schoolboy in the fifth or sixth grade, I remember driving with my grandfather from the little village where we lived to Rostoff-on-Don. It was a sultry, long, weary August day. Our eyes were dazzled, and our throats were parched by the heat, and the dry, burning wind kept whirling clouds of dust in our faces. We desired only not to open our eyes or to speak, and when the sleepy Little Russian driver Karpo flicked my cap, as he brandished his whip over his horse, I neither protested nor uttered a sound, but, waking from a half-doze, I looked meekly and listlessly into the distance, hoping to descry a village through the dust. We stopped to feed the horse at the house of a rich Armenian whom my grandfather knew in the large Armenian village of Baktchi-Salak. Never in my life have I seen anything more of a caricature, than our Armenian host. Picture to yourself a tiny, clean-shaven head, thick, overhanging eyebrows, a beak-like nose, a long, grey moustache, and a large mouth, out of which a long chibouk of cherrywood is hanging. This head was clumsily stuck on a stooping little body clothed in a fantastic costume consisting of a bobtailed red jacket and wide, bright blue breeches. The little man walked shuffling his slippers, with his feet far apart. He did not remove his pipe from his mouth when he spoke, and carried himself with true Armenian dignity, staring-eyed and unsmiling, doing his best to ignore his guests as much as possible.

Although there was neither wind nor dust in the Armenian's house, it was as uncomfortable and stifling and dreary in there as it had been on the road across the steppe. Dusty and heavy with the heat, I sat down on a green trunk in a corner. The wooden walls, the furniture, and the floor painted with yellow ochre smelled of dry wood blistering in the sun. Wherever the eye fell, were flies, flies, flies— My grandfather and the Armenian talked together in low voices of pasturage and fertilising and sheep. I knew that it would be an hour before the samovar would be brought, and that grandfather would then drink tea for at least an hour longer, after which he would lie down for a two or three hours' nap. A quarter of the day would thus be spent by me in waiting, after which we would resume the dust, the swelter, and the jolting of the road. I heard the two voices murmuring together, and began to feel as if I had been looking for ever at the Armenian, the china closet, the flies, and the windows through which the hot sun was pouring, and that I should only cease to look at them in the distant future.

I was seized with hatred of the steppe, the sun, and the flies.

A Little Russian woman, with a kerchief on her head, brought in first a tray of dishes, and then the samovar. The Armenian went without haste to the hall door, and called:

"Mashia! Come and pour the tea! Where are you, Mashia?"

We heard hurried footfalls, and a girl of sixteen in a plain cotton dress, with a white kerchief on her head, entered the room. Her back was turned toward me as she stood arranging the tea-things and pouring the tea, and all I could see was that she was slender and barefooted, and that her little toes were almost hidden by her long, full trousers.

Our host invited me to sit down at the table, and when I was seated, I looked into the girl's face as she handed me my glass. As I looked, I suddenly felt as if a wind had swept over my soul, blowing away all the impressions of the day with its tedium and dust. I beheld there the enchanting features of the most lovely face I had ever seen, waking or in my dreams. Before me stood a very beautiful girl; I recognised that at a glance, as one recognises a flash of lightning.

I am ready to swear that Masha—or, as her father called her, Mashia—was really beautiful, but I cannot prove it. Sometimes, in the evening, the clouds lie piled high on the horizon, and the sun, hidden behind them, stains them and the sky with a hundred colours, crimson, orange, gold, violet, and rosy pink. One cloud resembles a monk; another, a fish; a third, a turbaned Turk. The glow embraces one-third of the sky, flashing from the cross on the church, and the windows of the manor-house, lighting up the river and the meadows, and trembling upon the tree tops. Far, far away against the sunset a flock of wild ducks is winging its way to its night's resting-place. And the little cowherd with his cows, and the surveyor driving along the river dyke in his cart, and the inmates of the manor-house strolling in the evening air, all gaze at the sunset, and to each one it is supremely beautiful, but no one can say just where its beauty lies.

Not I alone found the young Armenian beautiful. My grandfather, an octogenarian, stern and indifferent to women and to the beauties of Nature, looked gently at Masha for a whole minute, and then asked:

"Is that your daughter, Avet Nazaritch?"

"Yes, that is my daughter," answered our host.

"She is a fine girl," the old man said heartily.

An artist would have called the Armenian's beauty classic and severe. It was the type of beauty in whose presence you feel that here are features of perfect regularity; that the hair, the eyes, the nose, the mouth, the chin, the neck, the breast, and every movement of the young body are merged into a perfect and harmonious chord, in which Nature has not sounded one false note. You somehow feel that a woman of ideal beauty should have just such a nose as Masha's, slender, with the slightest aquiline curve; just such large, dark eyes and long lashes; just such a languorous glance; that her dusky, curly hair and her black eyebrows match the delicate, tender white tint of her forehead and cheeks as green reeds match the waters of a quiet river. Masha's white throat and young breast were scarcely developed, and yet it seemed as if to chisel them one would have had to possess the highest creative genius. You looked at her, and little by little the longing seized you to say something wonderfully kind to her; something beautiful and true; something as beautiful as the girl herself.

I was hurt and humiliated at first that Masha should keep her eyes fixed on the ground as she did and fail to notice me. I felt as if a strange atmosphere of happiness and pride were blowing between us, sighing jealously at every glance of mine.

"It is because I am all sunburned and dusty," I thought. "And because I am still a boy."

But later I gradually forgot my feelings, and abandoned myself to her beauty heart and soul. I no longer remembered the dust and tedium of the steppe, nor heard the buzzing of the flies; I did not taste the tea, and only felt that there, across the table, stood that lovely girl.

Her beauty had a strange effect upon me. I experienced neither desire, nor rapture, nor pleasure, but a sweet, oppressive sadness, as vague and undefinable as a dream. I was sorry for myself, and for my grandfather, and for the Armenian, and for the girl herself, and felt as if each one of us had lost something significant and essential to our lives, which we could never find again. Grandfather, too, grew sad and no longer talked of sheep and pasturage, but sat in silence, his eyes resting pensively on Masha.

When tea was over, grandfather lay down to take his nap, and I went out and sat on the little porch at the front door. Like all the other houses in Baktchi-Salak, this one stood in the blazing sun; neither trees nor eaves threw any shade about it. The great courtyard, all overgrown with dock and nettles, was full of life and gaiety in spite of the intense heat. Wheat was being threshed behind one of the low wattle fences that intersected it in various places, and twelve horses were trotting round and round a post that had been driven into the middle of the threshing-floor. A Little Russian in a long, sleeveless coat, and wide breeches, was walking beside the horses cracking his whip over them, and shouting as if to excite them, and at the same time to vaunt his mastery over them.

"Ah—ah—ah—you little devils! Ah—ah, the cholera take you! Are you not afraid of me?"

Not knowing why they were being forced to trot round in a circle, trampling wheat straw under their feet, the horses—bay, white and piebald—moved unwillingly and wearily, angrily switching their tails. The wind raised clouds of golden chaff under their hoofs, and blew it away across the fence. Women with rakes were swarming among the tall stacks of fresh straw, tip-carts were hurrying to and fro, and behind the stacks in an adjoining courtyard another dozen horses were trotting around a post, and another Little Russian was cracking his whip and making merry over them.

The steps on which I was sitting were fiery hot, the heat had drawn drops of resin from the slender porch railing and the window-sills, and swarms of ruddy little beetles were crowded together in the strips of shade under the blinds and steps. The sun's rays were beating on my head, and breast, and back, but I was unconscious of them, and only felt that there, behind me, those bare feet were pattering about on the deal floor. Having cleared away the tea things, Masha ran down the steps, a little gust sweeping me as she passed, and flew like a bird into a small, smoky building that was no doubt the kitchen, from which issued a smell of roasting mutton and the angry tones of an Armenian voice. She vanished into the dark doorway, and in her stead there appeared on the threshold an old, humpbacked Armenian crone, in green trousers. The old woman was in a rage, and was scolding some one. Masha soon came out on the threshold again, flushed with the heat of the kitchen, bearing a huge loaf of black bread on her shoulder. Bending gracefully under its weight, she ran across the court in the direction of the threshing-floor, leaped over the fence, and plunged into the clouds of golden chaff. The Little Russian driver lowered his whip, stopped his cries, and gazed after her for a moment; then, when the girl appeared again beside the horses, and jumped back over the fence, he followed her once more with his eyes, and cried to his horses in a tone of affliction:

"Ah—ah—the Evil One fly away with you!"

From then on I sat and listened to the unceasing fall of her bare feet, and watched her whisking about the courtyard, with her face so serious and intent. Now she would run up the steps, fanning me with a whirl of wind; now dart into the kitchen; now across the threshing-floor; now out through the front gate, and all so fast that I could barely turn my head quickly enough to follow her with my eyes.

And the oftener she flashed across my vision with her beauty, the more profound my sadness grew. I pitied myself, and her, and the Little Russian sadly following her with his eyes each time that she ran through the cloud of chaff and past the straw-stacks. Was I envious of her beauty? Did I regret that this girl was not and never could be mine, and that I must for ever remain a stranger to her? Did I dimly realise that her rare loveliness was a freak of nature, vain, perishable like everything else on earth? Or did my sadness spring from a feeling peculiar to every heart at the sight of perfect beauty? Who shall say?

The three hours of waiting passed before I was

aware. It seemed to me that I had scarcely had a chance to look at Masha, before Karpo rode down to the river to wash off his horse, and began to harness up. The wet animal whinnied with delight, and struck the shafts with his hoofs. Karpo shouted "Ba—ack!" Grandfather woke up. Masha threw open the creaking gates; we climbed into our carriage and drove out of the courtyard. We travelled in silence, as if there had been a quarrel between us.

Three hours later, when we could already see Rostoff in the distance, Karpo, who had not spoken since we left the Armenian village, looked round swiftly and said:

"That Armenian has a pretty daughter!"

And as he said this he lashed his horse.

II

Once again, when I was a student in college, I was on my way south by train. It was May. At one of the stations between Byelogorod and Kharkoff, I think it was, I got out of the train to walk up and down the platform.

The evening shadows were already lying on the little garden, the platform, and the distant fields. The sunlight had faded from the station, but by the rosy glow that shone on the highest puffs of steam from our engine we could tell that the sun had not yet sunk beneath the horizon.

As I strolled along the platform I noticed that most

of the passengers had gathered round one of the second-class carriages as if there were some well-known person inside. In that inquisitive crowd I found my travelling companion, a bright young artillery officer, warm-hearted and sympathetic as people are with whom one strikes up a chance acquaintanceship for a few hours on a journey.

"What are you looking at?" I asked.

He did not answer, but motioned me with his eyes toward a female figure standing alongside the train. She was a young girl of seventeen or eighteen, dressed in Russian costume, bareheaded, with a kerchief thrown carelessly over one shoulder. She was not a passenger on the train, but probably the daughter or the sister of the station superintendent. She was chatting at a window with an elderly woman. Before I could realise exactly what I was looking at, I was suddenly overwhelmed by the same sensation that I had experienced in the Armenian village.

The girl was extraordinarily beautiful, of this neither I nor any one of those who were looking at her could have the slightest doubt.

Were I to describe her lineaments in detail, as the custom is, the only really beautiful point I could ascribe to her would be her thick, curly, blond hair, caught up with a black ribbon. Her other features were either irregular or frankly commonplace. Whether from coquetry or short-sightedness, she kept her eyes half closed; her nose was vaguely tip-tilted; her mouth was small; her profile was weak and ill-defined; her shoulders were too narrow for her years. Nevertheless, the girl gave one the impression of being a great beauty, and as I looked at her I grew convinced that the Russian physiognomy does not demand severe regularity of feature to be beautiful; on the contrary, it seemed to me that, had this girl's nose been straight and classic as the Armenian's was, her face would have lost all its comeliness.

As she stood at the window chatting and shrinking from the evening chill, the girl now glanced back at us, now stuck her arms akimbo, now raised her hands to catch up a stray lock of hair, and, as she laughed and talked, the expression on her face varied between surprise and mimic horror. I do not remember one second when her features and body were at rest. The very mystery and magic of her loveliness lay in those indescribably graceful little motions of hers; in her smile; in the play of her features; in her swift glances at us; in the union of delicate grace, youth, freshness, and purity that rang in her voice and laughter. The charm of her was the frailty which we love in children, birds, fawns, and slender saplings.

Hers was the beauty of the butterfly that accords so well with waltzes, with flutterings about a garden, with laughter, and the merriment that admits neither thought, nor sadness, nor repose. It seemed that, should a strong gust of wind blow along the platform, or a shower of rain fall, this fragile figure must crumple to nothing, and this wayward beauty dissolve like the pollen of a flower.

"Well, well, well!" murmured the officer, sighing as we walked toward our compartment after the second starting-bell had rung.

What he meant by that "Well, well, well," I shall not attempt to decide.

Perhaps he was sad at leaving the lovely girl and the spring evening, and returning to the stuffy train, or perhaps he was sorry, as I was, for her, and for himself, and for me, and for all the passengers that were languidly and unwillingly creeping toward their several compartments. As we walked past a window at which a pale, red-haired telegraph operator was sitting over his instrument, the officer, seeing his pompadour curls, and his faded, bony face, sighed again, and said:

"I'll bet you that operator is in love with the little beauty. To live among these lonely fields, under the same roof with that lovely little creature, and not to fall in love with her would be superhuman. And, oh, my friend, what a misfortune, what a mockery, to be a round-shouldered, threadbare, colourless, earnest, sensible man and to fall in love with that beautiful, foolish child, who is not worth a thought from any one! Or, worse still, supposing this operator is in love with her, and at the same time married to a woman as round-shouldered. and threadbare, and colourless, and sensible as himself! What misery!"

Near our compartment the train conductor was

leaning against the platform railing, gazing in the direction of the beautiful girl. His flabby, dissipated, wrinkled face, haggard with the weariness of sleepless nights and the motion of the train, wore an expression of profoundest melancholy, as if in this girl he saw the spectre of his youth, his happiness, his sober ways, his wife, and his children. His heart was full of repentance, and he felt with his whole being that this girl was not for him and that, with his premature old age, his awkwardness, and his bloated face, every-day, human happiness was as far beyond his reach as was the sky.

The third bell clanged, the whistle blew, and the train moved slowly away. Past our windows flashed the conductor, the station superintendent, the garden, and at last the beautiful girl herself with her sweet, childishly cunning smile.

By leaning out of the window and looking back, I could see her walking up and down the platform in front of the window where the telegraph operator was sitting, watching the train and pinning up a stray lock of hair. Then she ran into the garden. The station was no longer kindled by the western light; though the fields were level and bare, the sun's rays had faded from them, and the smoke from our engine lay in black, rolling masses upon the green velvet of the winter wheat. A sense of sadness pervaded the spring air, the darkling sky, and the railway-carriage.

Our friend the conductor came into our compartment and lit the lamp.

LIGHT AND SHADOW

THE CHORUS GIRL

ONE day while she was still pretty and young and her voice was sweet, Nikolai Kolpakoff, an admirer of hers, was sitting in a room on the second floor of her cottage. The afternoon was unbearably sultry and hot. Kolpakoff, who had just dined and drunk a whole bottle of vile port, felt thoroughly ill and out of sorts. Both he and she were bored, and were waiting for the heat to abate so that they might go for a stroll.

Suddenly a bell rang in the hall. Kolpakoff, who was sitting in his slippers without a coat, jumped up and looked at Pasha with a question in his eyes.

"It is probably the postman or one of the girls," said the singer.

Kolpakoff was not afraid of the postman or of Pasha's girl friends, but nevertheless he snatched up his coat and disappeared into the next room while Pasha ran to open the door. What was her astonishment when she saw on the threshold, not the postman nor a girl friend, but an unknown woman, beautiful and young! Her dress was distinguished and she was evidently a lady.

The stranger was pale and was breathing heavily as if she were out of breath from climbing the stairs.

"What can I do for you?" Pasha inquired.

The lady did not reply at once. She took a step forward, looked slowly around the room, and sank into a chair as if her legs had collapsed under her from faintness or fatigue. Her pale lips moved silently, trying to utter words which would not come.

"Is my husband here?" she asked at last, raising her large eyes with their red and swollen lids to Pasha's face.

"What husband do you mean?" Pasha whispered, suddenly taking such violent fright that her hands and feet grew as cold as ice. "What husband?" she repeated beginning to tremble.

"My husband—Nikolai Kolpakoff."

"N-no, my lady. I don't know your husband."

A minute passed in silence. The stranger drew her handkerchief several times across her pale lips, and held her breath in an effort to subdue an inward trembling, while Pasha stood before her as motionless as a statue, gazing at her full of uncertainty and fear.

"So you say he is not here?" asked the lady. Her voice was firm now and a strange smile had twisted her lips.

"I—I—don't know whom you mean!"

"You are a revolting, filthy, vile creature!" muttered the stranger looking at Pasha with hatred and disgust. "Yes, yes, you are revolting. I am glad indeed that an opportunity has come at last for me to tell you this!"

Pasha felt that she was producing the effect of something indecent and foul on this lady in black, with the angry eyes and the long, slender fingers, and she was ashamed of her fat, red cheeks, the pock-mark on her nose, and the lock of hair on her forehead that would never stay up. She thought that if she were thin and her face were not powdered, and she had not that curl on her forehead, she would not feel so afraid and ashamed standing there before this mysterious, unknown lady.

"Where is my husband?" the lady went on. "However it makes no difference to me whether he is here or not, I only want you to know that he has been caught embezzling funds intrusted to him, and that the police are looking for him. He is going to be arrested. Now see what you have done!"

The lady rose and began to walk up and down in violent agitation. Pasha stared at her; fear rendered her uncomprehending.

"He will be found to-day and arrested," the lady repeated with a sob full of bitterness and rage. "I know who has brought this horror upon him! Disgusting, abominable woman! Horrible, bought creature! (Here the lady's lips curled and her nose wrinkled with aversion.) I am impotent. Listen to me, you low woman. I am impotent and you are stronger than I, but there is One who will avenge me and my children. God's eyes see all things. He is just. He will call you to account for every tear I have shed, every sleepless night I have passed. The time will come when you will remember me!"

Once more silence fell. The lady walked to and fro wringing her hands. Pasha continued to watch her dully, uncomprehendingly, dazed with doubt, waiting for her to do something terrible.

"I don't know what you mean, my lady!" she suddenly cried, and burst into tears.

"That's a lie!" screamed the lady, her eyes flashing with anger. "I know all about it! I have known about you for a long time. I know that he has been coming here every day for the last month."

"Yes—and what if he has? Is it my fault? I have a great many visitors, but I don't force any one to come. They are free to do as they please."

"I tell you he is accused of embezzlement! He has taken money that didn't belong to him, and for the sake of a woman like you—for your sake, he has brought himself to commit a crime! Listen to me," the lady said sternly, halting before Pasha. "You are an unprincipled woman, I know. You exist to bring misfortune to men, that is the object of your life, but I cannot believe that you have fallen so low as not to have one spark of humanity left in your breast. He has a wife, he has children, oh, remember that! There is one means of saving us from poverty and shame; if I can find nine hundred roubles to-day he will be left in peace. Only nine hundred roubles!"

THE CHORUS GIRL 139

"What nine hundred roubles?" asked Pasha feebly. "I—I don't know—I didn't take——"

"I am not asking you to give me nine hundred roubles, you have no money, and I don't want anything that belongs to you. It is something else that I ask. Men generally give presents of jewellery to women like you. All I ask is that you should give me back the things that my husband has given you."

"My lady, he has never given me anything!" wailed Pasha beginning to understand.

"Then where is the money he has wasted? He has squandered in some way his own fortune, and mine, and the fortunes of others. Where has the money gone? Listen, I implore you! I was excited just now and said some unpleasant things, but I ask you to forgive me! I know you must hate me, but if pity exists for you, oh, put yourself in my place! I implore you to give me the jewellery!"

"H'm—" said Pasha shrugging her shoulders. "I should do it with pleasure, only I swear before God he never gave me a thing. He didn't, indeed. But, no, you are right," the singer suddenly stammered in confusion. "He did give me two little things. Wait a minute, I'll fetch them for you if you want them."

Pasha pulled out one of the drawers of her bureau, and took from it a bracelet of hollow gold, and a narrow ring set with a ruby.

"Here they are!" she said, handing them to her visitor.

The lady grew angry and a spasm passed over her features. She felt that she was being insulted.

"What is this you are giving me?" she cried. "I'm not asking for alms, but for the things that do not belong to you, for the things that you have extracted from my weak and unhappy husband by your position. When I saw you on the wharf with him on Thursday you were wearing costly brooches and bracelets. Do you think you can play the innocent baby with me? I ask you for the last time: will you give me those presents or not?"

"You are strange, I declare," Pasha exclaimed, beginning to take offence. "I swear to you that I have never had a thing from your Nikolai, except this bracelet and ring. He has never given me anything, but these and some little cakes."

"Little cakes!" the stranger laughed suddenly. "His children are starving at home, and he brings you little cakes! So you won't give up the things?"

Receiving no answer, the lady sat down, her eyes grew fixed, and she seemed to be debating something.

"What shall I do?" she murmured. "If I can't get nine hundred roubles he will be ruined as well as the children and myself. Shall I kill this creature, or shall I go down on my knees to her?"

The lady pressed her handkerchief to her eyes and burst into tears.

"Oh, I beseech you!" she sobbed. "It is you who have disgraced and ruined my husband; now save him!

THE CHORUS GIRL 141

You can have no pity for him, I know; but the children, remember the children! What have they done to deserve this?"

Pasha imagined his little children standing on the street corner weeping with hunger, and she, too, burst into tears.

"What can I do, my lady?" she cried. "You say I am a wicked creature who has ruined your husband, but I swear to you before God I have never had the least benefit from him! Mota is the only girl in our chorus who has a rich friend, the rest of us all live on bread and water. Your husband is an educated, pleasant gentleman, that's why I received him. We can't pick and choose."

"I want the jewellery; give me the jewellery! I am weeping, I am humiliating myself; see, I shall fall on my knees before you!"

Pasha screamed with terror and waved her arms. She felt that this pale, beautiful lady, who spoke the same refined language that people did in plays, might really fall on her knees before her, and for the very reason that she was so proud and high-bred, she would exalt herself by doing this, and degrade the little singer.

"Yes, yes, I'll give you the jewellery!" Pasha cried hastily, wiping her eyes. "Take it, but it did not come from your husband! I got it from other visitors. But take it, if you want it!"

Pasha pulled out an upper drawer of the bureau,

and took from it a diamond brooch, a string of corals, two or three rings, and a bracelet. These she handed to the lady.

"Here is the jewellery, but I tell you again your husband never gave me a thing. Take it, and may you be the richer for having it!" Pasha went on, offended by the lady's threat that she would go down on her knees. "You are a lady and his lawful wife—keep him at home then! The idea of it! As if I had asked him to come here! He came because he wanted to!"

The lady looked through her tears at the jewellery that Pasha had handed her and said:

"This isn't all. There is scarcely five hundred roubles' worth here."

Pasha violently snatched a gold watch, a cigarette-case, and a set of studs out of the drawer and flung up her arms, exclaiming:

"Now I am cleaned out! Look for yourself!"

Her visitor sighed. With trembling hands she wrapped the trinkets in her handkerchief, and went out without a word, without even a nod.

The door of the adjoining room opened and Kolpakoff came out. His face was pale and his head was shaking nervously, as if he had just swallowed a very bitter draught. His eyes were full of tears.

"I'd like to know what you ever gave me!" Pasha attacked him vehemently. "When did you ever give me the smallest present?"

"Presents—they are a detail, presents!" Kolpakoff cried, his head still shaking. "Oh, my God, she wept before you, she abased herself!"

"I ask you again: what have you ever given me?" screamed Pasha.

"My God, she—a respectable, a proud woman, was actually ready to fall on her knees before—before this—wench! And I have brought her to this! I allowed it!"

He seized his head in his hands.

"No," he groaned out, "I shall never forgive myself for this—never! Get away from me, wretch!" he cried, backing away from Pasha with horror, and keeping her off with outstretched, trembling hands. "She was ready to go down on her knees, and before whom?— Before you! Oh, my God!"

He threw on his coat and, pushing Pasha contemptuously aside, strode to the door and went out.

Pasha flung herself down on the sofa and burst into loud wails. She already regretted the things she had given away so impulsively, and her feelings were hurt. She remembered that a merchant had beaten her three years ago for nothing, yes, absolutely for nothing, and at that thought she wept louder than ever.

THE FATHER OF A FAMILY

THIS is what generally follows a grand loss at cards or a drinking-bout, when his indigestion begins to make itself felt. Stepan Jilin wakes up in an uncommonly gloomy frame of mind. He looks sour, ruffled, and peevish, and his grey face wears an expression partly discontented, partly offended, and partly sneering. He dresses deliberately, slowly drinks his vichy water, and begins roaming about the house.

"I wish to goodness I knew what br-rute goes through here leaving all the doors open!" he growls angrily, wrapping his dressing-gown about him and noisily clearing his throat. "Take this paper away! What is it lying here for? Though we keep twenty servants, this house is more untidy than a hovel! Who rang the bell? Who's there?"

"Aunty Anfisa, who nursed our Fedia," answers his wife.

"Yes, loafing about, eating the bread of idleness!"

"I don't understand you, Stepan; you invited her here yourself and now you are abusing her!"

"I'm not abusing her. I'm talking! And you ought to find something to do, too, good woman, instead of sitting there with your hands folded, picking quarrels with your husband! I don't understand a woman like you, upon my word I don't! How can you let day after day go by without working? Here's your husband toiling and moiling like an ox, like a beast of burden, and there you are, his wife, his life's companion, sitting about like a doll without ever turning your hand to a thing, so bored that you must seize every opportunity of quarrelling with him. It's high time for you to drop those schoolgirlish airs, madam! You're not a child nor a young miss any longer. You're a woman, a mother! You turn away, eh? Aha! You don't like disagreeable truths, do you?"

"It's odd you only speak disagreeable truths when you have indigestion!"

"That's right, let's have a scene; go ahead!"

"Did you go to town yesterday or did you play cards somewhere?"

"Well, and what if I did? Whose business is it? Am I accountable to any one? Don't I lose my own money? All that I spend and all that is spent in this house is mine, do you hear that? Mine!"

And so he persists in the same strain. But Jilin is never so crotchety, so stern, so bristling with virtue and justice, as he is when sitting at dinner with his household gathered about him. It generally begins with the soup. Having swallowed his first spoonful, Jilin suddenly scowls and stops eating.

"What the devil—" he mutters. "So I'll have to go to the café for lunch——"

"What is it?" asks his anxious wife. "Isn't the soup good?"

"I can't conceive the swinish tastes a person must have to swallow this mess! It is too salty, it smells of rags, it is flavoured with bugs and not onions! Anfisa Pavlovna!" he cries to his guest. "It is shocking! I give them oceans of money every day to buy food with, I deny myself everything, and this is what they give me to eat! No doubt they would like me to retire from business into the kitchen and do the cooking myself!"

"The soup is good to-day," the governess timidly ventures.

"Is it? Do you find it so?" inquires Jilin scowling angrily at her. "Every one to his taste, but I must confess that yours and mine differ widely, Varvara Vasilievna. You, for instance, admire the behavior of that child there (Jilin points a tragic forefinger at his son). You are in ecstasies over him, but I—I am shocked! Yes, I am!"

Fedia, a boy of seven with a delicate, pale face, stops eating and lowers his eyes. His cheeks grow paler than ever.

"Yes, you are in ecstasies, and I am shocked. I don't know which of us is right, but I venture to think that I, as his father, know my own son better than you do. Look at the way he is sitting! Is that how well-behaved children should hold themselves? Sit up!"

Fedia raises his chin and sticks out his neck and thinks he is sitting up straighter. His eyes are filling with tears.

"Eat your dinner! Hold your spoon properly! Don't dare to snuffle! Look me in the face!"

Fedia tries to look at him, but his lips are quivering and the tears are trickling down his cheeks.

"Aha, so you're crying? You're naughty and that makes you cry, eh? Leave the table and go and stand in the corner, puppy!"

"But—do let him finish his dinner first!" his wife intercedes for the boy.

"No—no dinner! Such a—such a naughty brat has no right to eat dinner!"

Fedia makes a wry face, slides down from his chair, and takes his stand in a corner.

"That's the way to treat him," his father continues. "If no one else will take charge of his education I must do it myself. I won't have you being naughty and crying at dinner, sir! Spoiled brat! You ought to work, do you hear me? Your father works, and you must work, too! No one may sponge on others. Be a man, a M-A-N!"

"For Heaven's sake, hush!" his wife beseeches him in French. "At least don't bite our heads off in public! The old lady is listening to every word, and the whole town will know of this, thanks to her."

"I'm not afraid of the public!" retorts Jilin in Russian. "Anfisa Pavlovna can see for herself that

I'm speaking the truth. What, do you think I ought to be satisfied with that youngster there? Do you know how much he costs me? Do you know, you worthless boy, how much you cost me? Or do you think I can create money and that it falls into my lap of its own accord? Stop bawling! Shut up! Do you hear me or not? Do you want me to thrash you, little wretch?"

Fedia breaks into piercing wails and begins sobbing.

"Oh, this is absolutely unbearable!" exclaims his mother, throwing down her napkin and getting up from the table. "He never lets us have our dinner in peace. That's where that bread of yours sticks!"

She points to her throat and, putting her handkerchief to her eyes, leaves the dining-room.

"Her feelings are hurt," mutters Jilin, forcing a smile. "She has been too gently handled, Anfisa Pavlovna, and that's why she doesn't like to hear the truth. We are to blame!"

Several minutes elapse in silence. Jilin catches sight of the dinner-plates and notices that the soup has not been touched. He sighs deeply and glares at the flushed and agitated face of the governess.

"Why don't you eat your dinner, Varvara Vasilievna?" he demands. "You're offended, too, are you? I see, you don't like the truth either. Forgive me, but it is my nature never to be hypocritical. I always hit straight from the shoulder. (A sigh.) I see, though, that my company is distasteful to you.

THE FATHER OF A FAMILY

No one can speak or eat in my presence. You ought to have told me that sooner so that I could have left you to yourselves. I am going now."

Jilin rises and walks with dignity toward the door. He stops as he passes the weeping Fedia.

"After what has happened just now you are fr-ee!" he says to him with a lofty toss of the head. "I shall no longer concern myself with your education. I wash my hands of it. Forgive me if, out of sincere fatherly solicitude for your welfare, I interfered with you and your preceptresses. At the same time, I renounce forever all responsibility for your future."

Fedia wails and sobs more loudly than ever. Jilin turns toward the door with a stately air and walks off into his bedroom.

After his noonday nap Jilin is tormented by the pangs of conscience. He is ashamed of his behaviour to his wife, his son, and Anfisa Pavlovna, and feels extremely uncomfortable on remembering what happened at dinner. But his egotism is too strong for him and he is not man enough to be truthful, so he continues to grumble and sulk.

When he wakes up the following morning he feels in the gayest of moods and whistles merrily at his ablutions. On entering the dining-room for breakfast he finds Fedia. The boy rises at the sight of his father and gazes at him with troubled eyes.

"Well, how goes it, young man?" Jilin asks cheerfully as he sits down to table. "What's the news, old fellow? Are you all right, eh? Come here, you little roly-poly, and give papa a kiss."

Fedia approaches his father with a pale, serious face and brushes his cheek with trembling lips. Then he silently retreats and resumes his place at the table.

THE ORATOR

ONE Sunday morning they were burying the Collegiate Assessor Kiril Ivanovitch, who had died from the two ailments so common amongst us: drink and a scolding wife. While the funeral procession was crawling from the church to the cemetery, a certain Poplavski, a colleague of the defunct civil servant, jumped into a cab, and galloped off to fetch his friend Gregory Zapoikin, a young but already popular man. As many of my readers know, Zapoikin was the possessor of a remarkable talent for making impromptu orations at weddings, jubilee celebrations, and funerals. Whether he was half-asleep, or fasting, or dead drunk, or in a fever, he was always ready to make a speech. His words always flowed from his lips as smoothly and evenly and abundantly as water out of a rain-pipe, and there were more heartrending expressions in his oratorical vocabulary than there are black beetles in an inn. His speeches were always eloquent and long, so long that sometimes, especially at the weddings of merchants, the aid of the police had to be summoned to put a stop to them.

"I have come to carry you off with me, old chap," began Poplavski. "Put on your things this minute and come along. One of our colleagues has kicked the bucket and we are about to despatch him into the next world. We must have some sort of folderol to see him off with, you know! All our hopes are centred on you! If one of our little fellows had died, we shouldn't have troubled you; but, after all, this one was an Assessor, a pillar of the state, one might say. It wouldn't do to bury a big fish like him without some kind of an oration!"

"Ah, the Assessor is it?" yawned Zapoikin. "What, that old soak?"

"Yes, that old soak! There will be pancakes and caviar, you know, and you will get your cab-fare paid. Come along, old man! Spout some of your Ciceronian hyperboles over his grave and you'll see the thanks you'll get from us all!"

Zapoikin consented to go with alacrity. He ruffled his hair, veiled his features in gloom, and stepped out with Poplavski into the street.

"I know that Assessor of yours!" he said, as he took his seat in the cab. "He was a rare brute of a rascal, God bless his soul!"

"Come, let dead men alone, Grisha!"

"Oh, of course, *de mortuis nil nisi bonum*, but that doesn't make him any less a rascal!"

The friends overtook the funeral cortège. It was travelling so slowly that before it reached its destination they had time to dash into a café three times to drink a drop to the peace of the dead man's soul.

At the cemetery the litany had already been sung.

THE ORATOR

The mother-in-law, the wife, and the sister-in-law of the departed were weeping in torrents. The wife even shrieked as the coffin was lowered into the grave: "Oh, let me go with him!" But she did not follow her husband, probably because she remembered his pension in time. Zapoikin waited until every sound had ceased and then stepped forward, embraced the whole crowd at a glance and began:

"Can we believe our eyes and our ears? Is this not a terrible dream? What is this grave here? What are these tear-stained faces, these sobs, these groans? Alas, they are not a dream! He whom, but a short time since we saw before us so valiant and brave, endowed still with all the freshness of youth; he whom, before our eyes, like the untiring bee, we saw carrying his burden of honey to the universal hive of the sovereign good, he whom—this man has now become dust, a mirage! Pitiless death has laid his bony hand upon him at a time when, notwithstanding the weight of his years, he was still in the very bloom of his powers, and radiant with hope. We have many a good servant of the state here, but Prokofi Osipitch stood alone among them all. He was devoted body and soul to the accomplishment of his honourable duties; he spared not his strength, and it may well be said of him that he was always without fear and without reproach. Ah, how he despised those who desired to buy his soul at the expense of the public good; those who, with the seductive blessings of earth, would fain have enticed him into a betrayal of the trusts confided to him! Yea, before our very eyes we could see Prokofi Osipitch giving his mite, his all, to comrades poorer than himself, and you have heard for yourselves, but a few moments since, the cries of the widows and orphans who lived by the kindness of his great heart. Engrossed in the duties of his post and in deeds of charity, he knew no joy in this world. Yea, he even forswore the happiness of family life. You know that he remained a bachelor to the end of his days. Who will take the place of this comrade of ours? I can see at this moment his gentle, clean-shaven face turned toward us with a benevolent smile. I seem to hear the soft, friendly tones of his voice. Eternal repose be to your soul, Prokofi Osipitch! Rest in peace, noble, honourable toiler of ours!"

Zapoikin continued his oration, but his audience had begun to whisper among themselves. The speech pleased every one and called forth numerous tears, but it seemed a little strange to many who heard it. In the first place, they could not understand why the speaker had referred to the dead man as "Prokofi Osipitch" when his real name had been Kiril Ivanovitch. In the second place, they all knew that the departed and his wife had fought like cat and dog, and that therefore he could hardly have been called a bachelor. In the third place, he had worn a thick red beard, and had never shaved in his life, therefore they could not make out why their Demosthenes had spoken

THE ORATOR

of him as being clean-shaven. They wondered and looked at one another and shrugged their shoulders.

"Prokofi Osipitch!" the speaker continued with a rapt look at the grave. "Prokofi Osipitch! You were ugly of face, it is true, yea, you were almost uncouth; you were gloomy and stern, but well we knew that beneath that deceitful exterior of yours there beat a warm and affectionate heart!"

The crowd was now beginning to notice something queer about the orator himself. He was glaring intently at some object near him and was shifting his position uneasily. At last he suddenly stopped, his jaw dropped with amazement, and he turned to Poplavski.

"Look here, that man's alive!" he cried, his eyes starting out of his head with horror.

"Who's alive?"

"Why, Prokofi Osipitch! There he is now, standing by that monument!"

"Of course he is! It was Kiril Ivanovitch that died, not he!"

"But you said yourself it was the Assessor!"

"I know! And wasn't Kiril Ivanovitch the Assessor? Oh, you moon-calf! You have got them mixed up! Of course Prokofi Osipitch used to be the Assessor, but that was two years ago. He has been chief of a table in chancery now for two years!"

"It's simply the devil to keep up with all you chaps!"

"What are you stopping for? Go on! This is getting too awkward!"

Zapoikin turned toward the grave, and continued his oration with all his former eloquence. Yes, and there near the monument stood Prokofi Osipitch, an old civil servant with a clean-shaven face, frowning and glaring furiously at the speaker.

"How in the world did you manage to do that?" laughed the officials as they and Zapoikin drove home from the cemetery together. "Ha! Ha! Ha! A funeral oration for a live man!"

"You made a great mistake, young man!" growled Prokofi Osipitch. "Your speech may have been appropriate enough for a dead man, but for a live one it was—it was simply a joke. Allow me to ask you, what was it you said? 'Without fear and without reproach; he never took a bribe!' Why, you *couldn't* say a thing like that about a live man unless you were joking! And no one asked you to dwell upon my personal appearance, young gentleman! 'Ugly and uncouth,' eh! That may be quite true, but why did you drag it in before every one in the city? I call it an insult!"

IONITCH

IF newcomers to the little provincial city of S. complained that life there was monotonous and dull, its inhabitants would answer that, on the contrary, S. was a very amusing place, indeed, that it had a library and a club, that balls were given there, and finally, that very pleasant families lived there with whom one might become acquainted. And they always pointed to the Turkins as the most accomplished and most enlightened family of all.

These Turkins lived in a house of their own, on Main Street, next door to the governor. Ivan Turkin, the father, was a stout, handsome, dark man with sidewhiskers. He often organized amateur theatricals for charity, playing the parts of the old generals in them and coughing most amusingly. He knew a lot of funny stories, riddles, and proverbs, and loved to joke and pun with, all the while, such a quaint expression on his face that no one ever knew whether he was serious or jesting. His wife Vera was a thin, rather pretty woman who wore glasses and wrote stories and novels which she liked to read aloud to her guests. Katherine, the daughter, played the piano. In short, each member of the family had his or her special talent. The Turkins always welcomed their guests cordially and showed off their accomplishments to them with cheerful and genial simplicity. The interior of their large stone house was spacious, and, in summer, delightfully cool. Half of its windows looked out upon a shady old garden where, on spring evenings, the nightingales sang. Whenever there were guests in the house a mighty chopping would always begin in the kitchen, and a smell of fried onions would pervade the courtyard. These signs always foretold a sumptuous and appetising supper.

So it came to pass that when Dimitri Ionitch Startseff received his appointment as government doctor, and went to live in Dialij, six miles from S., he too, as an intelligent man, was told that he must not fail to make the Turkins' acquaintance. Turkin was presented to him on the street one winter's day; they talked of the weather and the theatre and the cholera, and an invitation from Turkin followed. Next spring, on Ascension Day, after he had received his patients, Startseff went into town for a little holiday, and to make some purchases. He strolled along at a leisurely pace (he had no horse of his own yet), and as he walked he sang to himself:

"Before I had drunk those tears from Life's cup——"

After dining in town he sauntered through the public gardens, and the memory of Turkin's invitation somehow came into his mind. He decided to go to their house and see for himself what sort of people they were.

"Be welcome, if you please!" cried Turkin, meeting him on the front steps. "I am delighted, delighted to see such a welcome guest! Come, let me introduce you to the missus. I told him, Vera," he continued, presenting the doctor to his wife, "I told him that no law of the Medes and Persians allows him to shut himself up in his hospital as he does. He ought to give society the benefit of his leisure hours, oughtn't he, dearest?"

"Sit down here," said Madame Turkin, beckoning him to a seat at her side. "You may flirt with me, if you like. My husband is jealous, a regular Othello, but we'll try to behave so that he shan't notice anything."

"Oh, you little wretch, you!" murmured Turkin, tenderly kissing her forehead. "You have come at a very opportune moment," he went on, addressing his guest. "My missus has just written a splendiferous novel and is going to read it aloud to-day."

"Jean," said Madame Turkin to her husband. "Dites que l'on nous donne du thé."

Startseff next made the acquaintance of Miss Katherine, an eighteen-year old girl who much resembled her mother. Like her, she was pretty and slender; her expression was childlike still, and her figure delicate and supple, but her full, girlish chest spoke of spring and of the loveliness of spring. They drank tea with jam, honey, and sweetmeats and ate delicious cakes that melted in the mouth. When evening came other guests began to arrive, and Turkin turned his laughing eyes on each one in turn exclaiming:

"Be welcome, if you please!"

When all had assembled, they took their seats in the drawing-room, and Madame Turkin read her novel aloud. The story began with the words: "The frost was tightening its grasp." The windows were open wide, and sounds of chopping could be heard in the kitchen, while the smell of fried onions came floating through the air. Every one felt very peaceful sitting there in those deep, soft armchairs, while the friendly lamplight played tenderly among the shadows of the drawing-room. On that evening of summer, with the sound of voices and laughter floating up from the street, and the scent of lilacs blowing in through the open windows, it was hard to imagine the frost tightening its grasp, and the setting sun illuminating with its bleak rays a snowy plain and a solitary wayfarer journeying across it. Madame Turkin read of how a beautiful princess had built a school, and hospital, and library in the village where she lived, and had fallen in love with a strolling artist. She read of things that had never happened in this world, and yet it was delightfully comfortable to sit there and listen to her, while such pleasant and peaceful dreams floated through one's fancy that one wished never to move again.

"Not baddish!" said Turkin softly. And one of the guests, who had allowed his thoughts to roam far, far afield, said almost inaudibly:

"Yes—it is indeed!"

One hour passed, two hours passed. The town band began playing in the public gardens, and a chorus of singers struck up "The Little Torch." After Madame Turkin had folded her manuscript, every one sat silent for five minutes, listening to the old folk-song telling of things that happen in life and not in story-books.

"Do you have your stories published in the magazines?" asked Startseff.

"No," she answered. "I have never had anything published. I put all my manuscripts away in a closet. Why should I publish them?" she added by way of explanation. "We don't need the money."

And for some reason every one sighed.

"And now, Kitty, play us something," said Turkin to his daughter.

Some one raised the top of the piano, and opened the music which was already lying at hand. Katherine struck the keys with both hands. Then she struck them again with all her might, and then again and again. Her chest and shoulders quivered, and she obstinately hammered the same place, so that it seemed as if she were determined not to stop playing until she had beaten the keyboard into the piano. The drawing-room was filled with thunder; the floor, the ceiling, the furniture, everything rumbled. Katherine played a long, monotonous piece, interesting only for its intricacy, and as Startseff listened, he imagined he saw endless rocks rolling down a high mountainside. He wanted them to stop rolling as quickly as possible, and at the same time Katherine pleased him immensely, she looked so energetic and strong, all rosy from her exertions, with a lock of hair hanging down over her forehead. After his winter spent among sick people and peasants in Dialij, it was a new and agreeable sensation to be sitting in a drawing-room watching that graceful, pure young girl and listening to those noisy, monotonous but cultured sounds.

"Well, Kitty, you played better than ever to-day!" exclaimed Turkin, with tears in his eyes when his daughter had finished and risen from the piano-stool. "Last the best, you know!"

The guests all surrounded her exclaiming, congratulating, and declaring that they had not heard such music for ages. Kitty listened in silence, smiling a little, and triumph was written all over her face.

"Wonderful! Beautiful!"

"Beautiful!" exclaimed Startseff, abandoning himself to the general enthusiasm. "Where did you study music? At the conservatory?" he asked Katherine.

"No, I haven't been to the conservatory, but I am going there very soon. So far I have only had lessons here from Madame Zakivska."

"Did you go to the high school?"

"Oh, dear no!" the mother answered for her daughter. "We had teachers come to the house for her. She might have come under bad influences at school, you know. While a girl is growing up she should be under her mother's influence only."

"I'm going to the conservatory all the same!" declared Katherine.

"No, Kitty loves her mamma too much for that; Kitty would not grieve her mamma and papa!"

"Yes, I am going!" Katherine insisted, playfully and wilfully stamping her little foot.

At supper it was Turkin who showed off his accomplishments. With laughing eyes, but with a serious face he told funny stories, and made jokes, and asked ridiculous riddles which he answered himself. He spoke a language all his own, full of laboured, acrobatic feats of wit, in the shape of such words as "splendiferous," "not baddish," "I thank you blindly," which had clearly long since become a habit with him.

But this was not the end of the entertainment. When the well-fed, well-satisfied guests had trooped into the front hall to sort out their hats and canes they found Pava the footman, a shaven-headed boy of fourteen, bustling about among them.

"Come now, Pava! Do your act!" cried Turkin to the lad.

Pava struck an attitude, raised one hand, and said in a tragic voice:

"Die, unhappy woman!"

At which every one laughed.

"Quite amusing!" thought Startseff, as he stepped out into the street.

He went to a restaurant and had a glass of beer, and then started off on foot for his home in Dialij. As he walked he sang to himself:

"Your voice so languorous and soft——"

He felt no trace of fatigue after his six-mile walk, and as he went to bed he thought that, on the contrary, he would gladly have walked another fifteen miles.

"Not baddish!" he remembered as he fell asleep, and laughed aloud at the recollection.

II

After that Startseff was always meaning to go to the Turkins' again, but he was kept very busy in the hospital, and for the life of him could not win an hour's leisure for himself. More than a year of solitude and toil thus went by, until one day a letter in a blue envelope was brought to him from the city.

Madame Turkin had long been a sufferer from headaches, but since Kitty had begun to frighten her every day by threatening to go away to the conservatory her attacks had become more frequent. All the doctors in the city had treated her and now, at last, it was the country doctor's turn. Madame Turkin wrote him a

moving appeal in which she implored him to come,
and relieve her sufferings. Startseff went, and after
that he began to visit the Turkins often, very often.
The fact was, he did help Madame Turkin a little, and
she hastened to tell all her guests what a wonderful
and unusual physician he was, but it was not Madame
Turkin's headaches that took Startseff to the house.

One evening, on a holiday, when Katherine had
finished her long, wearisome exercises on the piano,
they all went into the dining-room and had sat there
a long time drinking tea while Turkin told some
of those funny stories of his. Suddenly a bell rang.
Some one had to go to the front door to meet a newly
come guest, and Startseff took advantage of the momentary
confusion to whisper into Katherine's ear
with intense agitation:

"For heaven's sake come into the garden with me,
I beseech you! Don't torment me!"

She shrugged her shoulders as if in doubt as to
what he wanted of her, but rose, nevertheless, and
went out with him.

"You play for three or four hours a day on the
piano, and then go and sit with your mother, and I
never have the slightest chance to talk to you. Give
me just one quarter of an hour, I implore you!"

Autumn was approaching, and the old garden, its
paths strewn with fallen leaves, was quiet and melancholy.
The early twilight was falling.

"I have not seen you for one whole week," Startseff

went on. "If you only knew what agony that has been for me! Let us sit down. Listen to me!"

The favourite haunt of both was a bench under an old spreading maple-tree. On this they took their seats.

"What is it you want?" asked Katherine in a hard, practical voice.

"I have not seen you for one whole week. I have not heard you speak for such a long time! I long madly for the sound of your voice. I hunger for it! Speak to me now!"

He was carried away by her freshness and the candid expression of her eyes and cheeks. He even saw in the fit of her dress something extraordinarily touching and sweet in its simplicity and artless grace. And at the same time, with all her innocence, she seemed to him wonderfully clever and precocious for her years. He could talk to her of literature or art or anything he pleased and could pour out his complaints to her about the life he led and the people he met, even if she did sometimes laugh for no reason when he was talking seriously, or jump up and run into the house. Like all the young ladies in S., she read a great deal. Most people there read very little, and, indeed, it was said in the library that if it were not for the girls, and the young Jews, the building might as well be closed. This reading of Katherine's was an endless source of pleasure to Startseff. Each time he met her he would ask her with emotion what she had been reading, and would listen enchanted as she told him.

"What have you read this week since we last saw one another?" he now asked. "Tell me, I beg you."

"I have been reading Pisemski."

"What have you been reading of Pisemski's?"

"'The Thousand Souls,'" answered Kitty. "What a funny name Pisemski had: Alexei Theofilaktitch!"

"Where are you going?" cried Startseff in terror as she suddenly jumped up and started toward the house. "I absolutely must speak to you. I want to tell you something! Stay with me, if only for five minutes, I implore you!"

She stopped as if she meant to answer him, and then awkwardly slipped a note into his hand and ran away into the house where she took her seat at the piano once more.

"Meet me in the cemetery at Demetti's grave tonight at eleven," Startseff read.

"How absurd!" he thought, when he had recovered himself a little. "Why in the cemetery? What is the sense of that?"

The answer was clear: Kitty was fooling. Who would think seriously of making a tryst at night in a cemetery far outside the city when it would have been so easy to meet in the street or in the public gardens? Was it becoming for him, a government doctor and a serious-minded person, to sigh and receive notes and wander about a cemetery, and do silly things that even schoolboys made fun of? How would this little adventure end? What would his friends say if they knew of it? These were Startseff's reflections, as he wandered about among the tables at the club that evening, but at half past ten he suddenly changed his mind and drove to the cemetery.

He had his own carriage and pair now, and a coachman named Panteleimon in a long velvet coat. The moon was shining. The night was still and mellow, but with an autumnal softness. The dogs barked at him as he drove through the suburbs and out through the city gates. Startseff stopped his carriage in an alley on the edge of the town and continued his way to the cemetery on foot.

"Every one has his freaks," he reflected. "Kitty is freakish, too, and, who knows, perhaps she was not joking and may come after all."

He abandoned himself to this faint, groundless hope, and it intoxicated him.

He crossed the fields for half a mile. The dark band of trees in the cemetery appeared in the distance like a wood or a large garden, then a white stone wall loomed up before him, and soon, by the light of the moon, Startseff was able to read the inscription over the gate: "Thy hour also approacheth—" He went in through a little side gate, and his eye was struck first by the white crosses and monuments on either side of a wide avenue, and by their black shadows and the shadows of the tall poplars that bordered the walk. Around him, on all sides, he could see the same checkering of white and black, with the sleeping trees brooding over the white tombstones. The night did not seem so dark as it had appeared in the fields. The fallen leaves of the maples, like tiny hands, lay sharply defined upon the sandy walks and marble slabs, and the inscriptions on the tombstones were clearly legible. Startseff was struck with the reflection that he now saw for the first and perhaps the last time a world unlike any other, a world that seemed to be the very cradle of the soft moonlight, where there was no life, no, not a breath of it; and yet, in every dark poplar, in every grave he felt the presence of a great mystery promising life, calm, beautiful, and eternal. Peace and sadness and mercy rose with the scent of autumn from the graves, the leaves, and the faded flowers.

Profoundest silence lay over all; the stars looked down from heaven with deep humility. Startseff's footsteps sounded jarring and out of place. It was only when the church-bells began to ring the hour, and he imagined himself lying dead under the ground for ever, that some one seemed to be watching him, and he thought suddenly that here were not silence and peace, but stifling despair and the dull anguish of non-existence.

Demetti's grave was a little chapel surmounted by an angel. An Italian opera troupe had once come to S., and one of its members had died there. She had been buried here, and this monument had been erected to her memory. No one in the city any longer remembered her, but the shrine lamp hanging in the doorway sparkled in the moon's rays and seemed to be alight.

No one was at the grave, and who should come there at midnight? Startseff waited, and the moonlight kindled all the passion in him. He ardently painted in his imagination the longed-for kiss and the embrace. He sat down beside the monument for half an hour, and then walked up and down the paths with his hat in his hand, waiting and thinking. How many girls, how many women, were lying here under these stones who had been beautiful and enchanting, and who had loved and glowed with passion in the night under the caresses of their lovers! How cruelly does Mother Nature jest with mankind! How bitter to acknowledge it! So thought Startseff and longed to scream aloud that he did not want to be jested with, that he wanted love at any price. Around him gleamed not white blocks of marble, but beautiful human forms timidly hiding among the shadows of the trees. He felt keen anguish.

Then, as if a curtain had been drawn across the scene, the moon vanished behind a cloud and darkness fell about him. Startseff found the gate with difficulty in the obscurity of the autumn night, and then wandered about for more than an hour in search of the alley where he had left his carriage.

"I am so tired, I am ready to drop," he said to Panteleimon.

And, as he sank blissfully into his seat, he thought: "Oh dear, I must not get fat!"

III

On the evening of the following day Startseff drove to the Turkins' to make his proposal. But he proved to have come at an unfortunate time, as Katherine was in her room having her hair dressed by a coiffeur before going to a dance at the club.

Once more Startseff was obliged to sit in the dining-room for an age drinking tea. Seeing that his guest was pensive and bored, Turkin took a scrap of paper out of his waistcoat pocket, and read aloud a droll letter from his German manager telling how "all the disavowals on the estate had been spoiled and all the modesty had been shaken down."

"They will probably give her a good dowry," thought Startseff, listening vacantly to what was being read.

After his sleepless night he felt almost stunned, as if he had drunk some sweet but poisonous sleeping potion. His mind was hazy but warm and cheerful, though at the same time a cold, hard fragment of his brain kept reasoning with him and saying:

"Stop before it is too late! Is she the woman for you? She is wilful and spoiled; she sleeps until two every day, and you are a government doctor and a poor deacon's son."

"Well, what does that matter?" he thought. "What if I am?"

"And what is more," that cold fragment continued.

"If you marry her her family will make you give up your government position, and live in town."

"And what of that?" he thought. "I'll live in town then! She will have a dowry. We will keep house."

At last Katherine appeared, looking pretty and immaculate in her low-necked ball dress, and the moment Startseff saw her he fell into such transports that he could not utter a word and could only stare at her and laugh.

She began to say good-bye, and as there was nothing to keep him here now that she was going, he, too, rose, saying that it was time for him to be off to attend to his patients in Dialij.

"If you must go now," said Turkin, "you can take Kitty to the club; it is on your way."

A light drizzle was falling and it was very dark, so that only by the help of Panteleimon's cough could they tell where the carriage was. The hood of the victoria was raised.

"Roll away!" cried Turkin, seating his daughter in the carriage. "Rolling stones gather no moss! God speed you, if you please!"

They drove away.

"I went to the cemetery last night," Startseff began. "How heartless and unkind of you——"

"You went to the cemetery?"

"Yes, I did, and waited there for you until nearly two o'clock. I was very unhappy."

"Then be unhappy if you can't understand a joke!"

Delighted to have caught her lover so cleverly, and to see him so much in love, Katherine burst out laughing, and then suddenly screamed as the carriage tipped and turned sharply in at the club gates. Startseff put his arm around her waist, and in her fright the girl pressed closer to him. At that he could contain himself no longer, and passionately kissed her on the lips and on the chin, holding her tighter than ever.

"That will do!" she said drily.

And a moment later she was no longer in the carriage, and the policeman standing near the lighted entrance to the club was shouting to Panteleimon in a harsh voice:

"Move on, you old crow! What are you standing there for?"

Startseff drove home, but only to return at once arrayed in a borrowed dress suit and a stiff collar that was always trying to climb up off the collar-band. At midnight he was sitting in the reception-room of the club, saying passionately to Katherine:

"Oh, how ignorant people are who have never loved! No one, I think, has ever truly described love, and it would scarcely be possible to depict this tender, blissful, agonising feeling. He who has once felt it would never be able to put it into words. Do I need introductions and descriptions? Do I need oratory to tell me what it is? My love is unspeakable—I beg you, I implore you to be my wife!" cried Startseff at last.

"Dimitri Ionitch," said Katherine, assuming a very serious, thoughtful expression. "Dimitri Ionitch, I am very grateful to you for the honour you do me. I esteem you, but—" here she rose and stood before him. "But, forgive me, I cannot be your wife. Let us be serious. You know, Dimitri Ionitch, that I love art more than anything else in the world. I am passionately fond of, I adore, music, and if I could I would consecrate my whole life to it. I want to be a musician. I long for fame and success and freedom and you ask me to go on living in this town, and to continue this empty, useless existence which has become unbearable to me! You want me to marry? Ah no, that cannot be! One should strive for a higher and brighter ideal, and family life would tie me down for ever. Dimitri Ionitch—" (she smiled a little as she said these words, remembering Alexei Theofilaktitch) "Dimitri Ionitch, you are kind and noble and clever, you are the nicest man I know" (her eyes filled with tears). "I sympathise with you with all my heart, but—but you must understand——"

She turned away and left the room, unable to restrain her tears.

Startseff's heart ceased beating madly. His first action on reaching the street was to tear off his stiff collar and draw a long, deep breath. He felt a little humiliated, and his pride was stung, for he had not expected a refusal, and could not believe that all his hopes and pangs and dreams had come to such a silly ending; he might as well have been the hero of a playlet at a performance of amateur theatricals! He regretted his lost love and emotion, regretted it so keenly that he could have sobbed aloud or given Panteleimon's broad back a good, sound blow with his umbrella.

For three days after that evening his business went to ruin, and he could neither eat nor sleep, but when he heard a rumour that Katherine had gone to Moscow to enter the conservatory he grew calmer, and once more gathered up the lost threads of his life.

Later, when he remembered how he had wandered about the cemetery and rushed all over town looking for a dress suit, he would yawn lazily and say:

"What a business that was!"

IV

Four years went by. Startseff now had a large practice in the city. He hastily prescribed for his sick people every morning at Dialij, and then drove to town to see his patients there, returning late at night. He had grown stouter and heavier, and would not walk, if he could help it, suffering as he did from asthma. Panteleimon, too, had become stouter, and the more he grew in width the more bitterly he sighed and lamented his hard lot: he was so tired of driving!

Startseff was now an occasional guest at several houses, but he had made close friends with no one. The conversation, the point of view, and even the looks of the inhabitants of S. bored him. Experience had taught him that as long as he played cards, or dined with them, they were peaceful, good-natured, and even fairly intelligent folk, but he had only to speak of anything that was not edible, he had only to mention politics or science to them, for them to become utterly nonplussed, or else to talk such foolish and mischievous nonsense that there was nothing to be done but to shrug one's shoulders and leave them. If Startseff tried to say to even the most liberal of them that, for instance, mankind was fortunately progressing, and that in time we should no longer suffer under a system of passports and capital punishment, they would look at him askance, and say mistrustfully: "Then one will be able to kill any one one wants to on the street, will one?" Or if at supper, in talking about work, Startseff said that labour was a good thing, and every one should work, each person present would take it as a personal affront and begin an angry and tiresome argument. As they never did anything and were not interested in anything, and as Startseff could never for the life of him think of anything to say to them, he avoided all conversation and confined himself to eating and playing cards. If there was a family fête at one of the houses and he was asked to dinner, he would eat in silence with his eyes fixed on his plate, listening to all the uninteresting, false, stupid things that were being said around him and feeling irritated and bored. But he would remain silent, and because he always sternly held his tongue and never raised his eyes from his plate, he was known as "the puffed-up Pole," although he was no more of a Pole than you or I. He shunned amusements, such as theatres and concerts, but he played cards with enjoyment for two or three hours every evening. There was one other pleasure to which he had unconsciously, little by little, become addicted, and that was to empty his pockets every evening of the little bills he had received in his practice during the day. Sometimes he would find them scattered through all his pockets, seventy roubles' worth of them, yellow ones and green ones, smelling of scent, and vinegar, and incense, and kerosene. When he had collected a hundred or more he would take them to the Mutual Loan Society, and have them put to his account.

In all the four years following Katherine's departure, he had only been to the Turkins' twice, each time at the request of Madame Turkin, who was still suffering from headaches. Katherine came back every summer to visit her parents, but he did not see her once; chance, somehow, willed otherwise.

And so four years had gone by. One warm, still morning a letter was brought to him at the hospital. Madame Turkin wrote that she missed Dimitri Ionitch very much and begged him to come without fail and relieve her sufferings, especially as it happened to be her birthday that day. At the end of the letter was a postscript: "I join my entreaties to those of my mother. K."

Startseff reflected a moment, and in the evening he drove to the Turkins'.

"Ah, be welcome, if you please!" Turkin cried with smiling eyes. "Bonjour to you!"

Madame Turkin, who had aged greatly and whose hair was now white, pressed his hand and sighed affectedly, saying:

"You don't want to flirt with me I see, doctor, you never come to see me. I am too old for you, but here is a young thing, perhaps she may be more lucky than I am!"

And Kitty? She had grown thinner and paler and was handsomer and more graceful than before, but she was Miss Katherine now, and Kitty no longer. Her freshness, and her artless, childish expression were gone; there was something new in her glance and manner, something timid and apologetic, as if she no longer felt at home here, in the house of the Turkins.

"How many summers, how many winters have gone by!" she said, giving her hand to Startseff, and one could see that her heart was beating anxiously. She looked curiously and intently into his face, and continued: "How stout you have grown! You look browner and more manly, but otherwise you haven't changed much."

She pleased him now as she had pleased him before, she pleased him very much, but something seemed to be wanting in her—or was it that there was something about her which would better have been lacking? He could not say, but he was prevented, somehow, from feeling toward her as he had felt in the past. He did not like her pallor, the new expression in her face, her weak smile, her voice, and, in a little while, he did not like her dress and the chair she was sitting in, and something displeased him about the past in which he had nearly married her. He remembered his love and the dreams and hopes that had thrilled him four years ago, and at the recollection he felt awkward.

They drank tea and ate cake. Then Madame Turkin read a story aloud, read of things that had never happened in this world, while Startseff sat looking at her handsome grey head, waiting for her to finish.

"It is not the people who can't write novels who are stupid," he thought. "But the people who write them and can't conceal it."

"Not baddish!" said Turkin.

Then Katherine played a long, loud piece on the piano, and when she had finished every one went into raptures and overwhelmed her with prolonged expressions of gratitude.

"It's a good thing I didn't marry her!" thought Startseff.

She looked at him, evidently expecting him to invite her to go into the garden, but he remained silent.

"Do let us have a talk!" she said going up to him. "How are you? What are you doing? Tell me about it all! I have been thinking about you for three days," she added nervously. "I wanted to write you a letter, I wanted to go to see you myself at Dialij, and then changed my mind. I have no idea how you will treat me now. I was so excited waiting for you to-day. Do let us go into the garden!"

They went out and took their seats under the old maple-tree, where they had sat four years before. Night was falling.

"Well, and what have you been doing?" asked Katherine.

"Nothing much; just living somehow," answered Startseff.

And that was all he could think of saying. They were silent.

"I am so excited!" said Katherine, covering her face with her hands. "But don't pay any attention to me. I am so glad to be at home, I am so glad to see every one again that I cannot get used to it. How many memories we have between us! I thought you and I would talk without stopping until morning!"

He saw her face and her shining eyes more closely now, and she looked younger to him than she had in the house. Even her childish expression seemed to have returned. She was gazing at him with naïve curiosity, as if she wanted to see and understand more clearly this man who had once loved her so tenderly and so unhappily. Her eyes thanked him for his love. And he remembered all that had passed between them down to the smallest detail, remembered how he had wandered about the cemetery and had gone home exhausted at dawn. He grew suddenly sad and felt sorry to think that the past had vanished for ever. A little flame sprang up in his heart.

"Do you remember how I took you to the club that evening?" he asked. "It was raining and dark——"

The little flame was burning more brightly, and now he wanted to talk and to lament his dull life.

"Alas!" he sighed. "You ask what I have been doing! What do we all do here? Nothing! We grow older and fatter and more sluggish. Day in, day out our colourless life passes by without impressions, without thoughts. It is money by day and the club by night, in the company of gamblers and inebriates whom I cannot endure. What is there in that?"

"But you have your work, your noble end in life. You used to like so much to talk about your hospital. I was a queer girl then, I thought I was a great pianist. All girls play the piano these days, and I played, too; there was nothing remarkable about me. I am as much of a pianist as mamma is an author. Of course I didn't understand you then, but later, in Moscow, I often thought of you. I thought only of you. Oh, what a joy it must be to be a country doctor, to help the sick and to serve the people! Oh, what a joy!" Katherine repeated with exaltation. "When I thought of you while I was in Moscow you seemed to me to be so lofty and ideal——"

Startseff remembered the little bills which he took out of his pockets every evening with such pleasure, and the little flame went out.

He rose to go into the house. She took his arm.

"You are the nicest person I have ever known in my life," she continued. "We shall see one another and talk together often, shan't we? Promise me that! I am not a pianist, I cherish no more illusions about myself, and shall not play to you or talk music to you any more."

When they had entered the house, and, in the evening light, Startseff saw her face and her melancholy eyes turned on him full of gratitude and suffering, he felt uneasy and thought again:

"It's a good thing I didn't marry her!"

He began to take his leave.

"No law of the Medes and Persians allows you to go away before supper!" cried Turkin, accompanying him to the door. "It is extremely peripatetic on your part. Come, do your act!" he cried to Pava as they reached the front hall.

Pava, no longer a boy, but a young fellow with a moustache, struck an attitude, raised one hand, and said in a tragic voice:

"Die, unhappy woman!"

All this irritated Startseff, and as he took his seat in his carriage and looked at the house and the dark garden that had once been so dear to him, he was overwhelmed by the recollection of Madame Turkin's novels and Kitty's noisy playing and Turkin's witticisms and Pava's tragic pose, and, as he recalled them, he thought:

"If the cleverest people in town are as stupid as that, what a deadly town this must be!"

Three days later Pava brought the doctor a letter from Katherine.

"You don't come to see us; why?" she wrote. "I am afraid your feeling for us has changed, and the very thought of that terrifies me. Calm my fears; come and tell me that all is well! I absolutely must see you. Yours,

K. T."

He read the letter, reflected a moment, and said to Pava:

"Tell them I can't get away to-day, my boy. Tell them I'll go to see them in three days' time."

But three days went by, a week went by, and still he did not go. Every time that he drove past the Turkins' house he remembered that he ought to drop in there for a few minutes; he remembered it and— did not go.

He never went to the Turkins' again.

V

Several years have passed since then. Startseff is stouter than ever now, he is even fat. He breathes heavily and walks with his head thrown back. The picture he now makes, as he drives by with his troika and his jingling carriage-bells, is impressive. He is round and red, and Panteleimon, round and red, with a brawny neck, sits on the box with his arms stuck straight out in front of him like pieces of wood, shouting to every one he meets: "Turn to the right!" It is more like the passage of a heathen god than of a man. He has an immense practice in the city, there is no time for repining now. He already owns an estate in the country and two houses in town, and is thinking of buying a third which will be even more remunerative than the others. If, at the Mutual Loan Society, he hears of a house for sale he goes straight to it, enters it without more ado, and walks through all the rooms not paying the slightest heed to any women or children who may be dressing there, though they look at him with doubt and fear. He taps all the doors with his cane and asks:

"Is this the library? Is this a bedroom? And what is this?"

And he breathes heavily as he says it and wipes the perspiration from his forehead.

Although he has so much business on his hands, he

still keeps his position of government doctor at Dialij. His acquisitiveness is too strong, and he wants to find time for everything. He is simply called "Ionitch" now, both in Dialij and in the city. "Where is Ionitch going?" the people ask, or "Shall we call in Ionitch to the consultation?"

His voice has changed and has become squeaky and harsh, probably because his throat is obstructed with fat. His character, too, has changed and he has grown irascible and crusty. He generally loses his temper with his patients and irritably thumps the floor with his stick, exclaiming in his unpleasant voice:

"Be good enough to confine yourself to answering my questions! No conversation!"

He is lonely, he is bored, and nothing interests him.

During all his life in Dialij his love for Kitty had been his only happiness, and will probably be his last. In the evening he plays cards in the club, and then sits alone at a large table and has supper. Ivan, the oldest and most respectable of the waiters, waits upon him and pours out his glass of Lafitte No. 17. Every one at the club, the officers and the chef and the waiters, all know what he likes and what he doesn't like and strive with might and main to please him, for if they don't he will suddenly grow angry and begin thumping the floor with his cane.

After supper he occasionally relents and takes part in a conversation.

"What were you saying? What? Whom did you say?"

And if the conversation at a neighbouring table turns on the Turkins, he asks:

"Which Turkins do you mean? The ones whose daughter plays the piano?"

That is all that can be said of Startseff.

And the Turkins? The father has not grown old, and has not changed in any way. He still makes jokes and tells funny stories. The mother still reads her novels aloud to her guests, with as much pleasure and genial simplicity as ever. Kitty practises the piano for four hours every day. She has grown conspicuously older, is delicate, and goes to the Crimea every autumn with her mother. As he bids them farewell at the station, Turkin wipes his eyes and cries as the train moves away:

"God speed you, if you please!"

And he waves his handkerchief after them.

AT CHRISTMAS TIME

"WHAT shall I write?" asked Yegor, dipping his pen in the ink.

Vasilissa had not seen her daughter for four years. Efimia had gone away to St. Petersburg with her husband after her wedding, had written two letters, and then had vanished as if the earth had engulfed her, not a word nor a sound had come from her since. So now, whether the aged mother was milking the cow at daybreak, or lighting the stove, or dozing at night, the tenor of her thoughts was always the same: "How is Efimia? Is she alive and well?" She wanted to send her a letter, but the old father could not write, and there was no one whom they could ask to write it for them.

But now Christmas had come, and Vasilissa could endure the silence no longer. She went to the tavern to see Yegor, the innkeeper's wife's brother, who had done nothing but sit idly at home in the tavern since he had come back from military service, but of whom people said that he wrote the most beautiful letters, if only one paid him enough. Vasilissa talked with the cook at the tavern, and with the innkeeper's wife, and finally with Yegor himself, and at last they agreed on a price of fifteen copecks.

So now, on the second day of the Christmas festival, Yegor was sitting at a table in the inn kitchen with a pen in his hand. Vasilissa was standing in front of him, plunged in thought, with a look of care and sorrow on her face. Her husband, Peter, a tall, gaunt old man with a bald, brown head, had accompanied her. He was staring steadily in front of him like a blind man; a pan of pork that was frying on the stove was sizzling and puffing, and seeming to say: "Hush, hush, hush!" The kitchen was hot and close.

"What shall I write?" Yegor asked again.

"What's that?" asked Vasilissa, looking at him angrily and suspiciously. "Don't hurry me! You are writing this letter for money, not for love! Now then, begin. To our esteemed son-in-law, Andrei Khrisanfitch, and our only and beloved daughter Efimia, we send greetings and love, and the everlasting blessing of their parents."

"All right, fire away!"

"We wish them a happy Christmas. We are alive and well, and we wish the same for you in the name of God, our Father in heaven—our Father in heaven——"

Vasilissa stopped to think, and exchanged glances with the old man.

"We wish the same for you in the name of God, our Father in Heaven—" she repeated and burst into tears.

That was all she could say. Yet she had thought,

as she had lain awake thinking night after night, that ten letters could not contain all she wanted to say. Much water had flowed into the sea since their daughter had gone away with her husband, and the old people had been as lonely as orphans, sighing sadly in the night hours, as if they had buried their child. How many things had happened in the village in all these years! How many people had married, how many had died! How long the winters had been, and how long the nights!

"My, but it's hot!" exclaimed Yegor, unbuttoning his waistcoat. "The temperature must be seventy! Well, what next?" he asked.

The old people answered nothing.

"What is your son-in-law's profession?"

"He used to be a soldier, brother; you know that," replied the old man in a feeble voice. "He went into military service at the same time you did. He used to be a soldier, but now he is in a hospital where a doctor treats sick people with water. He is the doorkeeper there."

"You can see it written here," said the old woman, taking a letter out of her handkerchief. "We got this from Efimia a long, long time ago. She may not be alive now."

Yegor reflected a moment, and then began to write swiftly.

"Fate has ordained you for the military profession," he wrote, "therefore we recommend you to look into the articles on disciplinary punishment and penal laws of the war department, and to find there the laws of civilisation for members of that department."

When this was written he read it aloud whilst Vasilissa thought of how she would like to write that there had been a famine last year, and that their flour had not even lasted until Christmas, so that they had been obliged to sell their cow; that the old man was often ill, and must soon surrender his soul to God; that they needed money—but how could she put all this into words? What should she say first and what last?

"Turn your attention to the fifth volume of military definitions," Yegor wrote. "The word soldier is a general appellation, a distinguishing term. Both the commander-in-chief of an army and the last infantryman in the ranks are alike called soldiers——"

The old man's lips moved and he said in a low voice: "I should like to see my little grandchildren!"

"What grandchildren?" asked the old woman crossly. "Perhaps there are no grandchildren."

"No grandchildren? But perhaps there are! Who knows?"

"And from this you may deduce," Yegor hurried on, "which is an internal, and which is a foreign enemy. Our greatest internal enemy is Bacchus——"

The pen scraped and scratched, and drew long, curly lines like fish-hooks across the paper. Yegor wrote at full speed and underlined each sentence two or three times. He was sitting on a stool with his legs stretched far apart under the table, a fat, lusty creature with a fiery nape and the face of a bulldog. He was the very essence of coarse, arrogant, stiff-necked vulgarity, proud to have been born and bred in a pot-house, and Vasilissa well knew how vulgar he was, but could not find words to express it, and could only glare angrily and suspiciously at him. Her head ached from the sound of his voice and his unintelligible words, and from the oppressive heat of the room, and her mind was confused. She could neither think nor speak, and could only stand and wait for Yegor's pen to stop scratching. But the old man was looking at the writer with unbounded confidence in his eyes. He trusted his old woman who had brought him here, he trusted Yegor, and, when he had spoken of the hydropathic establishment just now, his face had shown that he trusted that, and the healing power of its waters.

When the letter was written, Yegor got up and read it aloud from beginning to end. The old man understood not a word, but he nodded his head confidingly, and said:

"Very good. It runs smoothly. Thank you kindly, it is very good."

They laid three five-copeck pieces on the table and went out. The old man walked away staring straight ahead of him like a blind man, and a look of utmost confidence lay in his eyes, but Vasilissa, as she left the tavern, struck at a dog in her path and exclaimed angrily:

"Ugh—the plague!"

All that night the old woman lay awake full of restless thoughts, and at dawn she rose, said her prayers, and walked eleven miles to the station to post the letter.

II

Doctor Moselweiser's hydropathic establishment was open on New Year's Day as usual; the only difference was that Andrei Khrisanfitch, the doorkeeper, was wearing unusually shiny boots and a uniform trimmed with new gold braid, and that he wished every one who came in a happy New Year.

It was morning. Andrei was standing at the door reading a paper. At ten o'clock precisely an old general came in who was one of the regular visitors of the establishment. Behind him came the postman. Andrei took the general's cloak, and said:

"A happy New Year to your Excellency!"

"Thank you, friend, the same to you!"

And as he mounted the stairs the general nodded toward a closed door and asked, as he did every day, always forgetting the answer:

"And what is there in there?"

"A room for massage, your Excellency."

When the general's footsteps had died away, Andrei looked over the letters and found one addressed to him. He opened it, read a few lines, and then, still looking at his newspaper, sauntered toward the little room down-stairs at the end of a passage where he and his family lived. His wife Efimia was sitting on the bed feeding a baby, her oldest boy was standing at her knee with his curly head in her lap, and a third child was lying asleep on the bed.

Andrei entered their little room, and handed the letter to his wife, saying:

"This must be from the village."

Then he went out again, without raising his eyes from his newspaper, and stopped in the passage not far from the door. He heard Efimia read the first lines in a trembling voice. She could go no farther, but these were enough. Tears streamed from her eyes and she threw her arms round her eldest child and began talking to him and covering him with kisses. It was hard to tell whether she was laughing or crying.

"This is from granny and granddaddy," she cried—"from the village—oh, Queen of Heaven!— Oh! holy saints! The roofs are piled with snow there now—and the trees are white, oh, so white! The little children are out coasting on their dear little sleddies—and granddaddy darling, with his dear bald head is sitting by the big, old, warm stove, and the little brown doggie—oh, my precious chickabiddies——"

Andrei remembered as he listened to her that his wife had given him letters at three or four different times, and had asked him to send them to the village, but important business had always interfered, and the letters had remained lying about unposted.

"And the little white hares are skipping about in the fields now—" sobbed Efimia, embracing her boy with streaming eyes. "Granddaddy dear is so kind and good, and granny is so kind and so full of pity. People's hearts are soft and warm in the village— There is a little church there, and the men sing in the choir. Oh, take us away from here, Queen of Heaven! Intercede for us, merciful mother!"

Andrei returned to his room to smoke until the next patient should come in, and Efimia suddenly grew still and wiped her eyes; only her lips quivered. She was afraid of him, oh, so afraid! She quaked and shuddered at every look and every footstep of his, and never dared to open her mouth in his presence.

Andrei lit a cigarette, but at that moment a bell rang up-stairs. He put out his cigarette, and assuming a very solemn expression, hurried to the front door.

The old general, rosy and fresh from his bath, was descending the stairs.

"And what is there in there?" he asked, pointing to a closed door.

Andrei drew himself up at attention, and answered in a loud voice:

"The hot douche, your Excellency."

IN THE COACH HOUSE

IT was ten o'clock at night. Stepan, the coachman, Mikailo the house porter, Aliosha the coachman's grandson who was visiting his grandfather, and the old herring-vender Nikander who came peddling his wares every evening were assembled around a lantern in the large coach house playing cards. The door stood open and commanded a view of the whole courtyard with the wide double gates, the manor-house, the ice and vegetable cellars, and the servants' quarters. The scene was wrapped in the darkness of night, only four brilliantly lighted windows blazed in the wing of the house, which had been rented to tenants. The carriages and sleighs, with their shafts raised in the air, threw from the walls to the door long, tremulous shadows which mingled with those cast by the players around the lantern. In the stables beyond stood the horses, separated from the coach house by a light railing. The scent of hay hung in the air, and Nikander exhaled an unpleasant odour of herring.

They were playing "Kings."

"I am king!" cried the porter, assuming a pose which he thought befittingly regal, and blowing his nose loudly with a red and white checked handkerchief. "Come on! Who wants to have his head cut off?"

Aliosha, a boy of eight with a rough shock of blond hair, who had lacked but two tricks of being a king himself, now cast eyes of resentment and envy at the porter. He pouted and frowned.

"I'm going to lead up to you, grandpa," he said, pondering over his cards. "I know you must have the queen of hearts."

"Come, little stupid, stop thinking and play!"

Aliosha irresolutely led the knave of hearts. At that moment a bell rang in the courtyard.

"Oh, the devil—" muttered the porter rising. "The king must go and open the gate."

When he returned a few moments later Aliosha was already a prince, the herring-man was a soldier, and the coachman was a peasant.

"It's a bad business in there," said the porter resuming his seat. "I have just seen the doctor off. They didn't get it out."

"Huh! How could they? All they did, I'll be bound, was to make a hole in his head. When a man has a bullet in his brain it's no use to bother with doctors!"

"He is lying unconscious," continued the porter. "He will surely die. Aliosha, don't look at my cards, lambkin, or you'll get your ears boxed. Yes, it was out with the doctor, and in with his father and mother; they have just come. The Lord forbid such a crying and moaning as they are carrying on! They keep saying that he was their only son. It's a pity!"

All, except Aliosha who was engrossed in the game, glanced up at the lighted windows.

"We have all got to go to the police station tomorrow," said the porter. "There is going to be an inquest. But what do I know about it? Did I see what happened? All I know is that he called me this morning, and gave me a letter and said: 'Drop this in the letter-box.' And his eyes were all red with crying. His wife and children were away; they had gone for a walk. So while I was taking his letter to the mail he shot himself in the forehead with a revolver. When I came back his cook was already shrieking at the top of her lungs."

"He committed a great sin!" said the herringman in a hoarse voice, wagging his head. "A great sin."

"He went crazy from knowing too much," said the porter, picking up a trick. "He used to sit up at night writing papers—play, peasant! But he was a kind gentleman, and so pale and tall and black-eyed! He was a good tenant."

"They say there was a woman at the bottom of it," said the coachman, slapping a ten of trumps on a king of hearts. "They say he was in love with another man's wife, and had got to dislike his own. That happens sometimes."

"I crown myself king!" exclaimed the porter.

The bell in the courtyard rang again. The victorious monarch spat angrily and left the coach house. Shadows like those of dancing couples were flitting to and fro across the windows of the wing. Frightened voices and hurrying footsteps were heard.

"The doctor must have come back," said the coachman. "Our Mikailo is running."

A strange, wild scream suddenly rent the air.

Aliosha looked nervously first at his grandfather, and then at the windows, and said:

"He patted me on the head yesterday, and asked me where I was from. Grandfather, who was that howling just now?"

His grandfather said nothing, and turned up the flame of the lantern.

"A man has died," he said with a yawn. "His soul is lost and his children are lost. This will be a disgrace to them for the rest of their lives."

The porter returned, and sat down near the lantern.

"He is dead!" he said. "The old women from the almshouse have been sent for."

"Eternal peace and the kingdom of heaven be his!" whispered the coachman crossing himself.

Aliosha also crossed himself with his eyes on his grandfather.

"You mustn't pray for souls like his," the herringman said.

"Why not?"

"Because it's a sin."

"That's the truth," the porter agreed. "His soul has gone straight to the Evil One in hell."

"It's a sin," repeated the herring-man. "Men like him are neither shriven nor buried in church, but shovelled away like carrion."

The old man got up, and slung his sack across his shoulder.

"It happened that way with our general's lady," he said, adjusting the pack on his back. "We were still serfs at that time, and her youngest son shot himself in the head just as this one did, from knowing too much. The law says that such people must be buried outside the churchyard without a priest or a requiem. But to avoid the disgrace, our mistress greased the palms of the doctors and the police, and they gave her a paper saying that her son had done it by accident when he was crazy with fever. Money can do anything. So he was given a fine funeral with priests and music, and laid away under the church that his father had built with his own money, where the rest of the family were. Well, friends, one month passed, and another month passed, and nothing happened. But during the third month our mistress was told that the church watchmen wanted to see her. 'What do they want?' she asked. The watchmen were brought to her, and they fell down at her feet. 'Your ladyship!' they cried. 'We can't watch there any longer. You must find some other watchmen, and let us go!' 'Why?' she asked. 'No!' they said. 'We can't possibly stay. Your young gentleman howls under the church all night long.'"

Aliosha trembled and buried his face in his grandfather's back so as not to see those shining windows.

"At first our mistress wouldn't listen to their complaints," the old man went on. "She told them they were silly to be afraid of ghosts, and that a dead man couldn't possibly howl. But in a few days the watchmen came back, and the deacon came with them. He, too, had heard the corpse howling. Our mistress saw that the business was bad, so she shut herself up in her room with the watchmen and said to them: 'Here are twenty-five roubles for you, my friends. Go into the church quietly at night when no one can hear you, and dig up my unhappy son, and bury him outside the churchyard.' And she probably gave each man a glass of something to drink. So the watchmen did as she told them. The tombstone with its inscription lies under the church to-day, but the general's son is buried outside the churchyard. Oh, Lord, forgive us poor sinners!" sighed the herring-man. "There is only one day a year on which one can pray for such souls as his, and that is on the Saturday before Trinity Sunday. It's a sin to give food to beggars in their name, but one may feed the birds for the peace of their souls. The general's widow used to go out to the crossroads every three days, and feed the birds. One day a black dog suddenly appeared at the crossroads, gobbled up the bread, and took to his heels.

She knew who it was! For three days after that our mistress was like a mad woman; she refused to take food or drink, and every now and then she would suddenly fall down on her knees in the garden, and pray. But I'll say good night now, my friends. God and the Queen of Heaven be with you! Come Mikailo, open the gate for me."

The herring-man and the porter went out, and the coachman and Aliosha followed them so as not to be left alone in the coach house.

"The man was living and now he is dead," the coachman reflected, gazing at the windows across which the shadows were still flitting. "This morning he was walking about the courtyard, and now he is lying there lifeless."

"Our time will come, too," said the porter as he walked away with the herring-man and was lost with him in the darkness.

The coachman, followed by Aliosha, timidly approached the house and looked in. A very pale woman, her large eyes red with tears, and a handsome grey-haired man were moving two card-tables into the middle of the room; some figures scribbled in chalk on their green baize tops were still visible. The cook who had shrieked so loudly that morning was now standing on tiptoe on a table trying to cover a mirror with a sheet.

"What are they doing, grandpa?" Aliosha asked in a whisper.

"They are going to lay him on those tables soon," answered the old man. "Come, child, it's time to go to sleep."

The coachman and Aliosha returned to the coach house. They said their prayers and took off their boots. Stepan stretched himself on the floor in a corner, and Aliosha climbed into a sleigh. The doors had been shut, and the newly extinguished lantern filled the air with a strong smell of smoking oil. In a few minutes Aliosha raised his head, and stared about him; the light from those four windows was shining through the cracks of the door.

"Grandpa, I'm frightened!" he said.

"There, there, go to sleep!"

"But I tell you I'm frightened!"

"What are you afraid of, you spoiled baby?"

Both were silent.

Suddenly Aliosha jumped out of the sleigh, burst into tears, and rushed to his grandfather weeping loudly.

"What is it? What's the matter?" cried the startled coachman, jumping up, too.

"He's howling!"

"Who's howling?"

"I'm frightened, grandpa! Can't you hear him?"

"That is some one crying," his grandfather answered. "Go back to sleep, little silly. They are sad and so they are crying."

"I want to go home!" the boy persisted, sobbing

and trembling like a leaf. "Grandpa, do let us go home to mamma. Let us go, dear grandpa! God will give you the kingdom of heaven if you will take me home!"

"What a little idiot it is! There, there, be still, be still. Hush, I'll light the lantern, silly!"

The coachman felt for the matches, and lit the lantern, but the light did not calm Aliosha.

"Grandpa, let's go home!" he implored, weeping. "I'm so frightened here! Oh, *oh*, I'm so frightened! Why did you send for me to come here, you hateful man?"

"Who is a hateful man? Are you calling your own grandfather names? I'll beat you for that!"

"Beat me, grandpa, beat me like Sidorov's goat, only take me back to mamma! Oh, do! do! . . ."

"There, there, child, hush!" the coachman whispered tenderly. "No one is going to hurt you, don't be afraid. Why, I'm getting frightened myself! Say a prayer to God!"

The door creaked and the porter thrust his head into the coach house.

"Aren't you asleep yet, Stepan?" he asked. "I can't get any sleep to-night, opening and shutting the gate every minute. Why, Aliosha, what are you crying about?"

"I'm frightened," answered the coachman's grandson.

Again that wailing voice rang out. The porter said:

"They are crying. His mother can't believe her eyes. She is carrying on terribly."

"Is the father there, too?"

"Yes, he's there, but he's quiet. He's sitting in a corner, and not saying a word. The children have been sent to their relatives. Well, Stepan, shall we have another game?"

"Come on!" the coachman assented. "Go and lie down, Aliosha, and go to sleep. Why you're old enough to think of getting married, you young rascal, and there you are bawling! Run along, child, run along!"

The porter's presence calmed Aliosha; he went timidly to his sleigh and lay down. As he fell asleep he heard a whispering:

"I take the trick," his grandfather murmured.

"I take the trick," the porter repeated.

The bell rang in the courtyard, the door creaked and seemed to say:

"I take the trick!"

When Aliosha saw the dead master in his dreams, and jumped up weeping for fear of his eyes, it was already morning. His grandfather was snoring, and the coach house no longer seemed full of terror.

LADY N——'S STORY

ONE late afternoon, ten years ago, the examining magistrate, Peter Sergeitch, and I rode to the station together at hay-making time to fetch the mail.

The weather was superb, but as we were riding home we heard thunder growling, and saw an angry black cloud coming straight toward us. The storm was approaching and we were riding into its very teeth. Our house and the village church were gleaming white upon its breast, and the tall, silvery poplars were glistening against it. The scent of rain and of new-mown hay hung in the air. My companion was in high spirits, laughing and talking the wildest nonsense.

"How splendid it would be," he cried, "if we should suddenly come upon some antique castle of the Middle Ages with towers battlemented, moss-grown, and owl-haunted, where we could take refuge from the storm and where a bolt of lightning would end by striking us!"

But at that moment the first wave swept across the rye and oat fields, the wind moaned, and whirling dust filled the air. Peter Sergeitch laughed and spurred his horse.

"How glorious!" he cried. "How glorious!"

His gay mood was infectious. I, too, laughed to

think that in another moment we should be wet to the skin, and perhaps struck by lightning.

The blast and the swift pace thrilled us, and set our blood racing; we caught our breath against the gale and felt like flying birds.

The wind had fallen when we rode into our courtyard, and heavy drops of rain were drumming on the roof and lawn. The stable was deserted.

Peter Sergeitch himself unsaddled the horses, and led them into their stalls. I stood at the stable door waiting for him, watching the descent of the slanting sheets of rain. The sickly sweet scent of hay was even stronger here than it had been in the fields. The air was dark with thunder-clouds and rain.

"What a flash!" cried Peter Sergeitch coming to my side after an especially loud, rolling thunderclap that, it seemed, must have cleft the sky in two. "Well?"

He stood on the threshold beside me breathing deeply after our swift ride, with his eyes fixed on my face. I saw that his glance was full of admiration.

"Oh, Natalia!" he cried. "I would give anything on earth to be able to stand here for ever looking at you. You are glorious to-day."

His look was both rapturous and beseeching, his face was pale, and drops of rain were glistening on his beard and moustache; these, too, seemed to be looking lovingly at me.

"I love you!" he cried. "I love you and I am happy because I can see you. I know that you cannot be my wife, but I ask nothing, I desire nothing; only know that I love you. Don't answer me, don't notice me, only believe that you are very dear to me, and suffer me to look at you."

His ecstasy communicated itself to me. I saw his rapt look, I heard the tones of his voice mingling with the noise of the rain, and stood rooted to the spot as if bewitched. I longed to look at those radiant eyes and listen to those words for ever.

"You are silent! Good!" said Peter Sergeitch. "Do not speak!"

I was very happy. I laughed with pleasure, and ran through the pouring rain into the house. He laughed too, and ran after me.

We burst in wet and panting and tramped noisily up-stairs like two children. My father and brother, unaccustomed to seeing me laughing and gay, looked at me in surprise and began to laugh with us.

The storm blew over, the thunder grew silent, but the rain-drops still glistened on Peter Sergeitch's beard. He sang and whistled and romped noisily with the dog all the evening, chasing him through the house and nearly knocking the butler carrying the samovar off his feet. He ate a huge supper, talking all kinds of nonsense the while, swearing that if you eat fresh cucumbers in winter you can smell the spring in your nostrils.

When I went to my room I lit the candle and threw the casement wide open. A vague sensation took hold of me. I remembered that I was free and healthy, well-born and rich, and that I was beloved, but chiefly that I was well-born and rich—well-born and rich! Goodness, how delightful that was! Later, shrinking into bed to escape the chill that came stealing in from the garden with the dew, I lay and tried to decide whether I loved Peter Sergeitch or not. Not being able to make head or tail of the question, I went to sleep.

Next morning when I awoke and saw the shadows of the lindens and the trembling patches of sunlight that played across my bed, the events of yesterday rose vividly before me. Life seemed rich, and varied, and full of beauty. I dressed quickly and ran singing into the garden.

And then, what happened? Nothing! When winter came and we moved to the city, Peter Sergeitch seldom came to see us. Country acquaintances are only attractive in the country. In town, in the winter, they lose half their charm. When they come to call they look as if they were wearing borrowed clothes, and they stir their tea much too long. Peter Sergeitch sometimes spoke of love, but his words did not sound as enchanting as they had in the country. Here we felt more keenly the barrier between us. I was titled and rich; he was poor and was not even a noble, but an examining magistrate, the son of a deacon. Both of us—I because I was very young, and he, heaven knows why—considered this barrier very great and very high. He smiled affectedly when he was with us in town and criticised high society; if any one beside himself was in the drawing-room he remained morosely silent. There is no barrier so high but that it may be surmounted, but, from what I have known of him, the modern hero of romance is too timid, too indolent and lazy, too finical and ready to accept the idea that he is a failure cheated by life, to make the struggle. Instead, he carps at the world, and calls it vile, forgetting that his own criticism at last becomes vile in itself.

I was beloved; happiness was near, seemed almost to be walking at my side; my path was strewn with roses, and I lived without trying to understand myself, not knowing what I was expecting nor what I demanded from life. And so time went on and on—Men with their love passed near me; bright days and warm nights flew by; the nightingales sang; the air was sweet with new-mown hay—all these things, so dear, so touching to remember, flashed by me swiftly, unheeded, as they do by every one, leaving no trace behind them, until they vanished like mist. Where is it all now?

My father died; I grew older. All that had been so enchanting, so gracious, so hope-inspiring; the sound of rain, the rolling of thunder, dreams of happiness, and words of love, all these grew to be a memory alone. I now see before me a level, deserted plain, bounded by a dark and terrible horizon, without a living soul upon it.

A bell rang. It was Peter Sergeitch. When I see the winter trees, remembering how they decked themselves in green for me in summer-time, I whisper:

"Oh, you darling things!"

And when I see the people with whom I passed my own springtime, my heart grows warm and sad, and I whisper the same words.

Peter Sergeitch had moved to the city long ago through the influence of my father. He was a little elderly now, and a little stooping. It was long since he had spoken any words of love, he talked no nonsense now, and was dissatisfied with his occupation. He was a little ailing, and a little disillusioned; he snapped his fingers at life, and would have been glad to have had it over. He took his seat in the chimney-corner and looked silently into the fire. Not knowing what to say, I asked:

"Well, what news have you?"

"None at all."

Silence fell once more. The ruddy firelight played across his melancholy features.

I remembered our past, and suddenly my shoulders shook; I bent my head and wept bitterly. I felt unbearably sorry for myself and for this man, and I longed passionately for those things which had gone by, and which life now denied us. I no longer cared for my riches or my title.

I sobbed aloud with my head in my hands murmuring: "My God, my God, our lives are ruined!"

He sat silent and did not tell me not to weep. He knew that tears must be shed, and that the time for them had come. I read his pity for me in his eyes, and I, too, pitied him and was vexed with this timid failure who had not been able to mould his life or mine aright.

As I bade him farewell in the hall he seemed purposely to linger there, putting on his coat. He kissed my hand in silence twice, and looked long into my tear-stained face. I was sure that he was remembering that thunder-storm, those sheets of rain, our laughter, and my face as it had then been. He tried to say something; he would have done so gladly, but nothing came. He only shook his head and pressed my hand— God bless him!

When he had gone, I went back into the study and sat down on the carpet before the fire. Grey ashes were beginning to creep over the dying embers. The wintry blast was beating against the windows more angrily than ever and chanting some tale in the chimney.

The maid servant came in and called my name, thinking that I had fallen asleep.

A JOURNEY BY CART

THEY left the city at half past eight.

The highway was dry and a splendid April sun was beating fiercely down, but the snow still lay in the woods and wayside ditches. The long, dark, cruel winter was only just over, spring had come in a breath, but to Maria Vasilievna driving along the road in a cart there was nothing either new or attractive in the warmth, or the listless, misty woods flushed with the first heat of spring, or in the flocks of crows flying far away across the wide, flooded meadows, or in the marvellous, unfathomable sky into which one felt one could sail away with such infinite pleasure. Maria Vasilievna had been a school teacher for thirty years, and it would have been impossible for her to count the number of times she had driven to town for her salary, and returned home as she was doing now. It mattered not to her whether the season were spring, as now, or winter, or autumn with darkness and rain; she invariably longed for one thing and one thing only: a speedy end to her journey.

She felt as if she had lived in this part of the world for a long, long time, even a hundred years or more, and it seemed to her that she knew every stone and

A JOURNEY BY CART

every tree along the roadside between her school and the city. Here lay her past and her present as well, and she could not conceive of a future beyond her school and the road and the city, and then the road and her school again, and then once more the road and the city.

Of her past before she had been a school teacher she had long since ceased to think—she had almost forgotten it. She had had a father and mother once, and had lived with them in a large apartment near the Red Gate in Moscow, but her recollection of that life was as vague and shadowy as a dream. Her father had died when she was ten years old, and her mother had soon followed him. She had had a brother, an officer, with whom she had corresponded at first, but he had lost the habit of writing to her after a while, and had stopped answering her letters. Of her former belongings her mother's photograph was now her only possession, and this had been so faded by the dampness of the school that her mother's features had all disappeared except the eyebrows and hair.

When they had gone three miles on their way old daddy Simon, who was driving the cart, turned round and said:

"They have caught one of the town officials and have shipped him away. They say he killed the mayor of Moscow with the help of some Germans."

"Who told you that?"

"Ivan Ionoff read it in the paper at the inn."

For a long time neither spoke. Maria Vasilievna was thinking of her school, and the coming examinations for which she was preparing four boys and one girl. And just as her mind was full of these examinations, a landholder named Khanoff drove up with a four-in-hand harnessed to an open carriage. It was he who had held the examination in her school the year before. As he drove up alongside her cart he recognised her, bowed, and exclaimed:

"Good morning! Are you on your way home, may I ask?"

Khanoff was a man of forty or thereabouts. His expression was listless and blasé, and he had already begun to age perceptibly, but he was handsome still and admired by women. He lived alone on a large estate; he had no business anywhere, and it was said of him that he never did anything at home but walk about and whistle, or else play chess with his old man servant. It was also rumoured that he was a hard drinker. Maria Vasilievna remembered that, as a matter of fact, at the last examination even the papers that he had brought with him had smelled of scent and wine. Everything he had had on that day had been new, and Maria Vasilievna had liked him very much, and had even felt shy sitting there beside him. She was used to receiving the visits of cold, critical examiners, but this one did not remember a single prayer, and did not know what questions he ought to ask. He had been extremely considerate and

A JOURNEY BY CART

polite, and had given all the children full marks for everything.

"I am on my way to visit Bakvist" he now continued to Maria Vasilievna. "Is it true that he is away from home?"

They turned from the highway into a lane, Khanoff in the lead, Simon following him. The four horses proceeded at a foot-pace, straining to drag the heavy carriage through the mud. Simon tacked hither and thither across the road, first driving round a bump, then round a puddle, and jumping down from his seat every minute or so to give his horse a helpful push. Maria Vasilievna continued to think about the school, and whether the questions at the examinations would be difficult or easy. She felt annoyed with the board of the zemstvo, for she had been there yesterday, and had found no one in. How badly it was managed! Here it was two years since she had been asking to have the school watchman discharged for loafing and being rude to her and beating her scholars, and yet no one had paid any heed to her request. The president of the board was hardly ever in his office, and when he was, would vow with tears in his eyes that he hadn't time to attend to her now. The school inspector came only three times a year, and knew nothing about his business anyway, as he had formerly been an exciseman, and had obtained the office of inspector through favour. The school board seldom met, and no one ever knew where their meetings were held. The warden was an illiterate peasant who owned a tannery, a rough and stupid man and a close friend of the watchman's. In fact, the Lord only knew whom one could turn to to have complaints remedied and wrongs put right!

"He really is handsome!" thought the schoolteacher glancing at Khanoff.

The road grew worse and worse. They entered a wood. There was no possibility of turning out of the track here, the ruts were deep and full of gurgling, running water. Prickly twigs beat against their faces.

"What a road, eh?" cried Khanoff laughing.

The school teacher looked at him and marvelled that this queer fellow should be living here.

"What good do his wealth, his handsome face, and his fine culture do him in this God-forsaken mud and solitude?" she thought. "He has abandoned any advantage that fate may have given him, and is enduring the same hardships as Simon, tramping with him along this impossible road. Why does any one live here who could live in St. Petersburg or abroad?"

And it seemed to her that it would be worth this rich man's while to make a good road out of this bad one, so that he might not have to struggle with the mud, and be forced to see the despair written on the faces of Simon and his coachman. But he only laughed, and was obviously absolutely indifferent to it all, asking for no better life than this.

"He is kind and gentle and unsophisticated," Maria Vasilievna thought again. "He does not understand the hardships of life any more than he knew the suitable prayers to say at the examination. He gives globes to the school and sincerely thinks himself a useful man and a conspicuous benefactor of popular education. Much they need his globes in this wilderness!"

"Sit tight, Vasilievna!" shouted Simon.

The cart tipped violently to one side and seemed to be falling over. Something heavy rolled down on Maria Vasilievna's feet, it proved to be the purchases she had made in the city. They were crawling up a steep, clayey hill now. Torrents of water were rushing noisily down on either side of the track, and seemed to have eaten away the road bed. Surely it would be impossible to get by! The horses began to snort. Khanoff jumped out of his carriage and walked along the edge of the road in his long overcoat. He felt hot.

"What a road!" he laughed again. "My carriage will soon be smashed to bits at this rate!"

"And who asked you to go driving in weather like this?" asked Simon sternly. "Why don't you stay at home?"

"It is tiresome staying at home, daddy. I don't like it."

He looked gallant and tall walking beside old Simon, but in spite of his grace there was an almost imperceptible something about his walk that betrayed a being already rotten at the core, weak, and nearing his downfall. And the air in the woods suddenly seemed to carry an odour of wine. Maria Vasilievna shuddered, and began to feel sorry for this man who for some unknown reason was going to his ruin. She thought that if she were his wife or his sister she would gladly give up her whole life to rescuing him from disaster. His wife? Alas! He lived alone on his great estate, and she lived alone in a forlorn little village, and yet the very idea that they might one day become intimate and equal seemed to her impossible and absurd. Life was like that! And, at bottom, all human relationships and all life were so incomprehensible that if you thought about them at all dread would overwhelm you and your heart would stop beating.

"And how incomprehensible it is, too," she thought, "that God should give such beauty and charm and such kind, melancholy eyes to weak, unhappy, useless people, and make every one like them so!"

"I turn off to the right here," Khanoff said, getting into his carriage. "Farewell! A pleasant journey to you!"

And once more Maria Vasilievna's thoughts turned to her scholars, and the coming examinations, and the watchman, and the school board, until a gust of wind from the right bringing her the rumbling of the departing carriage, other reveries mingled with these thoughts, and she longed to dream of handsome eyes and love and the happiness that would never be hers.

She, a wife! Alas, how cold her little room was early in the morning! No one ever lit her stove, because the watchman was always away somewhere. Her pupils came at daybreak, with a great noise, bringing in with them mud and snow, and everything was so bleak and so uncomfortable in her little quarters of one small bedroom which also served as a kitchen! Her head ached every day when school was over. She was obliged to collect money from her scholars to buy wood and pay the watchman, and then to give it to that fat, insolent peasant, the warden, and beg him for mercy's sake to send her a load of wood. And at night she would dream of examinations and peasants and snow drifts. This life had aged and hardened her, and she had grown plain and angular and awkward, as if lead had been emptied into her veins. She was afraid of everything, and never dared to sit down in the presence of the warden or a member of the school board. If she mentioned any one of them in his absence, she always spoke of him respectfully as "his Honour." No one found her attractive; her life was spent without love, without friendship, without acquaintances who interested her. What a terrible calamity it would be were she, in her situation, to fall in love!

"Sit tight, Vasilievna!"

Once more they were crawling up a steep hill.

She had felt no call to be a teacher; want had forced her to be one. She never thought about her mission in life or the value of education; the most important things to her were, not her scholars nor their instruction, but the examinations. And how could she think of a mission, and of the value of education? School teachers, and poor doctors, and apothecaries, struggling with their heavy labours, have not even the consolation of thinking that they are advancing an ideal, and helping mankind. Their heads are too full of thoughts of their daily crust of bread, their wood, the bad roads, and their sicknesses for that. Their life is tedious and hard. Only those stand it for any length of time who are silent beasts of burden, like Maria Vasilievna. Those who are sensitive and impetuous and nervous, and who talk of their mission in life and of advancing a great ideal, soon become exhausted and give up the fight.

To find a dryer, shorter road, Simon sometimes struck across a meadow or drove through a back-yard, but in some places the peasants would not let him pass, in others the land belonged to a priest; here the road was blocked, there Ivan Ionoff had bought a piece of land from his master and surrounded it with a ditch. In such cases they had to turn back.

They arrived at Nijni Gorodishe. In the snowy, grimy yard around the tavern stood rows of wagons laden with huge flasks of oil of vitriol. A great crowd of carriers had assembled in the tavern, and the air reeked of vodka, tobacco, and sheepskin coats. Loud talk filled the room, and the door with its weight and pulley banged incessantly. In the tap room behind a partition some one was playing on the concertina without a moment's pause. Maria Vasilievna sat down to her tea, while at a near-by table a group of peasants saturated with tea and the heat of the room were drinking vodka and beer.

A confused babel filled the room.

"Did you hear that, Kuzma? Ha! Ha! What's that? By God! Ivan Dementitch, you'll catch it for that! Look, brother!"

A small, black-bearded, pock-marked peasant, who had been drunk for a long time, gave an exclamation of surprise and swore an ugly oath.

"What do you mean by swearing, you!" shouted Simon angrily from where he sat, far away at the other end of the room. "Can't you see there's a lady here?"

"A lady!" mocked some one from another corner.

"You pig, you!"

"I didn't mean to do it—" faltered the little peasant with embarrassment. "Excuse me! My money is as good here as hers. How do you do?"

"How do you do?" answered the school teacher.

"Very well, thank you kindly."

Maria Vasilievna enjoyed her tea, and grew as flushed as the peasants. Her thoughts were once more running on the watchman and the wood.

"Look there, brother!" she heard a voice at the next table cry. "There's the schoolmarm from Viasovia! I know her! She's a nice lady."

"Yes, she's a nice lady."

The door banged, men came and went. Maria Vasilievna sat absorbed in the same thoughts that had occupied her before, and the concertina behind the partition never ceased making music for an instant. Patches of sunlight that had lain on the floor when she had come in had moved up to the counter, then to the walls, and now had finally disappeared. So it was afternoon. The carriers at the table next to hers rose and prepared to leave. The little peasant went up to Maria Vasilievna swaying slightly, and held out his hand. The others followed him; all shook hands with the school teacher, and went out one by one. The door banged and whined nine times.

"Get ready, Vasilievna!" Simon cried.

They started again, still at a walk.

"A little school was built here in Nijni Gorodishe, not long ago," said Simon, looking back. "Some of the people sinned greatly."

"In what way?"

"It seems the president of the school board grabbed one thousand roubles, and the warden another thousand, and the teacher five hundred."

"A school always costs several thousand roubles. It is very wrong to repeat scandal, daddy. What you have just told me is nonsense."

"I don't know anything about it. I only tell you what people say."

It was clear, however, that Simon did not believe the school teacher. None of the peasants believed her.

A JOURNEY BY CART

They all thought that her salary was too large (she got twenty roubles a month, and they thought that five would have been plenty), and they also believed that most of the money which she collected from the children for wood she pocketed herself. The warden thought as all the other peasants did, and made a little out of the wood himself, besides receiving secret pay from the peasants unknown to the authorities.

But now, thank goodness, they had finally passed through the last of the woods, and from here on their road would lie through flat fields all the way to Viasovia. Only a few miles more to go, and then they would cross the river, and then the railway track, and then they would be at home.

"Where are you going, Simon?" asked Maria Vasilievna. "Take the right-hand road across the bridge!"

"What's that? We can cross here. It isn't very deep."

"Don't let the horse drown!"

"What's that?"

"There is Khanoff crossing the bridge!" cried Maria Vasilievna, catching sight of a carriage and four in the distance at their right. "Isn't that he?"

"That's him all right. He must have found Bakvist away. My goodness, what a donkey to drive all the way round when this road is two miles shorter!"

They plunged into the river. In summer time it was a tiny stream, in late spring it dwindled rapidly to a fordable river after the freshets, and by August it was generally dry, but during flood time it was a torrent of swift, cold, turbid water some fifty feet wide. Fresh wheel tracks were visible now on the bank leading down to the water's edge; some one, then, must have crossed here.

"Get up!" cried Simon, madly jerking the reins and flapping his arms like a pair of wings. "Get up!"

The horse waded into the stream up to his belly, stopped, and then plunged on again, throwing his whole weight into the collar. Maria Vasilievna felt a sharp wave of cold water lap her feet.

"Go on!" she cried, rising in her seat. "Go on!"

They drove out on the opposite bank.

"Well, of all things! My goodness!" muttered Simon. "What a worthless lot those zemstvo people are——"

Maria Vasilievna's goloshes and shoes were full of water, and the bottom of her dress and coat and one of her sleeves were soaked and dripping. Her sugar and flour were wet through, and this was harder to bear than all the rest. In her despair she could only wave her arms, and cry:

"Oh, Simon, Simon! How stupid you are, really——"

The gate was down when they reached the railway crossing, an express train was leaving the station. They stood and waited for the train to go by, and Maria Vasilievna shivered with cold from head to foot.

A JOURNEY BY CART

Viasovia was already in sight; there was the school with its green roof, and there stood the church with its blazing crosses reflecting the rays of the setting sun. The windows of the station were flashing, too, and a cloud of rosy steam was rising from the engine. Everything seemed to the school teacher to be shivering with cold.

At last the train appeared. Its windows were blazing like the crosses on the church, and their brilliance was dazzling. A lady was standing on the platform of one of the first-class carriages. One glance at her as she slipped past, and Maria Vasilievna thought: "My mother!" What a resemblance there was! There was her mother's thick and luxuriant hair; there were her forehead and the poise of her head. For the first time in all these thirty years Maria Vasilievna saw in imagination her mother, her father, and her brother in their apartment in Moscow, saw everything down to the least detail, even to the globe of goldfish in the sitting-room. She heard the strains of a piano, and the sound of her father's voice, and saw herself young and pretty and gaily dressed, in a warm, brightly lighted room with her family about her. Great joy and happiness suddenly welled up in her heart, and she pressed her hands to her temples in rapture, crying softly with a note of deep entreaty in her voice:

"Mother!"

Then she wept, she could not have said why. At that moment Khanoff drove up with his four-in-hand,

and when she saw him she smiled and nodded to him as if he and she were near and dear to each other, for she was conjuring up in her fancy a felicity that could never be hers. The sky, the trees, and the windows of the houses seemed to be reflecting her happiness and rejoicing with her. No! Her mother and father had not died; she had never been a school teacher; all that had been a long, strange, painful dream, and now she was awake.

"Vasilievna! Sit down!"

And in a breath everything vanished. The gate slowly rose. Shivering and numb with cold Maria Vasilievna sat down in the cart again. The four-in-hand crossed the track and Simon followed. The watchman at the crossing took off his cap as they drove by.

"Here is Viasovia! The journey is over!"

THE PRIVY COUNCILLOR

EARLY in April in the year 1870, my mother, Klavdia Arhipovna, the widow of a lieutenant, received a letter from her brother Ivan, a privy councillor in St. Petersburg. Among other things the letter said:

"An affection of the liver obliges me to spend every summer abroad, but as I have no funds this year with which to go to Marienbad, it is very probable that I may spend the coming summer with you at Kotchneffka, dear sister——"

My mother turned pale and trembled from head to foot as she perused this epistle, and an expression both smiling and tearful came into her face. She began to weep and to laugh. This conflict between laughter and tears always reminds me of the glitter and shimmer that follow when water is spilled on a brightly burning candle. Having read the letter through twice, my mother summoned her whole household together, and in a voice quivering with excitement began explaining to them that there had been four brothers in the Gundasoff family; one had died when he was a baby; a second had been a soldier, and had also died; a third, she meant no offence to him in saying it, had become an actor, and a fourth——

"'The fourth brother is not of our world,' sobbed my mother. "He is my own brother, we grew up together, and yet I am trembling all over at the thought of him. He is a privy councillor, a general! How can I meet my darling? What can a poor, uneducated woman like me find to talk to him about? It is fifteen years since I saw him last. Andrusha, darling!" cried my mother turning to me. "Rejoice little stupid, it is for your sake that God is sending him here!"

When we had all heard the history of the Gundasoff family down to the smallest detail, there arose an uproar on the farm such as I had not been accustomed to hearing except before weddings. Only the vault of heaven, and the water in the river escaped; everything else was subjected to a process of cleaning, scrubbing, and painting. If the sky had been smaller and lower, and the river had not been so swift, they too would have been scalded with boiling water and polished with cloths. The walls were white as snow already, but they were whitewashed again. The floors shone and glistened, but they were scrubbed every day. Bobtail, the cat (so-called because I had chopped off a good portion of his tail with a carving-knife when I was a baby), was taken from the house into the kitchen and put in charge of Anfisa. Fedia was told that if the dogs came anywhere near the front porch, "God would punish him." But nothing caught it so cruelly as did the unfortunate sofas and carpets and chairs! Never before had they been so unmercifully beaten with sticks as they now were in expectation of our guest's arrival. Hearing the blows, my doves fluttered anxiously about, and at last flew away straight up into the very sky.

From Novostroevka came Spiridon, the only tailor in the district who ventured to sew for the gentry. He was a sober, hard-working, intelligent man, not without some imagination and feeling for the plastic arts, but he sewed abominably nevertheless. His doubts always spoiled everything, for the idea that his clothes were not fashionable enough made him cut everything over five times at least. He used to go all the way to the city on foot on purpose to see how the young dandies were dressed, and then decked us in costumes that even a caricaturist would have called an exaggeration and a joke. We sported impossibly tight trousers, and coats so short that we always felt embarrassed whenever any young ladies were present.

Spiridon slowly took my measurements. He measured me lengthways and crossways as if he were going to fit me with barrel hoops, then wrote at length upon a sheet of paper with a very thick pencil, and at last marked his yardstick from end to end with little triangular notches. Having finished with me, he began upon my tutor Gregory Pobedimski. This unforgettable tutor of mine was just at the age when men anxiously watch the growth of their moustaches, and are critical about their attire, so that you may imagine with what holy terror Spiridon approached his person! Pobedimski was made to throw his head back, and spread himself apart like a V upside down, now raising, now lowering his arms. Spiridon measured him several times, circling about him as a love-sick pigeon circles about his mate; then he fell down on one knee, and bent himself into the form of a hook. My mother, weary and worn with all this bustle and faint from the heat of her irons in the laundry, said as she watched all these endless proceedings:

"Take care, Spiridon, God will call you to account if you spoil the cloth! And you will be an unlucky man if you don't hit the mark this time!"

My mother's words first threw Spiridon into a sweat and then into a fever, for he was very sure that he would not hit the mark. He asked one rouble and twenty copecks for making my suit, and two roubles for making my tutor's. The cloth, the buttons, and the linings were supplied by us. This cannot but seem cheap enough, especially when you consider that Novostroevka was six miles away, and that he came to try on the clothes four different times. At these fittings, as we pulled on our tight trousers and coats all streaked with white basting threads, my mother would look at our clothes, knit her brows with dissatisfaction and exclaim:

"Goodness knows we have queer fashions these days! I am almost ashamed to look at you! If my brother did not live in St. Petersburg I declare I wouldn't have you dressed in the fashion!"

Spiridon, delighted that the fashions and not he

were catching the blame, would shrug his shoulders, and sigh, as much as to say:

"There is nothing to be done about it; it is the spirit of the times!"

The trepidation with which we awaited the arrival of our guest can only be compared to the excitement that prevails among spiritualists when they are awaiting the appearance of a spirit. My mother had a headache, and burst into tears every minute. I lost my appetite and my sleep, and did not study my lessons. Even in my dreams I was devoured by my longing to see a general, a man with epaulettes, an embroidered collar reaching to his ears, and a naked sword in his hand; in short, a person exactly like the general I saw hanging over the sofa in our drawing-room glaring so balefully with his terrible black eyes at any one who ventured to look at him. Pobedimski alone felt at ease. He neither trembled nor rejoiced, and all he said as he listened to my mother's stories of the Gundasoff family was:

"Yes, it will be pleasant to talk with somebody new."

My tutor was considered a very exceptional person on our farm. He was a young man of twenty or thereabouts, pimply, ragged, with a low forehead, and an uncommonly long nose. In fact, this nose of his was so long that if he wanted to look at anything closely he had to put his head on one side like a bird. He had gone through the six grades of the high school, and had then entered the Veterinary College, from which he had been expelled in less than six months. By carefully concealing the reason of his expulsion, my tutor gave every one who wished it an opportunity for considering him a much-enduring and rather mysterious person. He talked little, and when he did it was always on learned subjects; he ate meat on fast-days, and looked upon the life about him in a high and mighty, contemptuous fashion, which, however, did not prevent him from accepting presents from my mother in the shape of suits of clothes, or from painting funny faces with red teeth on my kites. My mother did not like him on account of his "pride," but she had a deep respect for his learning.

We had not long to wait for our guest. Early in May two wagons piled with huge trunks arrived from the station. These trunks looked so majestic that the coachman unconsciously took off his hat as he unloaded them from the wagons.

"They must be full of uniforms and gunpowder!" thought I.

Why gunpowder? Probably because in my mind the idea of a general was closely connected with powder and cannon.

When my nurse woke me on the morning of the tenth of May, she announced in a whisper that my "uncle had come!" I dressed hastily, washing anyhow and forgetting my prayers, and scampered out of my room. In the hall I ran straight into a tall, stout gentleman with fashionable side-whiskers and an elegant overcoat. Swooning with horror, I drew myself up before him, and remembering the ceremonial taught me by my mother, I bowed deeply and attempted to kiss his hand. But the gentleman would not give me his hand to kiss, and stated that he was not my uncle, but only Peter, my uncle's valet. The sight of this Peter, dressed a great deal better than Pobedimski and myself, filled me with the profoundest astonishment which, to tell the truth, has not left me to this day. Is it possible that such grave, respectable men as he, with such stern, intelligent faces can be servants? Why should they be?

Peter told me that my uncle and mother were in the garden, and I rushed thither as fast as my legs could carry me.

Not knowing the history of the Gundasoff family and my uncle's rank, Nature felt a great deal freer and less constrained than I did. There was an activity in the garden such as one only sees at a country fair. Countless magpies were cleaving the air and hopping along the garden paths, chasing the mayflies with noisy cries. A flock of crows was swarming in the lilac bushes that thrust their delicate, fragrant blossoms into my very face. From all sides came the songs of orioles and the pipings of finches and blackbirds. At any other time I should have darted off after the grasshoppers or thrown stones at a crow that was sitting on a low haycock under a wasp's nest turning its blunt bill from side to side. But this was no time for play. My heart was hammering and shivers were running up and down my back. I was about to see a man with epaulettes, a naked sword, and terrible eyes!

Imagine, then, my disappointment! A slender little dandy in a white silk shirt and a white military cap was walking through the garden at my mother's side. Every now and then he would run on ahead and, with his hands in his pockets and his head thrown back, he looked like quite a young man. There was so much life and vivacity in his whole figure that the treachery of old age only became apparent to me as I approached from behind, and, peeping under his cap, saw the white hairs glistening beneath the brim. Instead of a stolid, autocratic gravity I saw in him an almost boyish nimbleness, and instead of a collar to the ears he wore an ordinary light blue necktie. My mother and uncle were walking up and down the path, chatting together. I crept up softly from behind and waited for one of them to turn round and see me.

"What an enchanting place you have here, Klavdia!" my uncle exclaimed. "How sweet and lovely it all is! If I had known how beautiful it was nothing could have taken me abroad all these years!"

My uncle stooped abruptly, and put his nose to a tulip. Everything he saw was a source of curiosity and delight to him, as if he had never seen a garden, or a sunny day before in his life. The strange little man moved as if on springs and chattered incessantly, not giving my mother a chance to put in a word. All at once Pobedimski stepped out from behind an elder bush at a turn of the path. His appearance was so unexpected that my uncle started and fell back a step. My tutor was dressed in his gala overcoat with a cape, in which he looked exactly like a windmill, especially from behind. His mien was majestic and triumphant. With his hat held close to his chest in Spanish fashion he took a step toward my uncle, and bowed forward and slightly sideways like a marquis in a melodrama.

"I have the honour to present myself to your worshipful highness," he said in a loud voice. "I am a pedagogue, the instructor of your nephew, and a former student at the Veterinary College. My name is Gregory Pobedimski, Esquire."

My tutor's beautiful manners pleased my mother immensely. She smiled and fluttered with the sweet expectation of his next brilliant sally, but my tutor was waiting for my uncle to respond to his lofty bearing with something equally lofty, and thought that two fingers would be offered him with a "h'm—" befitting a general. In consequence, he lost all his presence of mind and was completely embarrassed when my uncle smiled cordially and heartily pressed his hand. Murmuring some incoherent phrases, my tutor coughed and retired.

"Ha! Ha! Isn't that beautiful?" laughed my uncle. "Look at him. He has put on his wings, and is thinking what a clever fellow he is! I like that, upon my word and honour, I do! What youthful aplomb, what life there is in those silly wings! And who is this boy?" he asked, suddenly turning round and catching sight of me.

"This is my little Andrusha," said my mother blushing. "The comfort of my life."

I put my foot behind me and bowed deeply.

"A fine little fellow, a fine little fellow!" murmured my uncle taking his hand away from my lips, and patting my head. "So your name is Andrusha? Well, well—yes—upon my word and honour. Do you go to school?"

My mother began to enumerate my triumphs of learning and behaviour, adding to them and exaggerating as all mothers do, while I walked at my uncle's side and did not cease from bowing deeply according to the ceremonial we had agreed upon. When my mother began hinting that with my remarkable attainments it would not be amiss for me to enter the military academy at the expense of the state, and when, according to our plan, I should have burst into tears and implored the patronage of my uncle, that relative suddenly stopped short and threw up his hands in astonishment.

"Heavens and earth, who is that?" he exclaimed.

Down the garden path came Tatiana, the wife of our manager, Theodore Petrovitch. She was carrying a white starched skirt and a long ironing board, and as she passed us she blushed and glanced shyly at our guest from under her long lashes.

"Worse and worse!" said my uncle under his breath, looking tenderly after her. "Why, sister, one can't take a step here without encountering some surprise, upon my word and honour!"

Not every one would have called Tatiana beautiful. She was a small, plump woman of twenty, graceful, black-eyed, and always rosy and sweet, but in all her face and figure there was not one strong feature, not one bold line for the eye to rest upon. It was as if in making her Nature had lacked confidence and inspiration. Tatiana was shy and timid and well behaved. She glided quietly along, saying little, seldom laughing; her life was as even and smooth as her face and her neatly brushed hair. My uncle half closed his eyes and smiled as he watched her. My mother looked intently at his smiling face and grew serious.

"Oh, brother, why have you never married?" she sighed.

"I have never married because——"

"Why not?" asked my mother softly.

"What shall I say? Because things did not turn out that way. When I was young I worked too hard to have time for enjoying life, and then, when I wanted to live—behold! I had put fifty years behind me! I was too slow. However, this is a tedious subject for conversation!"

My mother and uncle sighed simultaneously, and

walked on together while I stayed behind, and ran to find my tutor in order to share my impressions with him. Pobedimski was standing in the middle of the courtyard gazing majestically at the sky.

"He is obviously an enlightened man," he said, wagging his head. "I hope we shall become friends."

An hour later my mother came to us.

"Oh, boys, I'm in terrible trouble!" she began with a sigh. "My brother has brought a valet with him, you know, and he is not the sort of man, heaven help him, whom one can put in the hall or the kitchen, he absolutely must have a room of his own. Look here, my children, couldn't you move into the wing with Theodore and give the valet your room?"

We answered that we should be delighted to do so, for, we thought, life in the wing would be much freer than in the house under the eyes of my mother.

"Yes, I'm terribly worried!" my mother continued. "My brother says he doesn't want to have his dinner at noon, but at seven as they do in the city. I am almost distracted. Why, by seven the dinner in the stove will be burned to a crisp. The truth is men know nothing about housekeeping, even if they are very clever. Oh, misery me, I shall have to have two dinners cooked every day! You must have yours at noon as you always do, children, and let the old lady wait until seven for her brother."

My mother breathed a profound sigh, told me to please my uncle whom God had brought here especially for my benefit, and ran into the kitchen. Pobedimski and I moved into the wing that very same day. We were put in a passage between the hall and the manager's bedroom.

In spite of my uncle's arrival and our change of quarters, our days continued to trickle by in their usual way, more drowsily and monotonously than we had expected. We were excused from our lessons "because of our guest." Pobedimski, who never read or did anything, now spent most of his time sitting on his bed absorbed in thought, with his long nose in the air. Every now and then he would get up, try on his new suit, sit down again, and continue his meditations. One thing only disturbed him, and that was the flies, whom he slapped unmercifully with the palms of his hands. After dinner he would generally "rest," causing keen anguish to the whole household by his snores. I played in the garden from morning till night, or else sat in my room making kites. During the first two or three weeks we saw little of my uncle. He stayed in his room and worked for days on end, heeding neither the flies nor the heat.

His extraordinary power of sitting as if glued to his desk appeared to us something in the nature of an inexplicable trick. To lazybones like ourselves, who did not know the meaning of systematic work, his industry appeared positively miraculous. Getting up at nine, he would sit down at his desk, and not move until dinner time. After dinner he would go to work once more, and work until late at night. Whenever I peeped into his room through the keyhole I invariably saw the same scene. My uncle would be sitting at his desk and working. His work consisted of writing with one hand while turning over the pages of a book with the other, and strange as it may seem, he constantly wriggled all over, swinging one foot like a pendulum, whistling and nodding his head in time to the music he made. His appearance at these times was extraordinarily frivolous and careless, more as if he were playing at naughts and crosses than working. Each time I looked in I saw him wearing a dashing little coat and a dandified necktie, and each time, even through the keyhole, I could smell a sweet feminine perfume. He emerged from his room only to dine, and then ate scarcely anything.

"I can't understand my brother," my mother complained. "Every day I have a turkey or some pigeons killed especially for him, and stew some fruits for him myself, and yet he drinks a little bouillon and eats a piece of meat no larger than my finger, after which he leaves the table at once. If I beg him to eat more he comes back and drinks a little milk. What is there in milk? It is slop, nothing more! He will die of eating that kind of food! If I try to persuade him to change his ways, he only laughs and makes a joke of it! No, children, our fare doesn't suit him!"

Our evenings passed much more pleasantly than our days. As a rule the setting sun and the long shadows falling across the courtyard found Tatiana, Pobedimski, and me seated on the porch of our wing. We did not speak until darkness fell—what could we talk about when everything had already been said? There had been one novelty, my uncle's arrival, but that theme had soon become exhausted as well as the others. My tutor constantly kept his eyes fixed on Tatiana's face and fetched one deep sigh after another. At that time I did not understand the meaning of those sighs, and did not seek to inquire into their cause, but they explain much to me now.

When the shadows had merged into thick, black darkness Theodore would come home from the hunt or the field. This Theodore seemed to me to be a wild and even fearsome man. He was the son of a Russianised gipsy, and was swarthy and dark with large black eyes and a tangled curly beard, and he was never spoken of by our peasants as anything but "the demon." There was a great deal of the gipsy in him beside his appearance. For instance, he never could stay at home, and would vanish for days at a time, hunting in the forest or roaming in the fields. He was gloomy, passionate, taciturn, and fearless, and could never be brought to acknowledge the authority of any one. He spoke gruffly to my mother, addressed me familiarly as "thou," and treated Pobedimski's learning with contempt, but we forgave him everything, because we considered that he had a morbidly excitable nature. My mother liked him in spite of his gipsy ways, for he was ideally honest and hard working. He loved his Tatiana passionately, in gipsy style, but his love was a thing of gloom, almost of suffering. He never caressed her in our presence, and only stared at her fiercely with his mouth all awry.

On coming back from the fields he would furiously slam down his gun on the floor of his room, and come out on the porch to take his seat beside his wife. When he had rested a while he would ask her a few questions about the housekeeping, and then relapse into silence.

"Let's sing!" I used to suggest.

My tutor would tune his guitar, and in a thick, deaconly voice would drone: "In Level Valleys." We would all chime in. My tutor sang bass, Theodore an almost inaudible tenor, and I contralto in tune with Tatiana.

When all the sky was strewn with stars, and the frogs' voices were hushed, our supper would be brought to us from the kitchen, and we would go into the house and fall to. My tutor and the gipsy ate ravenously, munching so loudly that it was hard to tell whether the noise came from the bones they were crunching or the cracking of their jaws. Tatiana and I, on the contrary, could scarcely manage to finish our portions. After supper our wing of the house would sink into deep slumber.

One evening at the end of May we were sitting on the porch waiting for our supper. Suddenly a shadow flitted toward us, and Gundasoff appeared as if he had sprung from the ground. He stared at us for a long time, and then waved his hands and laughed gaily.

"How idyllic!" he cried. "Singing and dreaming under the moon! It is beautiful, upon my word and honour! May I sit here and dream with you?"

We silently looked at one another. My uncle sat down on the lowest step, yawned, and gazed at the sky. Pobedimski, who had long been intending to have a conversation with this "new person," was delighted at the opportunity that now presented itself, and was the first to break the silence. He had only one subject for learned discussions, and that was the epizooty. It sometimes happens that, out of a crowd of thousands of persons with whom one is thrown, one face alone remains fixed in the memory, and so it was with Pobedimski. Out of all he had learned at the Veterinary College he remembered only one sentence:

"Epizooty is the cause of much loss to the peasant farmers. Every community should join hands with the state in fighting this disease."

Before saying this to Gundasoff, my tutor cleared his throat three times, and excitedly wrapped his cape around him. When my uncle had been informed concerning the epizooty, he made a noise in his nose that sounded like a laugh.

"How charming, upon my word and honour!" he said under his breath, staring at us as if we were maniacs. "This is indeed life! This is real nature! Why don't you say something, Pelagia?" he asked of Tatiana.

Tatiana grew confused and coughed.

"Go on talking, friends! Sing! Play! Don't waste a moment! That rascal time goes fast and waits for no man. Upon my word and honour, old age will be upon you before you know it. It will be too late to enjoy life then; so come, Pelagia, don't sit there and say nothing!"

At this point our supper was brought from the kitchen. My uncle went into the house with us, and ate five curd fritters and a duck's wing for company. He kept his eyes fixed on us while he despatched his supper; we all filled his heart with enthusiasm and emotion. Whatever silliness that unforgettable tutor of mine was guilty of, whatever Tatiana did, was lovely and charming in his eyes. When Tatiana quietly took her knitting into a corner after supper, his eyes never left her little fingers, and he babbled without a moment's pause.

"Friends, you must hurry and begin to enjoy life as fast as you can!" he said. "For heaven's sake, don't sacrifice the present to the future! You have youth and health and passion now, and the future is deceitful—a vapour! As soon as your twentieth year knocks at the door, then begin to live!"

Tatiana dropped a needle. My uncle jumped up, picked it up, and handed it to her with a bow, at which I realised for the first time that there was some one in the world with manners more polished than Pobedimski's.

"Yes," my uncle continued. "Fall in love! Marry! Be silly! Silliness is much more healthy and natural than our toiling and striving to be sensible."

My uncle talked much and long, and I sat on a trunk in a corner listening to him and dozing. I felt hurt because he had never once paid the least attention to me. He left our wing of the house at two o'clock that night, when I had given up the battle, and sunk into profound slumber.

From that time on my uncle came to us every evening. He sang with us and sat with us each night until two o'clock, chatting without end always of the same thing. He ceased his evening and nocturnal labours, and by the end of July, when the privy councillor had learned to eat my mother's turkeys and stewed fruits, his daytime toil was also abandoned. My uncle had torn himself away from his desk and had entered into "real life." By day he walked about the garden whistling and keeping the workmen from their work by making them tell him stories. If he caught sight of Tatiana he would run up to her, and, if she were carrying anything, would offer to carry it for her, which always embarrassed her dreadfully.

The farther summer advanced toward autumn the more absent-minded and frivolous and lively my uncle became. Pobedimski lost all his illusions about him.

"He is too one-sided," he used to say. "Nothing about him shows that he stands on the highest rung of the official hierarchic ladder. He can't even talk properly. He says 'upon my word and honour' after every word. No, I don't like him!"

A distinct change came over my tutor and Theodore from the time that my uncle began to visit us in our wing. Theodore stopped hunting and began to come home early. He grew more silent and stared more ferociously than ever at his wife. My tutor stopped talking of the epizooty in my uncle's presence, and now frowned and even smiled derisively at sight of him.

"Here comes our little hop o'my thumb!" he once growled, seeing my uncle coming toward our part of the house.

This change in the behaviour of both men I explained by the theory that Gundasoff had hurt their feelings. My absent-minded uncle always confused their names, and on the day of his departure had not learned which was my tutor, and which was Tatiana's husband. Tatiana herself he sometimes called Nastasia, sometimes Pelagia, sometimes Evdokia. Full of affectionate enthusiasm as he was for us all, he laughed at us and treated us as if we had been children. All this, of course, might easily have offended the young men. But, as I now see, this was not a question of lacerated feelings; sentiments much more delicate were involved.

One night, I remember, I was sitting on the trunk contending with my longing for sleep. A heavy glue seemed to have fallen on my eyelids, and my body was drooping sideways, exhausted by a long day's playing, but I tried to conquer my sleepiness, for I wanted to see what was going on. It was nearly midnight. Gentle, rosy, and meek as ever, Tatiana was sitting at a little table sewing a shirt for her husband. From one corner of the room Theodore was staring sternly and gloomily at her, in another corner sat Pobedimski snorting angrily, his head half buried in his high coat collar. My uncle was walking up and down plunged in thought. Silence reigned, broken only by the rustling of the linen in Tatiana's hands. Suddenly my uncle stopped in front of Tatiana, and said:

"Oh, you are all so young and fresh and good, and you live so peacefully in this quiet place that I envy you! I have grown so fond of this life of yours that, upon my honour, my heart aches when I remember that some day I shall have to leave it all."

Sleep closed my eyes and I heard no more. I was awakened by a bang, and saw my uncle standing in front of Tatiana, looking at her with emotion. His cheeks were burning.

"My life is over and I have not lived," he was saying. "Your young face reminds me of my lost youth, and I should be happy to sit here looking at you until I died. I should like to take you with me to St. Petersburg."

"Why?" demanded Theodore in a hoarse voice.

"I should like to put you under a glass case on my desk; I should delight in contemplating you, and showing you to my friends. Do you know, Pelagia, that we don't have people like you where I live? We have wealth and fame and sometimes beauty, but we have none of this natural life and this wholesome peacefulness——"

My uncle sat down in front of Tatiana and took her hand.

"So you won't come with me to St. Petersburg?" he laughed. "Then at least let me take this hand away with me, this lovely little hand! You won't? Very well then, little miser, at least allow me to kiss it!"

I heard a chair crack. Theodore sprang to his feet and strode toward his wife with a heavy, measured tread. His face was ashy grey and quivering. He raised his arm and brought his fist down on the table with all his might, saying in a muffled voice:

"I won't allow it!"

At the same moment Pobedimski jumped out of his chair, and with a face as pale and angry as the other's, he also advanced toward Tatiana and banged the table with his fist.

"I—I won't allow it!" he cried.

"What? What's the matter," asked my uncle in astonishment.

"I won't allow it!" Theodore repeated, with another blow on the table.

My uncle jumped up and abjectly blinked his eyes. He wanted to say something, but surprise and fright held him tongue-tied. He gave an embarrassed smile and pattered out of the room with short, senile steps, leaving his hat behind him. When my startled mother came into the room a few moments later, Theodore and Pobedimski were still banging the table with their fists like blacksmiths hammering an anvil, and shouting:

"I won't allow it!"

"What has happened here?" demanded my mother. "Why has my brother fainted? What is the matter?"

When she saw the frightened Tatiana and her angry husband, my mother must have guessed what had been going on, for she sighed and shook her head.

"Come, come, stop thumping the table!" she commanded. "Stop, Theodore! And what are you hammering for, Gregory Pobedimski? What business is this of yours?"

Pobedimski recollected himself and blushed. Theodore glared intently first at him and then at his wife, and began striding up and down the room. After my mother had gone, I saw something that for a long time after I took to be a dream. I saw Theodore seize my tutor, raise him in the air, and fling him out of the door.

When I awoke next morning my tutor's bed was empty. To my inquiries, my nurse replied in a whisper that he had been taken to the hospital early that morning, to be treated for a broken arm. Saddened by this news, and recalling yesterday's scandal, I went out into the courtyard. The day was overcast. The sky was covered with storm-clouds, and a strong wind was blowing across the earth, whirling before it dust, feathers, and scraps of paper. One could feel the approaching rain, and bad humour was obvious in both men and beasts. When I went back to the house I was told to walk lightly, and not to make a noise because my mother was ill in bed with a headache. What could I do? I went out of the front gate, and, sitting down on a bench, tried to make out the meaning of what I had seen the night before. The road from our gate wound past a blacksmith's shop and around a damp meadow, turning at last into the main highway. I sat and looked at the telegraph poles around which the dust was whirling, and at the sleepy birds sitting on the wires until, suddenly, such ennui overwhelmed me that I burst into tears.

A dusty char-à-banc came along the highway filled with townspeople who were probably on a pilgrimage to some shrine. The char-à-banc was scarcely out of sight before a light victoria drawn by a pair of horses appeared. Standing up in the carriage and holding on to the coachman's belt was the rural policeman. To my intense surprise the victoria turned into our road and rolled past me through the gate. While I was still seeking an answer to the riddle of the police-

THE PRIVY COUNCILLOR

man's appearance at our farm, a troika trotted up harnessed to a landau, and in the landau sat the captain of police pointing out our gate to his coachman.

"What does this mean?" I asked myself. "Pobedimski must have complained to them about Theodore, and they have come to fetch him away to prison."

But the problem was not so easily solved. The policeman and the police captain were evidently but the forerunners of some one more important still, for five minutes had scarcely elapsed before a coach drove into our gate. It flashed by me so quickly that, as I glanced in at the window, I could only catch a glimpse of a red beard.

Lost in conjectures and foreseeing some disaster, I ran into the house. The first person I met in the hall was my mother. Her face was pale, and she was staring with horror at a door from behind which came the sound of men's voices. Some guests had arrived unexpectedly and at the very height of her headache.

"Who is here, mamma?" I asked.

"Sister!" we heard my uncle call. "Do give the governor and the rest of us a bite to eat!"

"That's easier said than done!" whispered my mother, collapsing with horror. "What can I give them at such short notice? I shall be disgraced in my declining years!"

My mother clasped her head with her hands and hurried into the kitchen. The unexpected arrival of the governor had turned the whole farm upside down.

A cruel holocaust immediately began to take place. Ten hens were killed and five turkeys and eight ducks, and in the hurly-burly the old gander was beheaded, the ancestor of all our flock and the favourite of my mother. The coachman and the cook seemed to have gone mad, and frantically slaughtered every bird they could lay hands upon without regard to its age or breed. A pair of my precious turtle doves, as dear to me as the gander was to my mother, were sacrified to make a gravy. It was long before I forgave the governor their death.

That evening, when the governor and his suite had dined until they could eat no more, and had climbed into their carriages and driven away, I went into the house to look at the remains of the feast. Glancing into the drawing-room from the hall, I saw my mother there with my uncle. My uncle was shrugging his shoulders, and nervously pacing round and round the room with his hands behind his back. My mother looked exhausted and very much thinner. She was sitting on the sofa following my uncle's movements with eyes of suffering.

"I beg your pardon, sister, but one cannot behave like that! I introduced the governor to you, and you did not even shake hands with him! You quite embarrassed the poor man. Yes, it was most unseemly. Simplicity is all very pretty, but even simplicity must not be carried too far, upon my word and honour— And then that dinner! How could you serve a dinner like that? What was that dish-rag you gave us for the fourth course?"

"That was duck with apple sauce," answered my mother faintly.

"Duck! Forgive me, sister, but—but—I have an attack of indigestion! I'm ill!"

My uncle pulled a sour, tearful face and continued.

"The devil the governor had to come here to see me! Much I wanted a visit from him! Ouch—oh, my indigestion! I—I can't work and I can't sleep. I'm completely run down. I don't see how in the world you can exist here in this wilderness without anything to do! There now, the pain is commencing in the pit of my stomach!"

My uncle knit his brows and walked up and down more swiftly than ever.

"Brother," asked my mother softly. "How much does it cost to go abroad?"

"Three thousand roubles at least!" wailed my uncle. "I should certainly go, but where can I get the money? I haven't a copeck! Ouch, what a pain!"

My uncle stopped in his walk and gazed with anguish through the window at the grey, cloudy sky.

Silence fell. My mother fixed her eyes for a long time on the icon as if she were debating something, and then burst into tears and exclaimed:

"I'll let you have three thousand, brother!"

Three days later the majestic trunks were sent to the station, and behind them rolled the carriage containing the privy councillor. He had wept as he bade farewell to my mother, and had held her hand to his lips for a long time. As he climbed into the carriage his face had shone with childish joy. Radiant and happy, he had settled himself more comfortably in his seat, kissed his hand to my weeping mother, and suddenly and unexpectedly turned his regard to me. The utmost astonishment had appeared on his features——

"What boy is this?" he had asked.

As my mother had always assured me that God had sent my uncle to us for my especial benefit, this question gave her quite a turn. But I was not thinking about the question. As I looked at my uncle's happy face I felt, for some reason, very sorry for him. I could not endure it, and jumped up into the carriage to embrace this man, so frivolous, so weak, and so human. As I looked into his eyes I wanted to say something pleasant, so I asked him:

"Uncle, were you ever in a battle?"

"Oh, my precious boy!" laughed my uncle kissing me. "My precious boy, upon my word and honour! How natural and true to life it all is, upon my word and honour!"

The carriage moved away. I followed it with my eyes, and long after it had disappeared I still heard ringing in my ears that farewell, "Upon my word and honour!"

ROTHSCHILD'S FIDDLE

IT was a tiny town, worse than a village, inhabited chiefly by old people who so seldom died that it was really vexatious. Very few coffins were needed for the hospital and the jail; in a word, business was bad. If Jacob Ivanoff had been a maker of coffins in the county town, he would probably have owned a house of his own by now, and would have been called Mr. Ivanoff, but here in this little place he was simply called Jacob, and for some reason his nickname was Bronze. He lived as poorly as any common peasant in a little old hut of one room, in which he and Martha, and the stove, and a double bed, and the coffins, and his joiner's bench, and all the necessities of housekeeping were stowed away.

The coffins made by Jacob were serviceable and strong. For the peasants and townsfolk he made them to fit himself and never went wrong, for, although he was seventy years old, there was no man, not even in the prison, any taller or stouter than he was. For the gentry and for women he made them to measure, using an iron yardstick for the purpose. He was always very reluctant to take orders for children's coffins, and made them contemptuously without taking any measurements at all, always saying when he was paid for them:

"The fact is, I don't like to be bothered with trifles."

Beside what he received for his work as a joiner, he added a little to his income by playing the violin. There was a Jewish orchestra in the town that played for weddings, led by the tinsmith Moses Shakess, who took more than half of its earnings for himself. As Jacob played the fiddle extremely well, especially Russian songs, Shakess used sometimes to invite him to play in his orchestra for the sum of fifty copecks a day, not including the presents he might receive from the guests. Whenever Bronze took his seat in the orchestra, the first thing that happened to him was that his face grew red, and the perspiration streamed from it, for the air was always hot, and reeking of garlic to the point of suffocation. Then his fiddle would begin to moan, and a double bass would croak hoarsely into his right ear, and a flute would weep into his left. This flute was played by a gaunt, red-bearded Jew with a network of red and blue veins on his face, who bore the name of a famous rich man, Rothschild. This confounded Jew always contrived to play even the merriest tunes sadly. For no obvious reason Jacob little by little began to conceive a feeling of hatred and contempt for all Jews, and especially for Rothschild. He quarrelled with him and abused him in ugly language, and once even tried to beat him, but Rothschild took offence at this, and cried with a fierce look:

"If I had not always respected you for your music, I should have thrown you out of the window long ago!"

Then he burst into tears. So after that Bronze was not often invited to play in the orchestra, and was only called upon in cases of dire necessity, when one of the Jews was missing.

Jacob was never in a good humour, because he always had to endure the most terrible losses. For instance, it was a sin to work on a Sunday or a holiday, and Monday was always a bad day, so in that way there were about two hundred days a year on which he was compelled to sit with his hands folded in his lap. That was a great loss to him. If any one in town had a wedding without music, or if Shakess did not ask him to play, there was another loss. The police inspector had lain ill with consumption for two years while Jacob impatiently waited for him to die, and then had gone to take a cure in the city and had died there, which of course had meant another loss of at least ten roubles, as the coffin would have been an expensive one lined with brocade.

The thought of his losses worried Jacob at night more than at any other time, so he used to lay his fiddle at his side on the bed, and when those worries came trooping into his brain he would touch the strings, and the fiddle would give out a sound in the darkness, and Jacob's heart would feel lighter.

Last year on the sixth of May, Martha suddenly fell ill. The old woman breathed with difficulty, staggered in her walk, and felt terribly thirsty. Nevertheless, she got up that morning, lit the stove, and even went for the water. When evening came she went to bed. Jacob played his fiddle all day. When it grew quite dark, because he had nothing better to do, he took the book in which he kept an account of his losses, and began adding up the total for the year. They amounted to more than a thousand roubles. He was so shaken by this discovery, that he threw the counting board on the floor and trampled it under foot. Then he picked it up again and rattled it once more for a long time, heaving as he did so sighs both deep and long. His face grew purple, and perspiration dripped from his brow. He was thinking that if those thousand roubles he had lost had been in the bank then, he would have had at least forty roubles interest by the end of the year. So those forty roubles were still another loss! In a word, wherever he turned he found losses and nothing but losses.

"Jacob!" cried Martha unexpectedly, "I am going to die!"

He looked round at his wife. Her face was flushed with fever and looked unusually joyful and bright. Bronze was troubled, for he had been accustomed to seeing her pale and timid and unhappy. It seemed to him that she was actually dead, and glad to have left this hut, and the coffins, and Jacob at last. She was staring at the ceiling, with her lips moving as if she saw her deliverer Death approaching and were whispering with him.

The dawn was just breaking and the eastern sky was glowing with a faint radiance. As he stared at the old woman it somehow seemed to Jacob that he had never once spoken a tender word to her or pitied her; that he had never thought of buying her a kerchief or of bringing her back some sweetmeats from a wedding. On the contrary, he had shouted at her and abused her for his losses, and had shaken his fist at her. It was true he had never beaten her, but he had frightened her no less, and she had been paralysed with fear every time he had scolded her. Yes, and he had not allowed her to drink tea because his losses were heavy enough as it was, so she had had to be content with hot water. Now he understood why her face looked so strangely happy, and horror overwhelmed him.

As soon as it was light he borrowed a horse from a neighbour and took Martha to the hospital. As there were not many patients, he had not to wait very long— only about three hours. To his great satisfaction it was not the doctor who was receiving the sick that day, but his assistant, Maksim Nicolaitch, an old man of whom it was said that although he quarrelled and drank, he knew more than the doctor did.

"Good morning, your Honour," said Jacob leading his old woman into the office. "Excuse us for intruding upon you with our trifling affairs. As you see, this subject has fallen ill. My life's friend, if you will allow me to use the expression——"

Knitting his grey eyebrows and stroking his whiskers, the doctor's assistant fixed his eyes on the old woman. She was sitting all in a heap on a low stool, and with her thin, long-nosed face and her open mouth, she looked like a thirsty bird.

"Well, well—yes—" said the doctor slowly, heaving a sigh. "This is a case of influenza and possibly fever; there is typhoid in town. What's to be done? The old woman has lived her span of years, thank God. How old is she?"

"She lacks one year of being seventy, your Honour."

"Well, well, she has lived long. There must come an end to everything."

"You are certainly right, your Honour," said Jacob, smiling out of politeness. "And we thank you sincerely for your kindness, but allow me to suggest to you that even an insect dislikes to die!"

"Never mind if it does!" answered the doctor, as if the life or death of the old woman lay in his hands. "I'll tell you what you must do, my good man. Put a cold bandage around her head, and give her two of these powders a day. Now then, good-by! Bon jour!"

Jacob saw by the expression on the doctor's face that it was too late now for powders. He realised clearly that Martha must die very soon, if not to-day, then to-morrow. He touched the doctor's elbow gently, blinked, and whispered:

"She ought to be cupped, doctor!"

"I haven't time, I haven't time, my good man. Take your old woman, and go in God's name. Good-by."

"Please, please, cup her, doctor!" begged Jacob. "You know yourself that if she had a pain in her stomach, powders and drops would do her good, but she has a cold! The first thing to do when one catches cold is to let some blood, doctor!"

But the doctor had already sent for the next patient, and a woman leading a little boy came into the room.

"Go along, go along!" he cried to Jacob, frowning. "It's no use making a fuss!"

"Then at least put some leeches on her! Let me pray to God for you for the rest of my life!"

The doctor's temper flared up and he shouted:

"Don't say another word to me, blockhead!"

Jacob lost his temper, too, and flushed hotly, but he said nothing and, silently taking Martha's arm, led her out of the office. Only when they were once more seated in their wagon did he look fiercely and mockingly at the hospital and say:

"They're a pretty lot in there, they are! That doctor would have cupped a rich man, but he even begrudged a poor one a leech. The pig!"

When they returned to the hut, Martha stood for

nearly ten minutes supporting herself by the stove. She felt that if she lay down Jacob would begin to talk to her about his losses, and would scold her for lying down and not wanting to work. Jacob contemplated her sadly, thinking that to-morrow was St. John the Baptist's day, and day after to-morrow was St. Nicholas the Wonder Worker's day, and that the following day would be Sunday, and the day after that would be Monday, a bad day for work. So he would not be able to work for four days, and as Martha would probably die on one of these days, the coffin would have to be made at once. He took his iron yardstick in hand, went up to the old woman, and measured her. Then she lay down, and he crossed himself and went to work on the coffin.

When the task was completed Bronze put on his spectacles and wrote in his book:

"To 1 coffin for Martha Ivanoff—2 roubles, 40 copecks."

He sighed. All day the old woman lay silent with closed eyes, but toward evening, when the daylight began to fade, she suddenly called the old man to her side.

"Do you remember, Jacob?" she asked. "Do you remember how fifty years ago God gave us a little baby with curly golden hair? Do you remember how you and I used to sit on the bank of the river and sing songs under the willow tree?" Then with a bitter smile she added: "The baby died."

Jacob racked his brains, but for the life of him he could not recall the child or the willow tree.

"You are dreaming," he said.

The priest came and administered the Sacrament and Extreme Unction. Then Martha began muttering unintelligibly, and toward morning she died.

The neighbouring old women washed her and dressed her, and laid her in her coffin. To avoid paying the deacon, Jacob read the psalms over her himself, and her grave cost him nothing, as the watchman of the cemetery was his cousin. Four peasants carried the coffin to the grave, not for money but for love. The old women, the beggars, and two village idiots followed the body, and the people whom they passed on the way crossed themselves devoutly. Jacob was very glad that everything had passed off so nicely and decently and cheaply, without giving offence to any one. As he said farewell to Martha for the last time he touched the coffin with his hand and thought:

"That's a fine job!"

But walking homeward from the cemetery he was seized with great distress. He felt ill, his breath was burning hot, his legs grew weak, and he longed for a drink. Beside this, a thousand thoughts came crowding into his head. He remembered again that he had never once pitied Martha or said a tender word to her. The fifty years of their life together lay stretched far, far behind him, and somehow, during all that time,

he had never once thought about her at all or noticed
her more than if she had been a dog or a cat. And
yet she had lit the stove every day, and had cooked
and baked and fetched water and chopped wood, and
when he had come home drunk from a wedding she
had hung his fiddle reverently on a nail each time, and
had silently put him to bed with a timid, anxious look
on her face.

But here came Rothschild toward him, bowing and
scraping and smiling.

"I have been looking for you, uncle!" he said.
"Moses Shakess presents his compliments and wants
you to go to him at once."

Jacob did not feel in a mood to do anything. He
wanted to cry.

"Leave me alone!" he exclaimed, and walked on.

"Oh, how can you say that?" cried Rothschild,
running beside him in alarm. "Moses will be very
angry. He wants you to come at once!"

Jacob was disgusted by the panting of the Jew,
by his blinking eyes, and by the quantities of reddish
freckles on his face. He looked with aversion at his
long green coat and at the whole of his frail, delicate
figure.

"What do you mean by pestering me, garlic?" he
shouted. "Get away!"

The Jew grew angry and shouted back:

"Don't yell at me like that or I'll send you flying
over that fence!"

"Get out of my sight!" bellowed Jacob, shaking his fist at him. "There's no living in the same town with swine like you!"

Rothschild was petrified with terror. He sank to the ground and waved his hands over his head as if to protect himself from falling blows; then he jumped up and ran away as fast as his legs could carry him. As he ran he leaped and waved his arms, and his long, gaunt back could be seen quivering. The little boys were delighted at what had happened, and ran after him screaming: "Sheeny! Sheeny!" The dogs also joined barking in the chase. Somebody laughed and then whistled, at which the dogs barked louder and more vigorously than ever.

Then one of them must have bitten Rothschild, for a piteous, despairing scream rent the air.

Jacob walked across the common to the edge of the town without knowing where he was going, and the little boys shouted after him. "There goes old man Bronze! There goes old man Bronze!" He found himself by the river where the snipe were darting about with shrill cries, and the ducks were quacking and swimming to and fro. The sun was shining fiercely and the water was sparkling so brightly that it was painful to look at. Jacob struck into a path that led along the river bank. He came to a stout, red-cheeked woman just leaving a bath-house. "Aha, you otter, you!" he thought. Not far from the bath-house some little boys were fishing for crabs with pieces of meat. When they saw Jacob they shouted mischievously: "Old man Bronze! Old man Bronze!" But there before him stood an ancient, spreading willow tree with a massive trunk, and a crow's nest among its branches. Suddenly there flashed across Jacob's memory with all the vividness of life a little child with golden curls, and the willow of which Martha had spoken. Yes, this was the same tree, so green and peaceful and sad. How old it had grown, poor thing!

He sat down at its foot and thought of the past. On the opposite shore, where that meadow now was, there had stood in those days a wood of tall birch-trees, and that bare hill on the horizon yonder had been covered with the blue bloom of an ancient pine forest. And sailboats had plied the river then, but now all lay smooth and still, and only one little birch-tree was left on the opposite bank, a graceful young thing, like a girl, while on the river there swam only ducks and geese. It was hard to believe that boats had once sailed there. It even seemed to him that there were fewer geese now than there had been. Jacob shut his eyes, and one by one white geese came flying toward him, an endless flock.

He was puzzled to know why he had never once been down to the river during the last forty or fifty years of his life, or, if he had been there, why he had never paid any attention to it. The stream was fine and large; he might have fished in it and sold the

fish to the merchants and the government officials and
the restaurant keeper at the station, and put the
money in the bank. He might have rowed in a boat
from farm to farm and played on his fiddle. People
of every rank would have paid him money to hear him.
He might have tried to run a boat on the river, that
would have been better than making coffins. Finally,
he might have raised geese, and killed them, and sent
them to Moscow in the winter. Why, the down alone
would have brought him ten roubles a year! But he
had missed all these chances and had done nothing.
What losses were here! Ah, what terrible losses! And,
oh, if he had only done all these things at the same
time! If he had only fished, and played the fiddle,
and sailed a boat, and raised geese, what capital he
would have had by now! But he had not even
dreamed of doing all this; his life had gone by without
profit or pleasure. It had been lost for a song.
Nothing was left ahead; behind lay only losses, and
such terrible losses that he shuddered to think of them.
But why shouldn't men live so as to avoid all this waste
and these losses? Why, oh, why, should those birch
and pine forests have been felled? Why should those
meadows be lying so deserted? Why did people always
do exactly what they ought not to do? Why had
Jacob scolded and growled and clenched his fists and
hurt his wife's feelings all his life? Why, oh why,
had he frightened and insulted that Jew just now?
Why did people in general always interfere with one

another? What losses resulted from this! What terrible losses! If it were not for envy and anger they would get great profit from one another.

All that evening and night Jacob dreamed of the child, of the willow tree, of the fish and the geese, of Martha with her profile like a thirsty bird, and of Rothschild's pale, piteous mien. Queer faces seemed to be moving toward him from all sides, muttering to him about his losses. He tossed from side to side, and got up five times during the night to play his fiddle.

He rose with difficulty next morning, and walked to the hospital. The same doctor's assistant ordered him to put cold bandages on his head, and gave him little powders to take; by his expression and the tone of his voice Jacob knew that the state of affairs was bad, and that no powders could save him now. As he walked home he reflected that one good thing would result from his death: he would no longer have to eat and drink and pay taxes, neither would he offend people any more, and, as a man lies in his grave for hundreds of thousands of years, the sum of his profits would be immense. So, life to a man was a loss—death, a gain. Of course this reasoning was correct, but it was also distressingly sad. Why should the world be so strangely arranged that a man's life which was only given to him once must pass without profit?

He was not sorry then that he was going to die, but when he reached home, and saw his fiddle, his heart ached, and he regretted it deeply. He would not be able to take his fiddle with him into the grave, and now it would be left an orphan, and its fate would be that of the birch grove and the pine forest. Everything in the world had been lost, and would always be lost for ever. Jacob went out and sat on the threshold of his hut, clasping his fiddle to his breast. And as he thought of his life so full of waste and losses he began playing without knowing how piteous and touching his music was, and the tears streamed down his cheeks. And the more he thought the more sorrowfully sang his violin.

The latch clicked and Rothschild came in through the garden-gate, and walked boldly half-way across the garden. Then he suddenly stopped, crouched down, and, probably from fear, began making signs with his hands as if he were trying to show on his fingers what time it was.

"Come on, don't be afraid!" said Jacob gently, beckoning him to advance. "Come on!"

With many mistrustful and fearful glances Rothschild went slowly up to Jacob, and stopped about two yards away.

"Please don't beat me!" he said with a ducking bow. "Moses Shakess has sent me to you again. 'Don't be afraid,' he said, 'go to Jacob,' says he, 'and say that we can't possibly manage without him.' There is a wedding next Thursday. Ye-es, sir. Mr. Shapovaloff is marrying his daughter to a very fine man. It will be an expensive wedding, ai, ai!" added the Jew with a wink.

"I can't go" said Jacob breathing hard. "I'm ill, brother."

And he began to play again, and the tears gushed out of his eyes over his fiddle. Rothschild listened intently with his head turned away and his arms folded on his breast. The startled, irresolute look on his face gradually gave way to one of suffering and grief. He cast up his eyes as if in an ecstasy of agony and murmured: "Ou—ouch!" And the tears began to trickle slowly down his cheeks, and to drip over his green coat.

All day Jacob lay and suffered. When the priest came in the evening to administer the Sacrament he asked him if he could not think of any particular sin.

Struggling with his fading memories, Jacob recalled once more Martha's sad face, and the despairing cry of the Jew when the dog had bitten him. He murmured almost inaudibly:

"Give my fiddle to Rothschild."

"It shall be done," answered the priest.

So it happened that every one in the little town began asking:

"Where did Rothschild get that good fiddle? Did he buy it or steal it or get it out of a pawnshop?"

Rothschild has long since abandoned his flute, and now only plays on the violin. The same mournful notes flow from under his bow that used to come from his flute, and when he tries to repeat what Jacob played as he sat on the threshold of his hut, the result is an air so plaintive and sad that every one who hears him weeps, and he himself at last raises his eyes and murmurs: "Ou—ouch!" And this new song has so delighted the town that the merchants and government officials vie with each other in getting Rothschild to come to their houses, and sometimes make him play it ten times in succession.

A HORSEY NAME

MAJOR–GENERAL BULDEEFF was suffering from toothache. He had rinsed his mouth with vodka and cognac; applied tobacco ashes, opium, turpentine, and kerosene to the aching tooth; rubbed his cheek with iodine, and put cotton wool soaked with alcohol into his ears, but all these remedies had either failed to relieve him or else had made him sick. The dentist was sent for. He picked at his tooth and prescribed quinine, but this did not help the general. Buldeeff met the suggestion that the tooth should be pulled with refusal. Every one in the house, his wife, his children, the servants, even Petka, the scullery boy, suggested some remedy. Among others his steward, Ivan Evceitch came to him, and advised him to try a conjuror.

"Your Excellency," said he, "ten years ago an exciseman lived in this county whose name was Jacob. He was a first-class conjuror for the toothache. He used simply to turn toward the window and spit, and the pain would go in a minute. That was his gift."

"Where is he now?"

"After he was dismissed from the revenue service, he went to live in Saratoff with his mother-in-law. He makes his living off nothing but teeth now. If

any one has a toothache, he sends for him to cure it.
The Saratoff people have him come to their houses,
but he cures people in other cities by telegraph. Send
him a telegram, your Excellency, say: 'I, God's servant
Alexei, have the toothache. I want you to cure me.'
You can send him his fee by mail."

"Stuff and nonsense! Humbug!"

"Just try it, your Excellency! He is fond of vodka,
it is true, and is living with some German woman instead of his wife, and he uses terrible language, but he
is a remarkable wonder worker."

"Do send him a telegram, Alexei!" begged the
general's wife. "You don't believe in conjuring, I
know, but I have tried it. Why not send him the mes-
sage, even if you don't believe it will do you any
good? It can't kill you!"

"Very well, then," Buldeeff consented. "I would
willingly send a telegram to the devil, let alone to an
exciseman. Ouch! I can't stand this! Come, where
does your conjuror live? What is his name?"

The general sat down at his desk, and took up a pen.

"He is known to every dog in Saratoff," said the
steward. "Just address the telegram to Mr. Jacob—
Jacob——"

"Well?"

"Jacob—Jacob—what? I can't remember his surname. Jacob—darn it, what is his surname? I thought
of it as I was coming along. Wait a minute!"

Ivan raised his eyes to the ceiling, and moved his

lips. Buldeeff and his wife waited impatiently for him to remember the name.

"Well then, what is it? Think harder."

"Just a minute! Jacob—Jacob—I can't remember it! It's a common name too, something to do with a horse. Is it Mayres? No it isn't Mayres— Wait a bit, is it Colt? No, it isn't Colt. I know perfectly well it's a horsey name, but it has absolutely gone out of my head!"

"It isn't Filley?"

"No, no—wait a jiffy. Maresfield, Maresden—Farrier—Harrier——"

"That's a doggy name, not a horsey one. Is it Foley?"

"No, no, it isn't Foley. Just a second—Horseman—Horsey—Hackney. No, it isn't any of those."

"Then how am I to send that telegram? Think a little harder!"

"One moment! Carter—Coltsford—Shafter——"

"Shaftsbury?" suggested the general's wife.

"No, no—Wheeler—no, that isn't it! I've forgotten it!"

"Then why on earth did you come pestering me with your advice, if you couldn't remember the man's name?" stormed the general. "Get out of here!"

Ivan went slowly out, and the general clutched his cheek, and went rushing through the house.

"Ouch! Oh Lord!" he howled. "Oh, mother! Ouch! I'm as blind as a bat!"

A HORSEY NAME

The steward went into the garden, and, raising his eyes to heaven, tried to remember the exciseman's name.

"Hunt—Hunter—Huntley. No, that's wrong! Cobb—Cobden—Dobbins—Maresly——"

Shortly afterward, the steward was again summoned by his master.

"Well, have you thought of it?" asked the general.

"No, not yet, your Excellency!"

"Is it Barnes?" asked the general. "Is it Palfrey, by any chance?"

Every one in the house began madly to invent names. Horses of every possible age, breed, and sex were considered; their names, hoofs, and harness were all thought of. People were frantically walking up and down in the house, garden, servants' quarters, and kitchen, all scratching their heads, and searching for the right name.

Suddenly the steward was sent for again.

"Is it Herder?" they asked him. "Hocker? Hyde? Groome?"

"No, no, no," answered Ivan, and, casting up his eyes, he went on thinking aloud.

"Steed—Charger—Horsely—Harness——"

"Papa!" cried a voice from the nursery. "Tracey! Bitter!"

The whole farm was now in an uproar. The impatient, agonised general promised five roubles to any one who would think of the right name, and a perfect mob began to follow Ivan Evceitch about.

"Bayley!" They cried to him. "Trotter! Hackett!"

Evening came at last, and still the name had not been found. The household went to bed without sending the telegram.

The general did not sleep a wink, but walked, groaning, up and down his room. At three o'clock in the morning he went out into the yard and tapped at the steward's window.

"It isn't Gelder, is it?" he asked almost in tears.

"No, not Gelder, your Excellency," answered Ivan, sighing apologetically.

"Perhaps it isn't a horsey name at all? Perhaps it is something entirely different?"

"No, no, upon my word, it's a horsey name, your Excellency, I remember that perfectly."

"What an abominable memory you have, brother! That name is worth more than anything on earth to me now! I'm in agony!"

Next morning the general sent for the dentist again.

"I'll have it out!" he cried. "I can't stand this any longer!"

The dentist came and pulled out the aching tooth. The pain at once subsided, and the general grew quieter. Having done his work and received his fee, the dentist climbed into his gig, and drove away. In the field outside the front gate he met Ivan. The

A HORSEY NAME

steward was standing by the roadside plunged in thought, with his eyes fixed on the ground at his feet. Judging from the deep wrinkles that furrowed his brow, he was painfully racking his brains over something, and was muttering to himself:

"Dunn—Sadler—Buckle—Coachman——"

"Hello, Ivan!" cried the doctor driving up. "Won't you sell me a load of hay? I have been buying mine from the peasants lately, but it's no good."

Ivan glared dully at the doctor, smiled vaguely, and without answering a word threw up his arms, and rushed toward the house as if a mad dog were after him.

"I've thought of the name, your Excellency!" he shrieked with delight, bursting into the general's study. "I've thought of it, thanks to the doctor. Hayes! Hayes is the exciseman's name! Hayes, your Honour! Send a telegram to Hayes!"

"Slow-coach!" said the general contemptuously, snapping his fingers at him. "I don't need your horsey name now! Slow-coach!"

THE PETCHENEG*

ONE hot summer's day Ivan Jmukin was returning from town to his farm in southern Russia. Jmukin was a retired old Cossack officer, who had served in the Caucasus, and had once been lusty and strong, but he was an old man now, shrivelled and bent, with bushy eyebrows and a long, greenish-grey moustache. He had been fasting in town, and had made his will, for it was only two weeks since he had had a slight stroke of paralysis, and now, sitting in the train, he was full of deep, gloomy thoughts of his approaching death, of the vanity of life, and of the transient quality of all earthly things. At Provalye, one of the stations on the Don railway, a fair-haired, middle-aged man, carrying a worn portfolio under his arm, entered the compartment and sat down opposite the old Cossack. They began talking together.

"No," said Jmukin gazing pensively out of the window. "It is never too late to marry. I myself was forty-eight when I married, and every one said it was too late, but it has turned out to be neither too late nor too early. Still, it is better never to marry at all. Every one soon gets tired of a wife, though

* Petchenegs, wild tribesmen of the Caucasus.

not every one will tell you the truth, because, you know, people are ashamed of their family troubles, and try to conceal them. It is often 'Manya, dear Manya,' with a man when, if he had his way, he would put that Manya of his into a sack, and throw her into the river. A wife is a nuisance and a bore, and children are no better, I can assure you. I have two scoundrels myself. There is nowhere they can go to school on the steppe, and I can't afford to send them to Novotcherkask, so they are growing up here like young wolf cubs. At any moment they may murder some one on the highway."

The fair-haired man listened attentively, and answered all questions addressed to him briefly, in a low voice. He was evidently gentle and unassuming. He told his companion that he was an attorney, on his way to the village of Duevka on business.

"Why, for heaven's sake, that's only nine miles from where I live!" cried Jmukin, as if some one had been disputing it. "You won't be able to get any horses at the station this evening. In my opinion the best thing for you to do is to come home with me, you know, and spend the night at my house, you know, and let me send you on to-morrow with my horses."

After a moment's reflection the attorney accepted the invitation.

The sun was hanging low over the steppe when they arrived at the station. The two men remained silent as they drove from the railway to the farm, for the jolting that the road gave them forbade conversation. The tarantass* bounded and whined and seemed to be sobbing, as if its leaps caused it the keenest pain, and the attorney, who found his seat very uncomfortable, gazed with anguish before him, hoping to descry the farm in the distance. After they had driven eight miles a low house surrounded by a dark wattle fence came into view. The roof was painted green, the stucco on the walls was peeling off, and the little windows looked like puckered eyes. The farmhouse stood exposed to all the ardour of the sun; neither trees nor water were visible anywhere near it. The neighbouring landowners and peasants called it "Petcheneg Grange." Many years ago a passing surveyor, who was spending the night at the farm, had talked with Jmukin all night, and had gone away in the morning much displeased, saying sternly as he left: "Sir, you are nothing but a Petcheneg!" So the name "Petcheneg Grange" had been given to the farm, and had stuck to it all the more closely as Jmukin's boys began to grow up, and to perpetrate raids on the neighbouring gardens and melon fields. Jmukin himself was known as "old man you know," because he talked so much, and used the words "you know" so often.

Jmukin's two sons were standing in the courtyard, near the stables, as the tarantass drove up. One was about nineteen, the other was a hobbledehoy of a few years younger; both were barefoot and hatless. As

* A rough carriage used in southern Russia.

the carriage went by the younger boy threw a hen high up over his head. It described an arc in the air, and fluttered cackling down till the elder fired a shot from his gun, and the dead bird fell to earth with a thud.

"Those are my boys learning to shoot birds on the wing," Jmukin said.

The travellers were met in the front entry by a woman, a thin, pale-faced little creature, still pretty and young, who, from her dress, might have been taken for a servant.

"This," said Jmukin, "is the mother of those sons of guns of mine. Come on, Lyuboff!" he cried to his wife. "Hustle, now, mother, and help entertain our guest. Bring us some supper! Quick!"

The house consisted of two wings. On one side were the "drawing-room" and, adjoining it, the old man's bedchamber; close, stuffy apartments both, with low ceilings, infested by thousands of flies. On the other side was the kitchen, where the cooking and washing were done and the workmen were fed. Here, under benches, geese and turkeys were sitting on their nests, and here stood the beds of Lyuboff and her two sons. The furniture in the drawing-room was unpainted and had evidently been made by a country joiner. On the walls hung guns, game bags, and whips, all of which old trash was rusty and grey with dust. Not a picture was on the walls, only a dark, painted board that had once been an icon hung in one corner of the room.

A young peasant woman set the table and brought in ham and borstch.* Jmukin's guest declined vodka, and confined himself to eating cucumbers and bread.

"And what about the ham?" Jmukin asked.

"No, thank you, I don't eat ham," answered his guest. "I don't eat meat of any kind."

"Why not?"

"I'm a vegetarian. It's against my principles to kill animals."

Jmukin was silent for a moment, and then said slowly, with a sigh:

"I see—yes. I saw a man in town who didn't eat meat either. It is a new religion people have. And why shouldn't they have it? It's a good thing. One can't always be killing and shooting; one must take a rest sometimes and let the animals have a little peace. Of course it's a sin to kill, there's no doubt about that. Sometimes, when you shoot a hare, and hit him in the leg he will scream like a baby. So it hurts him!"

"Of course it hurts him! Animals suffer pain just as much as we do."

"That's a fact!" Jmukin agreed. "I see that perfectly," he added pensively. "Only there is one thing that I must say I can't quite understand. Suppose, for instance, you know, every one were to stop eating meat, what would become of all our barnyard fowls, like chickens and geese?"

* Borstch: the national soup of Little Russia.

"Chickens and geese would go free just like all other birds."

"Ah! Now I understand. Of course. Crows and magpies get on without us all right. Yes. And chickens and geese and rabbits and sheep would all be free and happy, you know, and would praise God, and not be afraid of us any more. So peace and quiet would reign upon earth. Only one thing I can't understand, you know," Jmukin continued, with a glance at the ham. "Where would all the pigs go to? What would become of them?"

"The same thing that would become of all the other animals, they would go free."

"I see—yes. But, listen, if they were not killed, they would multiply, you know, and then it would be good-by to our meadows and vegetable gardens! Why, if a pig is turned loose and not watched, it will ruin everything for you in a day! A pig is a pig, and hasn't been called one for nothing!"

They finished their supper. Jmukin rose from the table, and walked up and down the room for a long time, talking interminably. He loved to think of and discuss deep and serious subjects, and was longing to discover some theory that would sustain him in his old age, so that he might find peace of mind, and not think it so terrible to die. He desired for himself the same gentleness and self-confidence and peace of mind which he saw in this guest of his, who had just eaten his fill of cucumbers and bread, and was a better man for it, sitting there on a bench so healthy and fat, patiently bored, looking like a huge heathen idol that nothing could move from his seat.

"If a man can only find some idea to hold to in life, he will be happy," Jmukin thought.

The old Cossack went out on the front steps, and the attorney could hear him sighing and repeating to himself:

"Yes—I see——"

Night was falling, and the stars were shining out one by one. The lamps in the house had not been lit. Some one came creeping toward the drawing-room as silently as a shadow, and stopped in the doorway. It was Lyuboff, Jmukin's wife.

"Have you come from the city?" she asked timidly, without looking at her guest.

"Yes, I live in the city."

"Maybe you know about schools, master, and can tell us what to do if you will be so kind. We need advice."

"What do you want?"

"We have two sons, kind master, and they should have been sent to school long ago, but nobody ever comes here and we have no one to tell us anything. I myself know nothing. If they don't go to school, they will be taken into the army as common Cossacks. That is hard, master. They can't read or write, they are worse off than peasants, and their father himself despises them, and won't let them come into the house.

Is it their fault? If only the younger one, at least, could be sent to school! It's a pity to see them so!" she wailed, and her voice trembled. It seemed incredible that a woman so little and young could already have grown-up children. "Ah, it is such a pity!" she said again.

"You know nothing about it, mother, and it's none of your business," said Jmukin, appearing in the doorway. "Don't pester our guest with your wild talk. Go away, mother!"

Lyuboff went out, repeating once more in a high little voice as she reached the hall:

"Ah, it is such a pity!"

A bed was made up for the attorney on a sofa in the drawing-room, and Jmukin lit the little shrine lamp, so that he might not be left in the dark. Then he lay down in his own bedroom. Lying there he thought of many things: his soul, his old age, and his recent stroke which had given him such a fright and had so sharply reminded him of his approaching death. He liked to philosophise when he was alone in the dark, and at these times he imagined himself to be a very deep and serious person indeed, whose attention only questions of importance could engage. He now kept thinking that he would like to get hold of some one idea unlike any other idea he had ever had, something significant that would be the lodestar of his life. He wanted to think of some law for himself, that would make his life as serious and deep as he himself personally was. And here was an idea! He could go without meat now, and deprive himself of everything that was superfluous to his existence! The time would surely come when people would no longer kill animals or one another, it could not but come, and he pictured this future in his mind's eye, and distinctly saw himself living at peace with all the animal world. Then he remembered the pigs again, and his brain began to reel.

"What a muddle it all is!" he muttered, heaving a deep sigh.

"Are you asleep?" he asked.

"No."

Jmukin rose from his bed, and stood on the threshold of the door in his nightshirt, exposing to his guest's view his thin, sinewy legs, as straight as posts.

"Just look, now," he began. "Here is all this telegraph and telephone business, in a word, all these marvels, you know, and yet people are no more virtuous than they used to be. It is said that when I was young, thirty or forty years ago, people were rougher and crueller than they are now, but aren't they just the same to-day? Of course, they were less ceremonious when I was a youngster. I remember how once, when we had been stationed on the bank of a river in the Caucasus for four months without anything to do, quite a little romance took place. On the very bank of the river, you know, where our regiment was encamped, we had buried a prince whom we had killed not long before. So at night, you know, his princess used to come down to the grave and cry. She screamed and screamed, and groaned and groaned until we got into such a state that we couldn't sleep a wink. We didn't sleep for nights. We grew tired of it. And honestly, why should we be kept awake by that devil of a voice? Excuse the expression! So we took that princess and gave her a good thrashing, and she stopped coming to the grave. There you are! Nowadays, of course, men of that category don't exist any more. People don't thrash one another, and they live more cleanly and learn more lessons than they used to, but their hearts haven't changed one bit, you know. Listen to this, for instance. There is a landlord near here who owns a coal mine, you know. He has all sorts of vagabonds and men without passports working for him, men who have nowhere else to go. When Saturday comes round the workmen have to be paid, and their employer never wants to do that, he is too fond of his money. So he has picked out a foreman, a vagabond, too, though he wears a hat, and he says to him: 'Don't pay them a thing,' says our gentleman, 'not even a penny. They will beat you, but you must stand it. If you do, I'll give you ten roubles every Saturday.' So every week, regularly, when Saturday evening comes round the workmen come for their wages, and the foreman says: 'There aren't any wages!' Well, words follow, and then come abuse, and a drubbing. They beat him and kick him, for the men are wild with hunger, you know; they beat him until he is unconscious, and then go off to the four winds of heaven. The owner of the mine orders cold water to be thrown over his foreman, and pitches him ten roubles. The man takes the money, and is thankful, for the fact is he would agree to wear a noose round his neck for a penny! Yes, and on Monday a new gang of workmen arrives. They come because they have nowhere else to go. On Saturday there is the same old story over again."

The attorney rolled over, with his face toward the back of the sofa, and mumbled something incoherent.

"Take another example, for instance," Jmukin went on. "When we had the Siberian cattle plague here, you know, the cattle died like flies, I can tell you. The veterinary surgeons came, and strictly ordered all infected stock that died to be buried as far away from the farm as possible, and to be covered with lime and so on, according to the laws of science. Well, one of my horses died. I buried it with the greatest care, and shovelled at least ten poods* of lime on top of it, but what do you think? That pair of young jackanapes of mine dug up the horse one night, and sold the skin for three roubles! There now, what do you think of that?"

Flashes of lightning were gleaming through the cracks of the shutters on one side of the room. The air was sultry before the approaching storm, and the

* Pood: Russian measure of weight = 40 pounds.

THE PETCHENEG

mosquitoes had begun to bite. Jmukin groaned and sighed, as he lay meditating in his bed, and kept repeating to himself:

"Yes—I see——"

Sleep was impossible. Somewhere in the distance thunder was growling.

"Are you awake?"

"Yes," answered his guest.

Jmukin rose and walked with shuffling slippers through the drawing-room, and hall, and into the kitchen to get a drink of water.

"The worst thing in the world is stupidity," he said, as he returned a few minutes later with a dipper in his hand. "That Lyuboff of mine gets down on her knees and prays to God every night. She flops down on the floor and prays that the boys may be sent to school, you know. She is afraid they will be drafted into the army as common Cossacks, and have their backs tickled with sabres. But it would take money to send them to school, and where can I get it? What you haven't got you haven't got, and it's no use crying for the moon! Another reason she prays is because, like all women, you know, she thinks she is the most unhappy creature in the world. I am an outspoken man, and I won't hide anything from you. She comes of a poor priest's family—of church-bell stock, one might say—and I married her when she was seventeen. They gave her to me chiefly because times were hard, and her family were in want and had nothing to eat, and when all is said and done I do own some land, as you see, and I am an officer of sorts. She felt flattered at the idea of being my wife, you know. But she began to cry on the day of our wedding, and has cried every day since for twenty years; her eyes must be made of water! She does nothing but sit and think. What does she think about, I ask you? What can a woman think about? Nothing! The fact is, I don't consider women human beings."

The attorney jumped up impetuously, and sat up in bed.

"Excuse me, I feel a little faint," he said. "I am going out-of-doors."

Jmukin, still talking about women, drew back the bolts of the hall door, and both men went out together. A full moon was floating over the grange. The house and stables looked whiter than they had by day, and shimmering white bands of light lay among the shadows on the lawn. To the right lay the steppe, with the stars glowing softly over it; as one gazed into its depths, it looked mysterious and infinitely distant, like some bottomless abyss. To the left, heavy thunder-clouds lay piled one upon another. Their margins were lit by the rays of the moon, and they resembled dark forests, seas, and mountains with snowy summits. Flashes of lightning were playing about their peaks, and soft thunder was growling in their depths; a battle seemed to be raging among them.

Quite near the house a little screech owl was crying monotonously:

"Whew! Whew!"

"What time is it?" asked the attorney.

"Nearly two o'clock."

"What a long time yet until dawn!"

They re-entered the house and lay down. It was time to go to sleep, and sleep is usually so sound before a storm, but the old man was pining for grave, weighty meditations, and he not only wanted to think, he wanted to talk as well. So he babbled on of what a fine thing it would be if, for the sake of his soul, a man could shake off this idleness that was imperceptibly and uselessly devouring his days and years one after another. He said he would like to think of some feat of strength to perform, such as making a long journey on foot or giving up meat, as this young man had done. And once more he pictured the future when men would no longer kill animals; he pictured it as clearly and precisely as if he himself had lived at that time, but suddenly his thoughts grew confused, and again he understood nothing.

The thunder-storm rolled by, but one corner of the cloud passed over the grange, and the rain began to drum on the roof. Jmukin got up, sighing with age and stretching his limbs, and peered into the drawing-room. Seeing that his guest was still awake, he said:

"When we were in the Caucasus, you know, we had a colonel who was a vegetarian as you are. He never ate meat and never hunted or allowed his men to fish. I can understand that, of course. Every animal has a right to enjoy its life and its freedom. But I can't understand how pigs could be allowed to roam wherever they pleased without being watched——"

His guest sat up in bed; his pale, haggard face was stamped with vexation and fatigue. It was plain that he was suffering agonies, and that only a kind and considerate heart forbade him to put his irritation into words.

"It is already light," he said briefly. "Please let me have a horse now."

"What do you mean? Wait until the rain stops!"

"No, please!" begged the guest in a panic. "I really must be going at once!"

And he began to dress quickly.

The sun was already rising when a horse and carriage were brought to the door. The rain had stopped, the clouds were skimming across the sky, and the rifts of blue were growing wider and wider between them. The first rays of the sun were timidly lighting up the meadows below. The attorney passed through the front entry with his portfolio under his arm, while Jmukin's wife, with red eyes, and a face even paler than it had been the evening before, stood gazing fixedly at him with the innocent look of a little girl. Her sorrowful face showed how much she envied her guest his liberty. Ah, with what joy she, too, would have left this place! Her eyes spoke of something she longed to say to him, perhaps some advice she wanted to ask him about her boys. How pitiful she was! She was not a wife, she was not the mistress of the house, she was not even a servant, but a miserable dependent, a poor relation, a nonentity wanted by no one. Her husband bustled about near his guest, not ceasing his talk for an instant, and at last ran ahead to see him into the carriage, while she stood shrinking timidly and guiltily against the wall, still waiting for the moment to come that would give her an opportunity to speak.

"Come again! Come again!" the old man repeated over and over again. "Everything we have is at your service, you know!"

His guest hastily climbed into the tarantass, obviously with infinite pleasure, looking as if he were afraid every second of being detained. The tarantass bounded and whined as it had done the day before, and a bucket tied on behind clattered madly. The attorney looked round at Jmukin with a peculiar expression in his eyes. He seemed to be wanting to call him a Petcheneg, or something of the sort, as the surveyor had done, but his kindness triumphed. He controlled himself, and the words remained unsaid. As he reached the gate, however, he suddenly felt that he could no longer contain himself; he rose in his seat, and cried out in a loud, angry voice:

"You bore me to death!"

And with these words he vanished through the gate.

Jmukin's two sons were standing in front of the stable. The older was holding a gun, the younger had in his arms a grey cock with a bright red comb. The younger tossed the cock into the air with all his might; the bird shot up higher than the roof of the house, and turned over in the air. The elder boy shot, and it fell to the ground like a stone.

The old man stood nonplussed, and unable to comprehend his guest's unexpected exclamation. At last he turned and slowly went into the house. Sitting down to his breakfast, he fell into a long reverie about the present tendency of thought, about the universal wickedness of the present generation, about the telegraph and the telephone and bicycles, and about how unnecessary it all was. But he grew calmer little by little as he slowly ate his meal. He drank five glasses of tea, and lay down to take a nap.

THE BISHOP

IT was on the eve of Palm Sunday; vespers were being sung in the Staro-Petrovski Convent. The hour was nearly ten when the palm leaves were distributed, and the little shrine lamps were growing dim; their wicks had burnt low, and a soft haze hung in the chapel. As the worshippers surged forward in the twilight like the waves of the sea, it seemed to his Reverence Peter, who had been feeling ill for three days, that the people who came to him for palm leaves all looked alike, and, men or women, old or young, all had the same expression in their eyes. He could not see the doors through the haze; the endless procession rolled toward him, and seemed as if it must go on rolling for ever. A choir of women's voices was singing and a nun was reading the canon.

How hot and close the air was, and how long the prayers! His Reverence was tired. His dry, parching breath was coming quickly and painfully, his shoulders were aching, and his legs were trembling. The occasional cries of an idiot in the gallery annoyed him. And now, as a climax, his Reverence saw, as in a delirium, his own mother whom he had not seen for nine years coming toward him in the crowd. She, or an old woman exactly like her, took a palm leaf from

his hands, and moved away looking at him all the
while with a glad, sweet smile, until she was lost in
the crowd. And for some reason the tears began to
course down his cheeks. His heart was happy and
peaceful, but his eyes were fixed on a distant part of the
chapel where the prayers were being read, and where
no human being could be distinguished among the
shadows. The tears glistened on his cheeks and beard.
Then some one who was standing near him began to
weep, too, and then another, and then another, until
little by little the chapel was filled with a low sound of
weeping. Then the convent choir began to sing, the
weeping stopped, and everything went on as before.

Soon afterward the service ended. The fine, jubilant
notes of the heavy chapel-bells were throbbing through
the moonlit garden as the bishop stepped into his coach
and drove away. The white walls, the crosses on the
graves, the silvery birches, and the far-away moon
hanging directly over the monastery, all seemed to be
living a life of their own, incomprehensible, but very
near to mankind. It was early in April, and a chilly
night had succeeded a warm spring day. A light frost
was falling, but the breath of spring could be felt in
the soft, cool air. The road from the monastery was
sandy, the horses were obliged to proceed at a walk,
and, bathed in the bright, tranquil moonlight, a stream
of pilgrims was crawling along on either side of the
coach. All were thoughtful, no one spoke. Everything around them, the trees, the sky, and even the

THE BISHOP

moon, looked so young and intimate and friendly that they were reluctant to break the spell which they hoped might last for ever.

Finally the coach entered the city, and rolled down the main street. All the stores were closed but that of Erakin, the millionaire merchant. He was trying his electric lights for the first time, and they were flashing so violently that a crowd had collected in front of the store. Then came wide, dark streets in endless succession, and then the highway, and fields, and the smell of pines. Suddenly a white crenelated wall loomed before him, and beyond it rose a tall belfry flanked by five flashing golden cupolas, all bathed in moonlight. This was the Pankratievski Monastery where his Reverence Peter lived. Here, too, the calm, brooding moon was floating directly above the monastery. The coach drove through the gate, its wheels crunching on the sand. Here and there the dark forms of monks started out into the moonlight and footsteps rang along the flagstone paths.

"Your mother has been here while you were away, your Reverence," a lay brother told the bishop as he entered his room.

"My mother? When did she come?"

"Before vespers. She first found out where you were, and then drove to the convent."

"Then it was she whom I saw just now in the chapel! Oh, Father in heaven!"

And his Reverence laughed for joy.

"She told me to tell you, your Reverence," the lay brother continued, "that she would come back tomorrow. She had a little girl with her, a grandchild, I think. She is stopping at Ovsianikoff's inn."

"What time is it now?"

"It is after eleven."

"What a nuisance!"

His Reverence sat down irresolutely in his sitting-room, unwilling to believe that it was already so late. His arms and legs were racked with pain, the back of his neck was aching, and he felt uncomfortable and hot. When he had rested a few moments he went into his bedroom and there, too, he sat down, and dreamed of his mother. He heard the lay brother walking away and Father Sisoi the priest coughing in the next room. The monastery clock struck the quarter.

His Reverence undressed and began his prayers. He spoke the old, familiar words with scrupulous attention, and at the same time he thought of his mother. She had nine children, and about forty grandchildren. She had lived from the age of seventeen to the age of sixty with her husband the deacon in a little village. His Reverence remembered her from the days of his earliest childhood, and, ah, how he had loved her! Oh, that dear, precious, unforgettable childhood of his! Why did those years that had vanished for ever seem so much brighter and richer and gayer than they really had been? How tender and kind his mother had been when he was ill in his childhood and youth!

His prayers mingled with the memories that burned ever brighter and brighter in his heart like a flame, but they did not hinder his thoughts of his mother.

When he had prayed he lay down, and as soon as he found himself in the dark there rose before his eyes the vision of his dead father, his mother, and Lyesopolye, his native village. The creaking of wagon wheels, the bleating of sheep, the sound of church-bells on a clear summer morning, ah, how pleasant it was to think of these things! He remembered Father Simeon, the old priest at Lyesopolye, a kind, gentle, good-natured old man. He himself had been small, and the priest's son had been a huge strapping novice with a terrible bass voice. He remembered how this young priest had scolded the cook once, and had shouted: "Ah, you she-ass of Jehovah!" And Father Simeon had said nothing, and had only been mortified because he could not for the life of him remember reading of an ass of that name in the Bible!

Father Simeon had been succeeded by Father Demian, a hard drinker who sometimes even went so far as to see green snakes. He had actually borne the nickname of "Demian the Snake-Seer" in the village. Matvei Nikolaitch had been the schoolmaster, a kind, intelligent man, but a hard drinker, too. He never thrashed his scholars, but for some reason he kept a little bundle of birch twigs hanging on his wall, under which was a tablet bearing the absolutely unintelligible inscription: "Betula Kinderbalsamica Secuta."

He had had a woolly black dog whom he called "Syntax."

The bishop laughed. Eight miles from Lyesopolye lay the village of Obnino possessing a miraculous icon. A procession started from Obnino every summer bearing the wonder-working icon and making the round of all the neighbouring villages. The church-bells would ring all day long first in one village, then in another, and to Little Paul (his Reverence was called Little Paul then) the air itself seemed tremulous with rapture. Barefoot, hatless, and infinitely happy, he followed the icon with a naïve smile on his lips and naïve faith in his heart.

Until the age of fifteen Little Paul had been so slow at his lessons that his parents had even thought of taking him out of the ecclesiastical school and putting him to work in the village store.

The bishop turned over so as to break the train of his thoughts, and tried to go to sleep.

"My mother has come!" he remembered, and laughed.

The moon was shining in through the window, and the floor was lit by its rays while he lay in shadow. A cricket was chirping. Father Sisoi was snoring in the next room, and there was a forlorn, friendless, even a vagrant note in the old man's cadences.

Sisoi had once been the steward of a diocesan bishop and was known as "Father Former Steward." He was seventy years old, and lived sometimes in a

THE BISHOP

monastery sixteen miles away, sometimes in the city, sometimes wherever he happened to be. Three days ago he had turned up at the Pankratievski Monastery, and the bishop had kept him here in order to discuss with him at his leisure the affairs of the monastery.

The bell for matins rang at half past one. Father Sisoi coughed, growled something, and got up.

"Father Sisoi!" called the bishop.

Sisoi came in dressed in a white cassock, carrying a candle in his hand.

"I can't go to sleep," his Reverence said. "I must be ill. I don't know what the matter is; I have fever."

"You have caught cold, your Lordship. I must rub you with tallow."

Father Sisoi stood looking at him for a while and yawned: "Ah-h—the Lord have mercy on us!"

"Erakin has electricity in his store now—I hate it!" he continued.

Father Sisoi was aged, and round-shouldered, and gaunt. He was always displeased with something or other, and his eyes, which protruded like those of a crab, always wore an angry expression.

"I don't like it at all," he repeated—"I hate it."

II

Next day, on Palm Sunday, his Reverence officiated at the cathedral in the city. Then he went to the diocesan bishop's, then to see a general's wife who was very ill, and at last he drove home. At two o'clock two beloved guests were having dinner with him, his aged mother, and his little niece Kitty, a child of eight. The spring sun was peeping cheerily in through the windows as they sat at their meal, and was shining merrily on the white tablecloth, and on Kitty's red hair. Through the double panes they heard the rooks cawing, and the magpies chattering in the garden.

"It is nine years since I saw you last," said the old mother, "and yet when I caught sight of you in the convent chapel yesterday I thought to myself: God bless me, he has not changed a bit! Only perhaps you are a little thinner than you were, and your beard has grown longer. Oh, holy Mother, Queen of Heaven! Everybody was crying yesterday. As soon as I saw you, I began to cry myself, I don't know why. His holy will be done!"

In spite of the tenderness with which she said this, it was clear that she was not at her ease. It was as if she did not know whether to address the bishop by the familiar "thee" or the formal "you," and whether she ought to laugh or not. She seemed to feel herself more of a poor deacon's wife than a mother in his presence. Meanwhile Kitty was sitting with her eyes glued to the face of her uncle the bishop as if she were trying to make out what manner of man this was. Her hair had escaped from her comb and her bow of velvet ribbon, and was standing straight up around her head like a halo. Her eyes were foxy and bright.

She had broken a glass before sitting down, and now, as she talked, her grandmother kept moving first a glass, and then a wine glass out of her reach. As the bishop sat listening to his mother, he remembered how, many, many years ago, she had sometimes taken him and his brothers and sisters to visit relatives whom they considered rich. She had been busy with her own children in those days, and now she was busy with her grandchildren, and had come to visit him with Kitty here.

"Your sister Varenka has four children"—she was telling him—"Kitty is the oldest. God knows why, her father fell ill and died three days before Assumption. So my Varenka has been thrown out into the cold world."

"And how is my brother Nikanor?" the bishop asked.

"He is well, thank the Lord. He is pretty well, praise be to God. But his son Nikolasha wouldn't go into the church, and is at college instead learning to be a doctor. He thinks it is best, but who knows? However, God's will be done!"

"Nikolasha cuts up dead people!" said Kitty, spilling some water into her lap.

"Sit still child!" her grandmother said, quietly taking the glass out of her hands.

"How long it is since we have seen one another!" exclaimed his Reverence, tenderly stroking his mother's shoulder and hand. "I missed you when I was abroad, I missed you dreadfully."

"Thank you very much!"

"I used to sit by my window in the evening listening to the band playing, and feeling lonely and forlorn. Sometimes I would suddenly grow so homesick that I used to think I would gladly give everything I had in the world for a glimpse of you and home."

His mother smiled and beamed, and then immediately drew a long face and said stiffly:

"Thank you very much!"

The bishop's mood changed. He looked at his mother, and could not understand where she had acquired that deferential, humble expression of face and voice, and what the meaning of it might be. He hardly recognised her, and felt sorrowful and vexed. Besides, his head was still aching, and his legs were racked with pain. The fish he was eating tasted insipid and he was very thirsty.

After dinner two wealthy lady landowners visited him, and sat for an hour and a half with faces a mile long, never uttering a word. Then an archimandrite, a gloomy, taciturn man, came on business. Then the bells rang for vespers, the sun set behind the woods, and the day was done. As soon as he got back from church the bishop said his prayers, and went to bed, drawing the covers up closely about his ears. The moonlight troubled him, and soon the sound of voices came to his ears. Father Sisoi was talking politics with his mother in the next room.

"There is a war in Japan now," he was saying.

THE BISHOP

"The Japanese belong to the same race as the Montenegrins. They fell under the Turkish yoke at the same time."

And then the bishop heard his mother's voice say:

"And so, you see, when we had said our prayers, and had our tea, we went to Father Yegor——"

She kept saying over and over again that they "had tea," as if all she knew of life was tea-drinking.

The memory of his seminary and college life slowly and mistily took shape in the bishop's mind. He had been a teacher of Greek for three years, until he could no longer read without glasses, and then he had taken the vows, and had been made an inspector. When he was thirty-two he had been made the rector of a seminary, and then an archimandrite. At that time his life had been so easy and pleasant, and had seemed to stretch so far, far into the future that he could see absolutely no end to it. But his health had failed, and he had nearly lost his eyesight. His doctors had advised him to give up his work and go abroad.

"And what did you do next?" asked Father Sisoi in the adjoining room.

"And then we had tea," answered his mother.

"Why, Father, your beard is green!" exclaimed Kitty suddenly. And she burst out laughing.

The bishop remembered that the colour of Father Sisoi's beard really did verge on green, and he, too, laughed.

"My goodness! What a plague that child is!"

cried Father Sisoi in a loud voice, for he was growing angry. "You're a spoiled baby you are! Sit still!"

The bishop recalled the new white church in which he had officiated when he was abroad, and the sound of a warm sea. Eight years had slipped by while he was there; then he had been recalled to Russia, and now he was already a bishop, and the past had faded away into mist as if it had been but a dream.

Father Sisoi came into his room with a candle in his hand.

"Well, well!" he exclaimed, surprised. "Asleep already, your Reverence?"

"Why not?"

"It's early yet, only ten o'clock! I bought a candle this evening and wanted to rub you with tallow."

"I have a fever," the bishop said, sitting up. "I suppose something ought to be done. My head feels so queer."

Sisoi began to rub the bishop's chest and back with tallow.

"There—there—" he said. "Oh, Lord God Almighty! There! I went to town to-day, and saw that—what do you call him?—that archpresbyter Sidonski. I had tea with him. I hate him! Oh, Lord God Almighty! There! I hate him!"

III

The diocesan bishop was very old and very fat, and had been ill in bed with gout for a month. So his Reverence Peter had been visiting him almost every day, and had received his suppliants for him. And now that he was ill he was appalled to think of the futilities and trifles they asked for and wept over. He felt annoyed at their ignorance and cowardice. The very number of all those useless trivialities oppressed him, and he felt as if he could understand the diocesan bishop who had written "Lessons in Free Will" when he was young, and now seemed so absorbed in details that the memory of everything else, even of God, had forsaken him. Peter must have grown out of touch with Russian life while he was abroad, for it was hard for him to grow used to it now. The people seemed rough, the women stupid and tiresome, the novices and their teachers uneducated and often disorderly. And then the documents that passed through his hands by the hundreds of thousands! The provosts gave all the priests in the diocese, young and old, and their wives and children marks for good behaviour, and he was obliged to talk about all this, and read about it, and write serious articles on it. His Reverence never had a moment which he could call his own; all day his nerves were on edge, and he only grew calm when he found himself in church.

He could not grow accustomed to the terror which he involuntarily inspired in every breast in spite of his quiet and modest ways. Every one in the district seemed to shrivel and quake and apologise as soon as he looked at them. Every one trembled in his presence; even the old archpresbyters fell down at his feet, and not long ago one suppliant, the old wife of a village priest, had been prevented by terror from uttering a word, and had gone away without asking for anything. And he, who had never been able to say a harsh word in his sermons, and who never blamed people because he pitied them so, would grow exasperated with these suppliants, and hurl their petitions to the ground. Not a soul had spoken sincerely and naturally to him since he had been here; even his old mother had changed, yes, she had changed very much! Why did she talk so freely to Sisoi when all the while she was so serious and ill at ease with him, her own son? It was not like her at all! The only person who behaved naturally in his presence, and who said whatever came into his head was old man Sisoi, who had lived with bishops all his life, and had outlasted eleven of them. And therefore his Reverence felt at ease with Sisoi, even though he was, without doubt, a rough and quarrelsome person.

After morning prayers on Tuesday the bishop received his suppliants, and lost his temper with them. He felt ill, as usual, and longed to go to bed, but he had hardly entered his room before he was told that the young merchant Erakin, a benefactor of the monastery, had called on very important business. The bishop was obliged to receive him. Erakin stayed about an hour talking in a very loud voice, and it was hard to understand what he was trying to say.

After he had gone there came an abbess from a distant convent, and by the time she had gone the bells were tolling for vespers; it was time for the bishop to go to church.

The monks sang melodiously and rapturously that evening; a young, black-bearded priest officiated. His Reverence listened as they sang of the Bridegroom and of the chamber swept and garnished, and felt neither repentance nor sorrow, but only a deep peace of mind. He sat by the altar where the shadows were deepest, and was swept in imagination back into the days of his childhood and youth, when he had first heard these words sung. The tears trickled down his cheeks, and he meditated on how he had attained everything in life that it was possible for a man in his position to attain; his faith was unsullied, and yet all was not clear to him; something was lacking, and he did not want to die. It still seemed to him that he was leaving unfound the most important thing of all. Something of which he had dimly dreamed in the past, hopes that had thrilled his heart as a child, a schoolboy, and a traveller in foreign lands, troubled him still.

"How beautifully they are singing to-day!" he thought. "Oh, how beautifully!"

IV

On Thursday he held a service in the cathedral. It was the festival of the Washing of Feet. When the service was over, and the people had gone to their several homes, the sun was shining brightly and cheerily, and the air was warm. The gutters were streaming with bubbling water, and the tender songs of larks came floating in from the fields beyond the city, bringing peace to his heart. The trees were already awake, and over them brooded the blue, unfathomable sky.

His Reverence went to bed as soon as he reached home, and told the lay brother to close his shutters. The room grew dark. Oh, how tired he was!

As on the day before, the sound of voices and the tinkling of glasses came to him from the next room. His mother was gaily recounting some tale to Father Sisoi, with many a quaint word and saying, and the old man was listening gloomily, and answering in a gruff voice:

"Well, I never! Did they, indeed? What do you think of that!"

And once more the bishop felt annoyed, and then hurt that the old lady should be so natural and simple with strangers, and so silent and awkward with her own son. It even seemed to him that she always tried to find some pretext for standing in his presence, as if she felt uneasy sitting down. And his father? If he had been alive, he would probably not have been able to utter a word when the bishop was there.

Something in the next room fell to the floor with a crash. Kitty had evidently broken a cup or a saucer, for Father Sisoi suddenly snorted, and cried angrily:

"What a terrible plague this child is! Merciful heavens! No one could keep her supplied with china!"

Then silence fell. When he opened his eyes again, the bishop saw Kitty standing by his bedside staring at him, her red hair standing up around her head like a halo, as usual.

"Is that you, Kitty?" he asked. "Who is that opening and shutting doors down there?"

"I don't hear anything."

He stroked her head.

"So your cousin Nikolasha cuts up dead people, does he?" he asked, after a pause.

"Yes, he is learning to."

"Is he nice?"

"Yes, very, only he drinks a lot."

"What did your father die of?"

"Papa grew weaker and weaker, and thinner and thinner, and then came his sore throat. And I was ill, too, and so was my brother Fedia. We all had sore throats. Papa died, Uncle, but we got well."

Her chin quivered, her eyes filled with tears.

"Oh, your Reverence!" she cried in a shrill voice, beginning to weep bitterly. "Dear Uncle, mother and all of us are so unhappy! Do give us a little money! Help us, Uncle darling!"

He also shed tears, and for a moment could not speak for emotion. He stroked her hair, and touched her shoulder, and said:

"All right, all right, little child. Wait until Easter comes, then we will talk about it. I'll help you."

His mother came quietly and timidly into the room, and said a prayer before the icon. When she saw that he was awake, she asked:

"Would you like a little soup?"

"No, thanks," he answered. "I'm not hungry."

"I don't believe you are well—I can see that you are not well. You really mustn't fall ill! You have to be on your feet all day long. My goodness, it makes one tired to see you! Never mind, Easter is no longer over the hills and far away. When Easter comes you will rest. God will give us time for a little talk then, but now I'm not going to worry you any more with my silly chatter. Come, Kitty, let his Lordship have another forty winks——"

And the bishop remembered that, when he was a boy, she had used exactly the same half playful, half respectful tone to all high dignitaries of the church. Only by her strangely tender eyes, and by the anxious look which she gave him as she left the room could any one have guessed that she was his mother. He shut his eyes, and seemed to be asleep, but he heard the clock strike twice, and Father Sisoi coughing next door. His mother came in again, and looked shyly at him. Suddenly there came a bang, and a door slammed; a vehicle of some kind drove up to the front steps. The lay brother came into the bishop's room, and called:

"Your Reverence!"

"What is it?"

"Here is the coach! It is time to go to our Lord's Passion——"

"What time is it?"

"Quarter to eight."

The bishop dressed, and drove to the cathedral. He had to stand motionless in the centre of the church while the twelve gospels were being read, and the first and longest and most beautiful of them all he read himself. A strong, valiant mood took hold of him. He knew this gospel, beginning "The Son of Man is risen to-day—," by heart, and as he repeated it, he raised his eyes, and saw a sea of little lights about him. He heard the sputtering of candles, but the people had disappeared. He felt surrounded by those whom he had known in his youth; he felt that they would always be here until—God knew when!

His father had been a deacon, his grandfather had been a priest, and his great grandfather a deacon. He sprang from a race that had belonged to the church since Christianity first came to Russia, and his love for the ritual of the church, the clergy, and the sound of church-bells was inborn in him, deeply, irradicably implanted in his heart. When he was in church, especially when he was taking part in the service himself, he felt active and valorous and happy. And so it was with him now. Only, after the eighth gospel had been read, he felt that his voice was becoming so feeble that even his cough was inaudible; his head was aching, and he began to fear that he might collapse. His legs were growing numb; in a little while he ceased to have any sensation in them at all, and could not imagine what he was standing on, and why he did not fall down.

It was quarter to twelve when the service ended. The bishop went to bed as soon as he reached home, without even saying his prayers. As he pulled his blanket up over him, he suddenly wished that he were abroad; he passionately wished it. He would give his life, he thought, to cease from seeing these cheap, wooden walls and that low ceiling, to cease from smelling the stale scent of the monastery.

If there were only some one with whom he could talk, some one to whom he could unburden his heart!

He heard steps in the adjoining room, and tried to recall who it might be. At last the door opened, and Father Sisoi came in with a candle in one hand, and a teacup in the other.

"In bed already, your Reverence?" he asked. "I have come to rub your chest with vinegar and vodka. It is a fine thing, if rubbed in good and hard. Oh, Lord God Almighty! There—there—I have just come from our monastery. I hate it. I am going away from here to-morrow, my Lord. Oh, Lord, God Almighty—there——"

Sisoi never could stay long in one place, and he now felt as if he had been in this monastery for a year. It was hard to tell from what he said where his home was, whether there was any one or anything in the world that he loved, and whether he believed in God or not. He himself never could make out why he had become a monk, but then, he never gave it any thought, and the time when he had taken the vows had long since faded from his memory. He thought he must have been born a monk.

"Yes, I am going away to-morrow. Bother this place!"

"I want to have a talk with you—I never seem to have the time—" whispered the bishop, making a great effort to speak. "You see, I don't know any one—or anything—here——"

"Very well then, I shall stay until Sunday, but no longer! Bother this place!"

"What sort of a bishop am I?" his Reverence went on, in a faint voice. "I ought to have been a village priest, or a deacon, or a plain monk. All this is choking me—it is choking me——"

"What's that? Oh, Lord God Almighty! There—go to sleep now, your Reverence. What do you mean? What's all this you are saying? Good night!"

All night long the bishop lay awake, and in the

morning he grew very ill. The lay brother took fright and ran first to the archimandrite, and then for the monastery doctor who lived in the city. The doctor, a stout, elderly man, with a long, grey beard, looked intently at his Reverence, shook his head, knit his brows, and finally said:

"I'll tell you what, your Reverence; you have typhoid."

The bishop grew very thin and pale in the next hour, his eyes grew larger, his face became covered with wrinkles, and he looked quite small and old. He felt as if he were the thinnest, weakest, puniest man in the whole world, and as if everything that had occurred before this had been left far, far behind, and would never happen again.

"How glad I am of that!" he thought. "Oh, how glad!"

His aged mother came into the room. When she saw his wrinkled face and his great eyes, she was seized with fear, and, falling down on her knees by his bedside, she began kissing his face, his shoulders, and his hands. He seemed to her to be the thinnest, weakest, puniest man in the world, and she forgot that he was a bishop, and kissed him as if he had been a little child whom she dearly, dearly loved.

"Little Paul, my dearie!" she cried. "My little son, why do you look like this? Little Paul, oh, answer me!"

Kitty, pale and severe, stood near them, and could

not understand what was the matter with her uncle, and why granny wore such a look of suffering on her face, and spoke such heartrending words. And he, he was speechless, and knew nothing of what was going on around him. He was dreaming that he was an ordinary man once more, striding swiftly and merrily through the open country, a staff in his hand, bathed in sunshine, with the wide sky above him, as free as a bird to go wherever his fancy led him.

"My little son! My little Paul! Answer me!" begged his mother.

"Don't bother his Lordship," said Sisoi. "Let him sleep. What's the matter?"

Three doctors came, consulted together, and drove away. The day seemed long, incredibly long, and then came the long, long night. Just before dawn on Saturday morning the lay brother went to the old mother who was lying on a sofa in the sitting-room, and asked her to come into the bedroom; his Reverence had gone to eternal peace.

Next day was Easter. There were forty-two churches in the city, and two monasteries, and the deep, joyous notes of their bells pealed out over the town from morning until night. The birds were carolling, the bright sun was shining. The big market place was full of noise; barrel organs were droning, concertinas were squealing, and drunken voices were ringing through the air. Trotting races were held in the main street that afternoon; in a word, all was merry and gay, as had been the year before and as, doubtless, it would be the year to come.

A month later a new bishop was appointed, and every one forgot his Reverence Peter. Only the dead man's mother, who is living now in a little country town with her son the deacon, when she goes out at sunset to meet her cow, and joins the other women on the way, tells them about her children and grandchildren, and her boy who became a bishop.

And when she mentions him she looks at them shyly, for she is afraid they will not believe her.

And, as a matter of fact, not all of them do.